Bunnies and Bowties

S.N. Moor

Contents

Hey Dad

W HELP! T HIS IS AWKWARD. To answer your question, yes... I will write another book you can read, but this is not it. Like not by a long shot. I love the support, but I implore you to put the book down now. Close it, put it on a shelf and then tell all your friends about the other books you're allowed to read. Not this book. Because likely, if I don't want you reading this book, it would be suuuuuper awkward if you recommended it to a friend. I want your friends to still engage in casual conversation with you. If they read this book, conversation will be awkward AF.

But because I know you're curious, I will give you a little recap of this book, so you can put it down. As you know from the last book, Everlee met some friends, but at the end left to try to protect herself from getting hurt. Boo. But she still misses them, so two month later she sees them again and is like woooah. But she is going away for the weekend to see her parents for Easter. Hello adult competitive easter egg hunting! While home, her mom sets her up on a date with a nice gentleman, but.... something happens. Just say wow! Can you believe that happened? Some other things happen yada yada yada and you're left feeling happy. So that's it, you're welcome!

The End!

For all those girls who want to be told STFUATOCLAGG

Content Warning

THIS IS THE 2ND book. It is highly recommended you read Cupid's Contract/Hearts and Arrows first.

Please do not let the cover fool you. This is a 'ghost pepper level' spicy holiday romance.

If you like your books with DVP, DOP, Dom/Sub, Praise, throat grabbing, anal play, salad tossing, cooking, kayaking, swords crossing, and hilarity then this book is for you ;)

Recap

In **<u>Cupid's Contract/Hearts and Arrows</u>**, Everlee meets her four delicious men who give her the time of her life and the confidence she lost after dickface, Rich, destroys her. The only problem is the men make her agree to only sleep with them two times before they part ways. By the end of the arrangement, Everlee gets attached but doesn't know how the men feel, so she honors the agreement against her own desires and leaves. She's scared of getting hurt again, but at the same time doesn't know how to have a relationship with the men and her family. There are things she needs to figure out to protect everyone's hearts.

EVERLEE - IT'S HARD FINDING GOOD HELP OR A CHARGED VIBRATOR

"Now slip your fingers into your glistening pussy. I want to watch you make yourself come," the man's deep voice commands through my headphones with a thick accent. He could read the phone book with that voice and I'd probably come. I adjust the speed of the vibrator and plunge it back in. "That's right. Good girl."

The words hit differently than they did before, but they still cause a flutter in my stomach and a pang in my heart.

I hadn't planned on coming home to masturbate in my living room after work, but sometimes you read a good book and the next thing you know you're finger fucking yourself on the couch with one leg propped over the arm, hoping your little peeping tom neighbors in the apartment building beside you aren't chomping down on a handful of freshly popped popcorn watching the show. And then perhaps the other part of you is like fuck it, let them watch and you don't know what turns you on more.

"Move faster," he commands.

I pulse my bright pink and purple boyfriend in and out. It's the new one Lizzy bought me after... you know. It's not the biggest size cock on the market, but it does the job. My other boyfriends are on life support plugged in and this one was the only one up to the challenge, although I don't know how much life he has left in him. I call him BOB because he's my battery-operated boyfriend and I only need him just... a little... longer.

My back arches and then...

Silence.

No. No, no, no, no, no. I pull BOB out and look at him. He buzzes again, filling me with hope, then stops. He's on the fritz. The mother fucking fritz. "Come on BOB, you've been so good to me all these months. The one I could always count on."

Another quick buzz, then nothing.

"You're dead to me, BOB!" I yell out in frustration, tossing him to the ground. "I guess manual it is."

The girl is moaning in my ear as she's coming undone.

At least one of us can girlfriend.

Excited to experience my own release, I press my fingers against my clit and begin moving in circles, as the slickness heightens the sensation.

KNOCK! KNOCK!

My heart stops beating, and I freeze, my eyes fixed on the door.

KNOCK! KNOCK!

It's a Thursday night at nine o'clock. Who could be at my door?

KNOCK! KNOCK! KNOCK! KNOCK!

"Open up this door, bitch! I know you're inside!"

Lizzy.

With a chuckle, I stand from the couch and slip my pajama pants back on.

KNO-

Opening the door mid-knock, I'm greeted with a wide-eyed Lizzy, hand still in the air. She's wearing bunny ears on her head, with a light brown trench coat draped over her shoulders, eyeing me up and down with a large box in her hands.

"Nope," I say bluntly, cutting off any further discussion. Whatever she's trying to convince me to do will not be good.

"Oh stop. You don't even know why I'm here."

I move aside from the door, gesturing for her to come in. "You're here to convince me to go to some holiday party, probably at Vixen, if I had to guess."

She narrows her gaze on me. "Ok. Well, maybe you do. But come on," she pleads, dropping the box on the ground.

"Lizzy. I can't." Turning my back, I walk into the kitchen to grab a glass of water.

"You can. You're just choosing not to. It's been two months since you've gone out. You can't hide away forever."

"I'm not hid-"

The buzz of the vibrator reverberates against the floor, pulling our attention.

Well, shit.

She looks over and finds him laying by the couch. "I'm glad you're using the one I bought you." She smirks.

I roll my eyes.

"Let's go! This is an intervention. They probably don't even remember you."

"Lizzy!" I snap.

"You're right. That was mean and I'm sorry. They definitely remember you, because who wouldn't? You're a bad bitch who is gorgeous and stupid. I can't believe you walked away from them."

"Lizzy!" I snap again.

She holds her hands up. "I know, I know. I suck right now. I'm in unfamiliar territory. At least with dickface, he was a douche, so it was easy. It made sense. But these guys…"

"You aren't helping your case at all."

She puckers out her bottom lip. "Ok. Look. For real. I'm worried about you. You need to get back out there. How do you plan on meeting someone if you never put yourself out there?"

"I don't."

She huffs.

"Vixen is having a bunnies and bowties party tonight. I'm going, and really want you to come with me, but I won't force you."

She drops to her knees, and for a minute, I think she's about to beg. Instead, she opens the large box. "I got you an outfit in case you said yes. I thought we could be twinsies."

My eyes shift from the outfit to her, and I can feel my resolve weakening. I want to go. I want to see them, but I'm scared. What would it be like? Would they ignore me? Would they not? Would it be awkward?

Not a day has gone by since they came to my apartment, that I haven't thought about them, but my daydreams always end the same. Walking up to my parent's house with them behind me, introducing them as my boyfriends and then… sadness, regret. My mom falling to her knees with her face cupped in her hands with my dad pointing for us to leave- for *me* to leave. Even though it always ends the same, I still have it. One so I can try to change the outcome, but two, so I can see them again. My mind wanders, getting lost in their features and the way they look at me. I miss seeing them. It's been long enough. Perhaps it won't even be an issue.

Lizzy can sense my mind changing and starts getting all jittery. She holds up the white satin corset, bunny ears and little cotton tail.

"Fine," I huff. Add another point in the column for Lizzy getting her way.

She stands up and wraps her arms around me. "Oh thank you, thank you, thank you!"

"I don't understand why you're so excited."

"No reason."

"Lizzy," I groan.

"What? Can't a girl be excited about having her best friend in the world come to a nightclub with her?"

"Yes. But I don't trust you."

She bats the air. "Now, go get dressed!" She checks her watch, which makes me a little apprehensive.

Grabbing the box, I go into the bedroom and toss it on my bed. Panic prickles on my skin when I hear her moving around the kitchen, clinking glasses together, but have to assume she's making us some cocktails.

I slip the corset and tail on and look at myself in the mirror, then pull my boobs up a little to give them some more lift. If I'm going to do this, then damn it, I want to look good. I run the curler through my hair, giving a few twists and touch up my makeup before sliding the ears on. I rifle through my closet and find a pair of low heels and have a flashback to the last time I wore them. Memories flood my mind of that night at the guy's house and all the naked fun we had.

"What's taking so long?" Lizzy knocks on the bedroom door.

"Coming."

"I hope you do."

I open the door and glare at her.

"Too soon?"

I push past her, not answering her question, and grab the drink she's made off the counter in the kitchen.

"Cheers!" I say, holding up the glass to hers.

Lizzy smiles, clinking my glass. "To an unforgettable night."

"Yay," I say deadpan, tipping the drink back.

"Ok. Let's go. Our car is waiting downstairs."

"Waiting? Was it waiting this entire time?"

Lizzy smiles.

"You should have told me."

"It's fine. I gave them a big tip to wait."

"I hope they're still there."

"I'm sure she is."

"Give me one sec." I grab my vibrator off the floor and run into my room, plugging it in.

Gazing at my shelf of boyfriends, I bid them all a good night. I really hope I don't regret going.

EVERLEE - DON'T BE A BRIDEZILLA OR A CUNT BAG

WE'RE DOWNSTAIRS A FEW minutes later, walking to the car and I recognize the four-door blue sedan. When I crawl into the back seat, Betty turns around to look at us.

"So you got her to come?" Betty smiles.

"Betty, that's a personal question," Lizzy teases, handing her ten bucks.

Confused, I look curiously at Lizzy. She said a big tip, so I was expecting over ten dollars.

"I'm not going to take your money." Betty bats her hand away and starts pulling onto the road.

"Betty. A bet is a bet, and I lost," Lizzy insists.

"Oh, fine!" She huffs, reaching her hand back when we get to the stoplight. I watch her place it on the hundred-dollar bill, which I assume is the tip Lizzy gave her for waiting.

"How are you doing, darling?" Betty asks, looking at me in her rearview mirror.

"I'm doing good."

"She's not. She was masturbating in her living room when I got there."

"Fuck, Lizzy!" I smack her arm.

"What? Betty's part of the team."

"What team?"

"Team Everlee."

"I don't have a team."

Lizzy laughs. "Oh, darling."

"Had I known you two were going to team up against me, I'd have never connected you."

"I thought that's how you liked it..." Lizzy pumps her eyebrows and it takes everything inside of me not to punch her in the arm.

Betty laughs and diverts my attention. "Don't say that, Everlee. Lizzy has been keeping me busy." She turns to Lizzy. "Did Tony win the bid?"

"He did." Lizzy bounces up and down in her seat.

"That's great to hear. I know he was really nervous about it falling through at the end."

"It was touch and go there for a bit. They made some last-minute changes, but everything worked out."

"So good to hear! Is he still taking you to Bo La Vie to celebrate?"

Lizzy glances at me, and I raise my eyebrows. If we're about to go to their club, she can't feel weird talking about their restaurant in front of me. It's been months and I'm an adult. We can have conversations about them without it getting all weird.

"He is. We're going on Saturday night. They have a special Easter menu."

An Easter menu? I sigh, remembering my night with Lizzy at Bo's. It's Emmett's baby he recently opened up, and the food is divine. I miss it a lot and even though Emmett said I have a standing reservation every Monday at eight, I haven't gone. I can't. They'd all be there, because that's when they have their weekly meeting to discuss all their business ideas and such. Which I'm still not sure what all they have their hands in.

My stomach tightens into knots the closer we get to Vixen. I thought I was ready to see them, but I don't know. It's been two months, and now that's not feeling long enough. I mean, we weren't together for that long, but the sex. God, the sex. My stomach clenches just thinking about it.

I let myself get caught up in their world, and I loved it. They made me feel alive. Wanted. Confident. All the things I needed to help me get back to who I was after dickface. I hoped I'd have been able to go out after them, but every time I tried, I couldn't do it.

"Here we are, girls," Betty says, pulling up out front. There are several other ride shares dropping people off, so she pulls further down the curb, close to the road that leads to the back of the club.

Curiosity getting the better of me and perhaps a hidden masochistic kink, I look down the dimly lit alleyway. Callum's black Audi is parked beside the door, with Brady standing beside the car. He looks up at me and after a second, waves, so I wave back.

Shit.

My stomach twists into knots.

I'm going to see him tonight. My heart begins to pound a hole through my chest.

"Lizzy," I start, but my throat clamps and words stop coming out of my mouth.

She looks at me, and her smile drops as she sees the terror on my face. Gone is the in-your-face Lizzy, who will push you to the very edge and present is the Lizzy who is nurturing and caring. "You got this, and if you don't, we'll leave." Her words are sincere as she interlaces her fingers in mine.

I nod. "Ok." I can do this. I can go see three, maybe four, deliciously hot men I let sexually ravage and delight me. Men who I can't get off my mind, even though it's been months. Who I let myself get attached to. I can do this.

"Let's go find you a cock to ride, because I know you didn't finish earlier."

"You're like the sex whisperer."

She throws her head back, laughing as we walk past the very long line of people waiting to get in. "It was nicer when you were fucking them. At least we didn't have to wait in this line."

"That's the truth."

The weather is still cool, but not as bad as it was at Valentine's, so we leave our jackets in Betty's trunk since she's planning on coming back to pick us up.

We find the last spot, which is about fifty, maybe sixty, people from the door and wait, pressing up against the brick wall.

"I'm glad their business is doing so well," I say, looking down the long line before turning to see a large group of about twenty people walking up behind us. It looks to be a bachelorette party, because all the girls are wearing pink corsets except for the one rambling in the middle, wearing a white corset with a crown on her head.

"OMG, this line is so long, you guys," the assumed bride-to-be whines, walking up. "You should have called and told them we were coming. Gotten us VIP access or something."

One girl clasps her hands together. "We tried. We called, and they said their VIP section was already booked for the night."

Her nose wrinkles on her face like she just smelled a field of cow shit. "On a Thursday before Easter Sunday? Who would be here then?" she whines again, grating on my nerves.

Lizzy's eyes are enormous and I know we're both thinking the same thing. Who would be here? She is here! Why is she special?

The girl shuffles behind me, looking over my shoulder. "Ugh, this line is not moving."

"You're going to love it!" the one girl who spoke earlier says.

"I hope so. If not, you're no longer my maid of honor." I'd like to think she is kidding, but the tone in her voice and the gasp from her friend tells me she's serious.

I sign to Lizzy. *If you act like that, I will dump your ass.*

So no Bridezilla?

Hell to the no.

Lizzy laughs.

"Oh girls, look, they're deaf."

Rage boils under my skin, listening to her talk. The way she says it is as if we're some sort of attraction at the zoo. I want to punch her in the face.

She mumbles something about my shoes not looking right with my outfit and how she would have gone with a different heel and then mentions something about my age.

My eyebrows raise onto my forehead and I take in a deep breath, trying to calm the itch on my knuckles. Lizzy grabs my hand for good measure, but I'm not sure if it's to calm me or to prevent me from punching her. She's always been able to read me like an open book.

"Oh. Are they together?" she sighs. "Is this a gay bar?"

Trying to hold my words in, I bite my bottom lip.

"No. No. God no. We would never," the maid of honor rushes out.

The bride-to-be just moans, then looks over my shoulder again. "Oh good. Someone from the club is coming this way. Maybe they'll let us in because I'm getting married," she peeps with a grating cheerfulness.

"You think they'll let us all in?" another girl asks.

"I don't know!" Bridezilla snaps back.

Seriously, why do these girls stay around her? She's horrible.

As I glance down the sidewalk, my eyes lock onto a man dressed entirely in black, steadily making his way towards us. At first, when she mentioned someone from the club, my heart leapt, thinking it was Callum. But I don't recognize this man.

The bride-to-be is squealing behind me and I can tell she's bouncing up and down. "Girls, were you tricking me? He's coming over here. He's looking right at me."

The maid of honor nervously laughs and I feel bad for her.

The man stops beside us. "Everlee?"

Shocked, my eyes flitter to his face. "Yes?"

"Can you and your friend come with me?"

I mutter something, so Lizzy answers for us. "Yes. Yes, we can."

We step out of line and before we walk away, the bride-to-be calls out, "What about me? I'm getting married Saturday!"

The man in black turns to look at her and simply answers, "No."

"But." She stomps her foot, mumbling something about us.

Losing what little patience I have, I turn to look at her.

"Ev, don't," Lizzy pleads, grabbing for my arm.

"I'm good," I say before turning to look at the Bridezilla. "I feel bad for the man you're marrying. He's going to be miserable, because *you* are miserable."

"You don't know me."

"You're right. I don't. I only know the five minutes of you I've had to endure, and I can't imagine why these girls hang around you. You are a self-centered cunt bag and your maid of honor, whoever she is, deserves someone who actually appreciates her. And for the record, we aren't deaf. Surprise. Nor are we a couple, although if we were, I'd be one lucky girl. She was holding my hand, so I didn't turn around and punch you in the face for saying stupid shit."

She gasps and I turn to walk away.

The man in black looks at me with a smile tugging at his lips. "Are you ready?"

"Now, I am."

We get to the door and the bouncer looks at us, then unhooks the rope.

"Why did you get us?" Lizzy asks.

"Callum heard you were here and didn't want you both waiting outside."

My stomach flips and my pulse quickens. Suddenly, my lips are drier than the Sahara Desert, so I lick them, expecting to see him waiting for us when we walk in, but he's not there.

"You two have a good night." The man walks away, leaving Lizzy and me standing in the hall. Lizzy looks ready to party and I feel slightly dumbfounded and let down.

"Ok then," she says, looking around. "Bar or dance floor?"

"Bar."

EVERLEE - YOU SHOULD NEVER KISS A STRANGER IN THE DARK

NERVES COURSE THROUGH ME, like lightning trapped in a tube. I forgot about the guys for a second when we were waiting outside, because I was focused on that bridal hussy, but now it's just us, the music, and my thoughts. Callum knows I'm here. What does that mean? Why did he pull me out of line?

I feel myself being sucked down the dark and twisted hole I used to frequent with dickface. The hole that left me broken and achy inside, and doubting myself.

We walk to the bar and I automatically look for Emmett. When I don't see him, I'm equal parts sad and relieved because I want to see his beautiful face while at the same time, I don't.

"This isn't a good idea," I mumble to Lizzy. My hands are getting clammy and I feel a light sheen of perspiration glaze over my body.

"Let's just have a few drinks, then we'll leave. What time is your flight tomorrow?"

"Three in the afternoon."

"Thank you for clarifying in the afternoon. Without that, I may have thought you booked an unreasonably early flight in the morning." She looks at me coolly and I roll my eyes. She claps and continues, "This works out perfectly, though. You can get wasted and come home with me!"

"Lizzy..."

"What?" She pushes her way through the bar. "Two lemon drop shots-"

"And two pineapple martinis?" the bartender finishes. She's cute and edgy with a pixie haircut which has a fade on one side and streaks of purple and blue colored through-out. Her eyebrow, nose and lip are pierced, with several small tattoos scattered around her arms, neck and chest. "Haven't seen you here in a few weeks."

Confused, I start to answer before I'm cut off by Lizzy, "Yea. It's been super busy at work."

"Where's Tony tonight?"

"He's with his brother and sister."

"You should have told them to come here." She hands us the shots, then starts on the martinis. "Is his sister as attractive as he is?"

Listening to their conversation, I feel so completely out of the loop. It's only been a couple of months, but it also feels like a lifetime. The world did not stop moving when I holed myself up in my apartment and now here I am, feeling lost in my own skin.

"Low, I thought you were seeing that other chick. Rosy or something like that."

She sighs. "Yea. It fizzled out last week." She looks at me. "Who's your friend?"

"This is Everlee, but she loves cock. Everlee, this is Harlow."

"Bummer. Well, nice to meet you, Everlee. I've heard so much about you."

I panic for a moment, and Lizzy puts her hand on my arm. "Guilty. I may have told her all about you."

"Hopefully not everything." I smile. Like the part where I used to fuck all the owners of this club, I think to myself.

"No. Just the embarrassing parts."

"Perfect." I laugh. "Nice to meet you, Harlow."

"You can call me Low."

I smile as she hands us our drinks.

"Tab?"

"Yes, please," Lizzy says before we walk away.

I've already glanced up to the second floor three times, looking for any sign of Jax, Knox, Callum, or Emmett, but haven't seen them. I grab Lizzy's arm. "Let's sit over there." I point to the far corner of the room. From these seats, it will make it difficult to see anyone on the top floor.

The air is warm, and the lights dance all around us as the bass pumps through the air. A woman walks by in a black corset and black bunny ears and asks if we want a shot. It's some sort of liquid in a chocolate Easter egg shot glass. I, of course, have to try it.

"It's our special recipe. One of the owners created it," the woman chimes.

Emmett.

My heart aches.

"I'll take two then," I say, grabbing another off the tray. If Emmett made them, I know they're going to be dangerously good.

I tilt the first back and let out a moan. It's heaven. Some sort of vanilla vodka paired with the milk chocolate egg.

"Damn. Emmett knows what he's doing," Lizzy chimes, biting a piece of the egg.

"He does." There's a long silence between us, and then curiosity gets the better of me. "Have you seen them?"

"Not tonight."

"But you have other nights?"

She nods slowly.

I want to ask her if they've asked about me, but I can't get the words out. I want to know, but at the same time, don't. With a quick motion, I knock back the other shot and savor the vanilla and chocolate flavors. "Want to go dance?"

"Would love to," she peeps.

We walk onto the dance floor, and I fight the urge to look up again. Instead, I let the music flow through me, closing my eyes, and just let all the worry and pain go. The buzz from the drinks paired with the music thumping through my body makes me feel great.

I watched a show once that talked about how the beat of the music was extremely important to ensuring the dancer is having the best experience. Before the show, I'd never realized how much science went into EDM music.

"Hey girls!" An unfamiliar voice calls and I open my eyes to see a shirtless man wearing black satin boxers, a bow tie, and some bunny ears dancing over to us with absolutely no rhythm. He has golden blond shaggy locks and green eyes that look a little glassy, but his smile seems genuine.

"Hey there." I smile.

"My buddy's having a party up in VIP and wants some hot girls up there. You want to go up? There are free drinks."

"Yea!" Lizzy says, pumping her fist into the air without even looking at me.

I look at her curiously.

"Cool. My name is Mark."

"Hi, Mark. I'm Lizzy and this is Everlee!" she leans over and yells in his ear.

"Everlee. That's a cool name."

"Thanks!" I smile, cautiously. It always feels so weird having guys just walk up to you at the bar. I always feel guarded, which is probably why I haven't found anyone since dickface. It could also be because I'm looking in the wrong places.

"This will be fun!" Lizzy cheers.

Yeah. Fun for who? I'm trying to avoid seeing them and now I'm going to the place they will probably be. *Are you really trying to avoid them, though? You came to the club they own, to not see them?*

"Let's do this!" I should just go find them, say hello and get this over with. We could still be friends. Be civil. It's not like we dated for very long.

Long.

A memory of taking Callum's long cock in my mouth while the other guys watched flashes before me. Get it together, Everlee!

We follow Mark to the set of stairs, where he thumbs over his shoulder, letting the bouncer know we're with him.

Once upstairs, there are streamers and balloons all over the place with two enormous balloons with the numbers three and five. I quickly scan the floor, but still don't see any sign of my guys.

Lizzy grabs my hand and gives it a light, encouraging squeeze.

"Come to the dance floor. I'll introduce you to the birthday boy!" Mark calls out.

We follow him through the crowd to a man who is dancing with two other women. Mark taps him on the shoulder. "Hey Rich. I brought two more up."

My stomach drops.

Rich turns around and standing in front of me is Dick.

Lizzy looks from me to him, back to me.

"Everlee?" He smiles, leaning forward to give me a hug.

I awkwardly accept it, but don't return it. He moves to give Lizzy a hug, but she stiff arms him. "No, thanks."

"You know them? Wild!" Mark says, before mindlessly flitting away to go back downstairs.

"We can leave," I offer, thumbing over my shoulder.

"No. Don't be silly. Stay! Drinks are free up here!" Dick smiles while he continues to dance.

I study him for a minute, then turn to look at Lizzy.

She looks at him. "I will stay for the free drinks, but I'm not singing happy birthday to you."

Dick chuckles. "That's fair." His gaze settles on me. "You look good, Everlee."

"She knows!" Lizzy barks back.

He laughs, "I see you're protective as ever." He winks at me, then turns back to the girls and continues dancing.

"Let's get a drink," Lizzy mumbles and grabs my hand.

She drags me behind her as we move across the floor to the bar, and I can't help but glance over my shoulder to look at Dick. Of all the things I thought would happen tonight, ending up at Dick's birthday party never made the list. The last time I'd seen him was a few days after the Valentine's gala when he showed up at my doorstep and tried to get me to give him another chance. He said he was going to win me back, but it's been radio silence. It's probably a good thing, because I would have slipped. Not because I wanted to get back with him, but because I was sad and horny and he's someone I know. It would only be to fuck him, but that would open the door and I didn't feel like dealing with that baggage.

A squeal catches my attention and I turn to find Bridezilla dancing with Dick. I guess flies are attracted to shit, so it makes sense they'd find each other. They grind and dance, their hands moving in places they probably shouldn't be.

"I guess some things never change," Lizzy groans, staring at Dick.

"Good luck to that woman's groom," I grumble.

"Want to go dance? On the opposite side of the floor from him?"

"Sure."

We sit our empty glasses on the bar and walk, hand in hand, to the other side of the dance floor. All the other times I'd been up here, it had just been a few of us. It's weird to see it so busy, but I'm happy for them. The club looks like it's doing really well.

The song changes, just as we get on the floor, and it must be a popular song, because suddenly the floor is packed. A man pushes his way between Lizzy and me and starts dancing with us. I try not to think too much and just move my body, letting the beat take control.

A moment later, I feel a hand on my side. I lean back and close my eyes, dancing with this stranger, moving my hips, rubbing against him. I just want to have fun and let go of everything. Callum, Jax, Knox, Emmett, Dick.

The man's hand slips up to my waist, then back down to my hip. My body feels electrified right now. It's humming. The vibration from the bass and the drinks are probably helping. His head drops beside my face as he continues to grind into me. Our bodies moving together in perfect rhythm. It feels so right. So perfect. I snake my hand around his neck, holding him in place as his fingers fumble with my hair, moving it out of the way. His lips gently kiss my neck and a moan escapes my lips. I try not to cringe and ruin this moment. This is the first time in months I feel... free... happy. He smiles against my throat as he continues to nibble and suck on my fevered skin.

I turn my head to find his lips just as the lights go out, but our lips still connect. The kiss starts off soft, cautious, then quickly turns into something more. His tongue brushes across my lips and I open, letting our tongues dance. Needing more, I fully turn around, so I'm facing him chest to chest.

I want more.

I need more.

The crowd starts to sing happy birthday, but I don't care about anything but these lips on mine right now. It's like everything around us fades to black and white and it's just me and this stranger. These lips. This kiss. My insides tighten as I melt into him.

The song finishes and the lights click back on. I pull away and look at the man I've been kissing.

His bright blue eyes are on my face with a smile tugging on his lips while his hand rests on my cheek.

EVERLEE - MAKING UP... FOR LOST TIME

MY THROAT CLOSES, TRAPPING any words that I could and would say. Mouth hanging open, I blink twice, as if the man in front of me is a blurry image and I'm trying to make him clear.

"Everlee." His thumb gently caresses my cheekbone, sending a shiver down my spine.

"Callum," I breathe, reflexively pressing into his hand. "I should have known..."

He chuckles as his eyes settle on my face. "You kissed me first," he defends.

I push against him, his hard muscles twitching under my palm. "I don't think so, buddy. You were kissing my neck."

He lets out a low hum, tilting his head to the side in a flirtatious grin that makes my chest tighten. "I suppose that's true."

I can't help but smile looking at him. He's just as sexy as the last time I saw him, with maybe a few more strands of silver threaded through his dark hair.

"Are you here with Rich?" The inflection in his voice when he says Rich makes me smile.

"No. Some guy brought us up for his friend's birthday. Turned out to be Dick's, and he invited us to stay for the free drinks."

He hums, grabbing my hand and guiding me over to a booth in the corner. I catch Lizzy's eye, so she knows where I am, and her face glows with a shit-eating grin.

"How have you been?" he asks, sitting beside me, with his hand comfortably resting on my thigh.

"Good," I answer breathlessly. "You?"

His eyes bore holes into me, like he's trying to listen to my thoughts. Listen to the words I'm not saying.

The truth.

That I've been absolutely miserable these last few months.

The touch of his hand sets off a chain reaction in my body, like a symphony of sensations- my skin is on fire and my stomach clenches. "I've been better," he admits, and I can't help but wonder if I have something to do with that.

Shrugging, I admit, "I guess I've been better, as well."

His hand slides up my leg and a wanting breath escapes from between my lips, but he stops.

"Callum," I cry softly, begging him to continue. I want to feel his touch. Feel his lips.

"Everlee," his voice cracks.

He looks torn, so I place my hand on the side of his cheek and his eyes close slowly, savoring the feel of my touch. He turns his lips and presses them into the palm of my hand. "God, I miss the taste of you," he mumbles, more to himself than to me.

"So... fix it." I encourage.

His eyes shoot to mine as he holds my gaze for a moment.

"Come with me." Standing up from the couch, he makes his way towards a door nestled in the corner, the beat of the music matching the thump in my chest. He pulls his retractable ID from his clip and swipes it against the pad and pushes the door open. As soon as he pulls me in, he presses me against the door as his lips eagerly take mine. His hands tangle in my hair as need consumes him, like he can't get enough of my feel.

A moan escapes as my hands feverishly rake across his body, sliding his jacket off and fumbling with the buttons on his shirt.

"Everlee." He warns, his hands holding my wrists.

"Please. Just this once. I need you."

He swallows and moves his hands back to my corset and unties the ribbons in the front before painfully unhooking each of the clasps. I slip his shirt off and pull back from our kiss so I can admire his beautifully tattooed torso. I kiss his chest and hear him suck in a breath between his teeth.

His hands continue with the hooks. So many fucking hooks! I unhook the ones between my legs and slide the corset the rest of the way down. I'm standing in front of him completely naked, seconds later.

"Fuck Everlee. You're a goddamn vision." He moves in quickly and takes a breast in his mouth, while his hand cups the other. "And I see no panties again." He says in between switching breasts.

"Didn't really go with the outfit."

"No. I guess they don't," he says, dropping to his knees and throwing my leg over his shoulder. A second later, his tongue is swiping up my pussy from back to front before he plunges his tongue in.

"Callum," I moan out, pressing my back against the door, eyes fluttering up to the ceiling as the muscles in my body clench.

"I've missed your moans too."

"I've missed your mouth on my pussy," I say, tangling my fingers in his hair. He wraps his arms around me tightly and stands up, sliding me up the door. Throwing my other leg over his shoulder, I grip his head as he carries me to the couch, mesmerized by the ripple of the muscles in his back with each step. He lays back, so my knees press into the couch beside his cheeks.

"Fuck my face, Everlee."

A shiver runs through my body as I move my hips, relishing the sensation of his tongue exploring me. His groans of pleasure urge me to move faster, while his hand reaches around my leg to find my clit. The gentle pressure as he rubs in circles electrifies me to the core, like he's flipped a switch inside of me.

"Fuck Callum." I'm so close. My hands grip into his hair as I continue to gyrate on his face.

BEEP!

We freeze.

The door is unlocking.

Shit! Shit! Shit!

My clothes are across the room and there's nothing I can use to cover myself.

"Callum? Have you seen Ever-"

Jax.

Fuck me. He looks hot as ever.

He closes the door and looks at us, a smile tugging on his lips. "I guess that answers my question. Enjoying yourself, love?"

"Yes." I nod, removing my hands from my chest.

His teeth scrape across his bottom lip as his eyes rake across my naked body.

Feeling extra bold and high on desire, I ask, "Do you want to watch or do you want to join?"

"What do you want?" he asks, tilting his head to the side.

Smiling, I say, "I want your cock in my mouth while Callum fucks my pussy."

"I see your mouth isn't any less filthy," Jax says, running his hand over the growing bulge in his pants.

"No." I rock on Callum's face again as he continues rubbing my clit. Running my hands over my breasts, I look at the ceiling and moan out. "I'm going to come, Callum." I was almost there before the door opened, and now having Jax watch me is like adding fuel to the fire.

When I look at Jax, his eyes are almost animalistic. Wild.

"Oh, fuck!" I cry out.

Callum grabs both of my legs, pulling me down on his face, tongue spearing me as I ride out my orgasm. The seductive, wet sounds of my juices unleash a torrent of desire within me, much like a dam breaking free. My heart is pounding and my body is on fire as he holds me there, eagerly lapping all he can as my pussy pulses around his tongue.

"I've fucking missed you," I growl, pushing off his face.

"Samesies." Jax says, walking over with his hand, stroking his cock.

"Ass." Climbing off Callum, I meet Jax in the middle of the room. I shove against his hard chest, but he grabs me by the throat, his eyes locked on mine before he claims my mouth with his. He pushes us towards Callum, who's waiting on the couch, slowly stroking himself.

Jax pulls away from our kiss, but his hand remains clamped under my jaw. "I can't wait to feel your lips around my cock. It's missed you." He kisses me one more time, then drops his hand.

"Do you have a condom?" I turn to Callum. "I don't need your come dripping down my leg the rest of the night."

It's been two months without them and yet it feels like it's been days... hours even. Slipping in right where we left off. Everything just feels so right... so natural with them. Even from the second I felt Callum's hand on me on the dance floor before I knew it was him.

He smiles. "I guess." He flicks his hand up with a condom pressed between his index and middle finger. "Though I would love to see my release all over you, and for everyone to know, I just fucked you."

He slips the condom on and, without hesitation, I climb on top of him and sink down, letting him fill me. It's been months since I've had an actual dick inside of me, so it takes a minute to stretch around him. But he feels like heaven. A tingle moves up my spine as my body appreciates this feeling.

"Goddamn you're so tight."

"I've not had sex in a while." I look at him and his chin tilts up.

"Then let's give you all we have tonight." His hands clamp around my legs, pulling me down further onto his cock while he slowly rocks his hips, pressing deep inside of me. My pussy feels tight, appreciating the full size of his cock, and my skin tingles with excitement as desire pulses through me.

"You feel so good," I whimper, running my fingers over my body, meeting Jax's gaze with a satisfied smile.

He walks over and wraps his hand around the back of my head and guides me towards his cock. No words, just lust and need fill the air. Wrapping my fingers around the base one at a time, I run my tongue up the underside before swirling it around his head, licking the arousal off the tip. I suck just the head into my mouth, while I continue to rock on Callum, savoring the taste, the feel of both of them.

This is definitely not how I pictured my night going when I left work this afternoon.

"You're teasing me," Jax growls.

Looking up at him, I suck him into my mouth, taking him as deep as I can. A nonverbal dare for him to say something else. His eyes roll into the back of his head before he looks at me with a smile curling on his lips. With a firm grip, I stroke his cock up and down, cheeks hollowing out around him, never breaking eye contact. I want to watch him watch me. I want to see the fire in his eyes. The longing to have my lips around him.

"Damn Everlee." His hand grips tighter in my hair as his hips rock into me, hitting the back of my throat.

He is perfection. His teeth clamp tight on his bottom lip as his eyes remain locked on mine. Drinking me up.

Callum's finger rubs on my clit, eliciting another moan from me, this time around Jax's cock. Wanting to feel Callum fuck me from underneath, I barely press up on my knees, hovering over him. I need him to claim me.

"Do you want it hard, Everlee?" Callum asks, as if reading my thoughts.

I hum a yes.

"Hold up Jax. Let's change," Callum commands.

Jax sighs and pulls away, wiping his finger across my lips before taking my mouth in a quick kiss.

"Jax," Callum warns.

"Sorry. I just missed her lips." With a playful wink, he sends a jolt of anticipation through me, causing my stomach to tighten and my insides to melt.

I'm a pile of mush. Put a pin in me, I'm done.

Callum points for Jax to stand at the end of the couch. I get up on all fours and Callum moves around behind me. "There. Now I can fuck you the way you deserve to be fucked." Callum lines up his cock at my entrance before plunging into me.

A grunt escapes and a trickle of pain radiates through me as he pushes in deep, but I don't care. I love the feel of him. His hands grip onto my hips and I push back, my body needing more. "Harder," I assert. I don't wait for him to speak before I grab Jax and bring him to my mouth. A deep swell of passion, of fire, races through me. I've missed these guys with every fiber of my being and I was so stupid for walking away.

It takes a couple of thrusts, but we get into a rhythm where Jax and Callum are fucking me from both ends.

"That's my good girl," Callum says, running his hand down my spine.

Like a cat looking for affection, my back arches as my ass lifts into the air.

"Our good girl," Jax corrects.

My eyes flutter as my stomach clenches. Their words are going to make me come before their cocks do. Why did I ever leave them? We can find a way to make this work. They are worth it and so are their cocks.

Jax's hands clamp tighter in my hair, holding me in place. He's getting close and so am I.

"Callum?" Jax asks.

"Almost."

Callum's hand slips around my hip and begins circling my clit. "She's so fucking wet, I keep slipping."

"You're out of practice, brother."

Out of practice? Does that mean they haven't slept with anyone either? No. That can't be. No. I'm thinking too much and just need to focus on them. On right now.

"Come on, baby. Come for me." Callum changes the angle of his thrusts, rubbing on all the right spots as his speed picks up.

"Give her what she wants," Jax hums, rocking into me.

A second later, something wet hits my back, then I feel Callum's finger swipe over my tight hole.

Fuck.

"Oh, she's getting excited," Jax says.

A garbled groan escapes at the same time Callum slips his finger in. I clench around Callum's cock and squeeze onto Jax's.

"Shit!" Jax shouts before a warm saltiness explodes in my mouth, but I don't let up on the thrusts, hollowing my cheeks out around him. "Damn it, Everlee!" He spits, frustrated that I made him break his rule.

A second later, I release Jax and he rubs his hand over his cock, watching us finish. Callum's other hand moves around to my clit and he circles. Am I holding myself back from my orgasm because I don't want this to end?

"Your tits look so perfect," Jax says, watching them swing, fire still in his eyes.

"Here, brother." Callum sits back, bringing me with him, so I'm sitting on his lap with my back pressed to his chest.

"Yes." Jax walks over and sits on the couch in front of us. Callum pauses, letting me sink on him while Jax takes my neck in his mouth, biting and sucking. His one hand plays with my nipple while the other slides down and begins rubbing my clit. Soft, slow.

I slowly grind my hips against Callum, savoring the intimate connection.

"You like that?" Jax asks.

"Mmhmm." I let my head fall to the side, giving him more access.

"You want more of this?"

"Yes."

He pinches my nipple between his fingers, causing a ripple of pain mixed with pleasure to move down my body to between my legs. I rock faster as Jax's finger presses harder on my clit while he leans down and takes a breast in his mouth.

"You should have never left us Everlee," Callum says.

"I know. I'm sorry."

And I *am* sorry. Fear of getting hurt made me walk away, but that fixed nothing. I still hurt these last two months, and had no sex. Stupid me.

"She's getting close," Callum says, pressing his hands to my legs, holding me down so he can grind further into me.

Jax's finger moves faster as he sucks my breast, rubbing his teeth over my nipple.

"Fuck!" I cry out. My orgasm hits me hard. A low grumble echoes from deep inside as Jax's mouth slides over mine, swallowing the noises falling from my mouth. With two final pumps, Callum finishes, leaving me feeling like a limp noodle. Jax's kiss changes from hard and fast to slower and more passionate.

I whimper out one more time and Jax pulls back and swipes his thumb across my bottom lip. "Beautiful." He gives me a quick peck on the end of my nose before walking over to the desk.

After I climb off Callum, I walk across the room to grab the tissue from Jax.

"Well, Knox and Emmett are going to be pissed," Jax huffs, pulling his pants back up and fixing his belt.

I scrunch my face. "How are they?"

"They miss you. They kept hoping you would stop by Bo's on Mondays."

"We all missed you," Callum corrects, walking over, grabbing another tissue.

"I missed you guys, too," I admit, grabbing my outfit near the door and sliding it back on. "I just... I knew you had your rules, and we were technically done."

"Technically?"

"What happened to rules are meant to be broken?" Jax asks.

"I wanted the rules to be broken..." I adjust the bunny ears on my head. "I was scared you all didn't and... that was going to hurt. And then the other part of me was scared you wanted to change the rules, but even then, wouldn't because of societal pressures. And then there was–is– my family."

Callum and Jax both watch me move across the room to stand in front of the mirror. My eyes meet theirs behind me and my heart tightens in my chest. Blinking hard, I look at my reflection and give my lips a soft rub. They're swollen, just fucked lips. There's no way I'll be able to hide this from Lizzy. Hopefully, she can keep her composure and not make a big fuss in front of everyone.

I look between the both of them.

"Are you drooling?" Jax asks.

"Shut up." I laugh. "I was just trying to figure out how mental I was to walk away from you all."

Jax chuckles. "We were all fighting each other, trying not to knock down your door and bring you back to us. There were a few times we were close."

"You were outside of my office a couple of weeks ago, weren't you?"

"No!" Callum spits too quickly, looking guilty.

"Callum?" Jax warns.

"Fine. I wasn't going to kidnap you... I think. I just wanted to see you." He turns to Jax. "It's not like you weren't camped out in front of her apartment for several nights," Callum tattles.

Jax's lips pucker.

"Well, I visited Lizzy a couple of times and showed up early and waited outside, in hopes you'd be driving down the road at the same time and see me." I point. "You didn't, so I sat there freezing my ass off." I laugh, awkwardly.

"You could have always come down to Vixen, like you did tonight."

"I could have, but I was scared. I almost didn't come tonight."

"Glad we could help." They wink.

I smile. "Well, that kind of come... yes, thank you... but..."

"Does Lizzy know about us?"

I scrunch my nose. I don't know what prompts the question. Perhaps she had said or done something one of the times she was here?

"We couldn't be mad at you if we wanted," Callum offers, trying to coax the answer from me.

"After everything happened, I needed to talk to someone. I made her sign an NDA, though, if that makes it better."

Callum shakes his head, smiling. "Well, that's something."

"Speak of the devil..." Jax says, looking at the cameras just before a knock thumps on the door.

"Lizzy?" I ask Jax before walking over.

He nods.

I open the door and she peeks her head in before stepping in. "Wanted to make sure you dirty fuckers were all dressed. Although I wouldn't hate to see what you hide under those shirts." She points at Jax and Callum with a devious smile.

"Lizzy..." I blush.

"Hello Lizzy," Jax drones, face lacking amusement.

"Guys." She nods to them both before running her hand from my cheek to chin. "Thank you for taking care of her. She needed a good fuck."

"Lizzy!" I snap.

"She really does have a gift." Jax smiles, impressed.

"It can be a pain in the ass sometimes."

"Oh, but you love me."

"Yes. I do."

"Are you ready to go?" she asks.

"Yes." I look longingly at Jax and Callum. What do I say? Where do we go from here?

Callum walks over and slips his arm around me, giving me a kiss on the top of my head. "We need to talk, but the next couple of days aren't good. Are you free next week?"

I meet Jax's intense gaze, his eyes locked onto mine.

"Yes. I'm free."

"Perfect. We'll call to set up a time." Callum puts his hands in his front pockets.

"So formal," I tease.

"We could just kidnap you if you prefer?" Jax smiles.

"Kinky."

He shakes his head.

"You girls have a good rest of the night. Your tab from downstairs has been comped," Callum informs.

"You didn't have to do that." Lizzy bats her hand in the air.

Callum winks at me. "Have a good night."

Lizzy and I walk out of their office and down the stairs. I ignore the glance from dickface as he watches us leave their office, no doubt wondering what was happening in there.

"Queen." Lizzy grabs my arm when we get outside.

I blush again, laughing awkwardly.

"Quueeenn."

"Stop."

"Well, I'm glad you got some dick tonight."

"It was so good, Lizzy."

"I take it you got both."

I smile.

"I try not to be a jealous woman, but damn girl. You got me in my feels."

Betty pulls up before I can respond. As I step into the car, I look back at Vixen one more time.

"Did you both have a lovely night?"

"Yes, we did," Lizzy answers for both of us, fortunately not elaborating.

I decide to stay at my house since I'm not drunk, plus it would give me more time to think about our meeting next week. Fortunately, I'll be out of town for the long weekend to spend some time with my family. Maybe I can figure out a way to talk to them about this and see where they stand. Time by the lake always seems to help set my mind right, and I need it after tonight.

No Vixen. No Lizzy. No Guys.

CALLUM - WHEN YOU FUCK THE FORBIDDEN FRUIT, DON'T TRUST JAX NOT TO TOSS A GRENADE

Walking behind the desk, I flip to the screen to watch Lizzy and Everlee leave. Jax sits on the couch, legs parted with his hands dangling over his knees, and chuckles coolly.

His eyes glance up to meet mine. "The boys are going to be pissed they weren't here tonight."

I smack my lips. "Yea. But fuck. I saw her." I sigh. "At first I didn't really know it was her and then I did and then... so many thoughts..." I say, trying to formulate a sentence. "Why was she here? Up here with him? I knew it was her ex as soon as I saw him show up tonight for the party. But then, the way he was dancing with all those girls, there was no way they were together."

"So you did what any rational person would have done and walked over to her and invited her into the office for some kinky fuckery?"

"Not exactly." A flurry of emotions tear through me and all I can do is hit the table. "She's like a fucking drug. I don't get it. Why can't I just walk away from her? Ever since I saw her that first night when we opened."

"Sounds like you have it bad..."

"Don't say that. I don't. I can't." Right? Falling for the girl isn't allowed. Sure, we all like to fuck them, but is that what Everlee is? I slap myself in the head because I know that's not the case. She's more than that.

"What are you going to tell the boys?" Jax asks.

"Me? You aren't innocent in this." I huff.

"Mine was more by happenstance. I walked in on you two."

"Fuck."

"I mean, I'm not mad." He walks over to the door. "She looked good."

"That fucking bunny costume." I smile, shaking my head. I've always had a weakness for costumes.

"That, too. I mean, she always looks fucking delicious, but I don't know. Something else about her... she just seemed good. Strong. Confident. She's always had a bit of that, but there was always a fractured piece of her you could see behind her eyes. I don't really see that anymore."

"Yea, I noticed it too." I sigh. "I want to call her so fucking bad."

"Don't. Not yet."

"What if she changes her mind and doesn't meet with us?"

Jax laughs. "Then we will go kidnap her."

"We were close a couple of times before, weren't we?" I tease.

"We had to make sure she was ok," he tries to justify.

It's been hell since we walked out of her apartment two months ago. We went to get her back after we got her note, but I realized when we were talking to her how selfish we were being. She's close to her family, and asking her to give them up... we couldn't do that. It was infuriating, but it was the right thing. The rule breaker was the one following the rules.

It's easier for us. We have no family. We are our family. With all our parents either dead, unknown, or not wanting anything to do with us, it makes our lifestyle easy. She's not like us, though. They are an enormous chunk of her life and to ask her to live two separate lives... it wasn't fair.

So we left.

It was the hardest fucking thing we ever did.

The ache. The physical pain of not being around her. Seeing her. Talking to her. That was all real.

I turn back to the cameras hoping to get one more glimpse of her, but she's gone. If it wasn't for the taste of her on my lips, I would think I dreamed her up tonight. My mind twists in torture, coming up with a list of reasons she won't answer our call or texts.

That night, when Jax and I get home, Knox and Emmett are on the roof.

"Hey boys. How was the night?" Emmett asks, his arms spread on either side of the hot tub.

Jax takes his clothes off and slips in, while I walk over to the bar and pour me a bourbon neat.

"That bad?" Knox asks.

"I'll let Callum tell you."

I roll my eyes, but no one sees, then turn around and pull up a seat by the hot tub. "We saw her tonight."

"Everlee?" They both ask, sitting up. Body tense. Brows raised.

"Yes."

"How did she look? Was she with anyone?" Knox asks with a hint of worry weaved through his words.

"She looked... fucking fantastic. She was wearing this satin bunny corset outfit with these bunny ears. It was sexy as fuck."

"I meant, how did she seem?"

"Good." I lift the glass to my lips and let the warmness of the bourbon burn down the back of my throat.

"Callum fucked her." Jax drops the grenade.

The boy's eyes expand in shock as they nearly climb out of the water.

"Thanks, Jax," I say deadpan. "He was there too."

"You both got to?" Emmett nearly whines.

"It wasn't planned. It just sort of happened," I retort.

Knox bats the water. "Damn it! I knew I should have been there tonight!"

"If you booked our flights like you said you did a couple of months ago, then you wouldn't have had to scramble."

"Thank you, daddy." Knox pumps his eyebrows.

I shiver. "Don't."

"Did you get us tickets?" Jax asks, ignoring Knox's feeble attempt to get under his skin.

"One better. Our buddy, Mr. Michael Dufrey, has a little plane he uses for some of his contract work," Knox says in an all-to-proud voice.

Michael did a tour with Jax, Knox, and Brady and currently works as a contractor handling off the books government ops or private sector ops. He reached out to Jax several times to bring him in on a mission, but Jax always declined. He never approached Knox, which I don't think bothered him. While Jax and Knox both served together, they were cut from a different cloth. Knox is too much of a lover and an overall optimist. Jax... is not. He does a good job hiding it, but...

"He's ok letting us use it this weekend?" Jax asks, interrupting my thoughts.

"Yea. He's on another mission with a buddy, so he won't be needing it."

"Good job, Knox." Jax bats his hand across the water, sending it into Knox's face.

"Thank you, Daddy." He claws at the air playfully and Jax shakes his head.

Emmett interjects. "We aren't done talking about Everlee. Don't think you two can try to change the topic. You fucked her. Seriously?"

"She's coming over next week to talk through things."

"This is going to be the longest fucking weekend," he groans.

"But we get to see Mrs. Mary and celebrate all of her contributions to the community," I say, trying to cheer him up.

Mrs. Mary is the foster mother who raised us. Loved us. Emmett is probably the closest to her, sharing her love of cooking. He would always stay back to help her in the kitchen or clean around the house. He latched onto her and never let go. She's probably the reason he's such an excellent cook today, finding that spark within him and fanning it until it burst into a flame. It's the same things she did with all of her children. She never once let the fact we were her foster children stop her from loving us fully and giving us everything we could ever want or need.

He smiles. "That will be nice. I haven't been checking in with her as much since opening Bo's. I can't wait to tell her all about it."

The room falls to a natural hush as we all escape to different thoughts. Once I finish my drink, I clean out the glass and put it back on its shelf, before saying goodnight to the men. I'm tired, but more than that, I'm mentally exhausted. Since I saw Everlee, it's like my brain hasn't stopped flipping through all the possibilities of our conversation next week.

"So early?" Jax asks, holding his arm to the water.

"I'm heading by the club in the morning to work with Low. I want to make sure she's ready for tomorrow night."

"How's she working out?" Emmett asks.

"You did good. She's smart and works hard. Also, doesn't take shit from anyone." He nods, satisfied.

After my shower, I lay in bed mindlessly flipping through the pages on my e-reader as my thoughts drift back to Everlee, and that kiss, and her pussy- the taste, the feel.

I'm getting hard with each passing second and before I know it, I'm grabbing lube out of my drawer and pumping my cock as images of her float around in my head moving so fast from one to the other that it's like my personal porno video. The same and only video I've been watching since she walked out. It wasn't that I couldn't find anyone else, because plenty of girls have made passes at the club, but I didn't *want* anyone else, and maybe on some level I thought, rather, hoped, this was not over with us.

With another pump and a jerk, I cover my chest and hand in my come. After a minute passes, I climb out of bed and head to the shower for a quick rinse and again, memories flood my mind.

Fuck!

I just need to get through this weekend, I encourage myself.

EVERLEE—HOME SWEET HOME

THE SPRING SUN WARMS my face when I step outside of the airport. Closing my eyes and tilting my head up towards the sky, I soak in the rays and feel the temperature on my skin. It's at least twenty degrees warmer here than it was at home yesterday, which in part is because of the weather system moving through, but also because I'm further south. Warmer weather and humidity. My shoulders give a light shake to the thin cape of moisture that has settled around me.

A flurry of people walk up and down the sidewalk, looking for their ride among the row of cars lined up. Stepping forward and leaning over the curb, I look for my brother in the sea of cars. Not finding him, I shift my carry-on bag to pull my phone out of my back pocket to text him at the same time a horn honks, and a silver SUV speeds to a stop in front of me. Sitting in the driver's seat is Beckett and his mop of brown hair, wearing a schmedium mint green shirt, hugging his chest and biceps tightly, with some logo on it. I don't recognize it, but that's the case most of the time now, since he makes his own shirts. He got a Cricut for Christmas and now designs all sorts of logos and designs for shirts, cups, laptops, and anything else he can put stickers on. If I get one more cup that has my name on it, I'm going to scream!

"Get in the car! It's freezing!" He yells through his passenger window, rubbing his hands together for extra emphasis.

Laughing and rolling my eyes, I walk around to his trunk and wait for him to open it. I toss my bags into the immaculate space and can't help but compare it to Lizzy's wreck of a space. My luggage barely fit in Lizzy's and here in Beckett's, it's sprawled out like a starfish on the beach.

When I climb into the passenger's seat, I reach across to give him a hug. After a moment, he pulls back and runs his hands around my hair and cheeks, then asks without hesitation, "Who's the man?"

Fucking two of them. I can't escape their sex wizardry. "Who's your man? You seem extra giddy and these muscles. Hubba hubba." I fire back, squeezing his arms.

"Oh stop. We're not talking about any guys I'm seeing. We're talking about you right now."

"Why?"

"You've been fucked recently."

"Are you kidding me right now? Do I have 'ask me about my sex life' stamped across my forehead?"

He stares at me down his nose without speaking.

All I can do is shake my head and look out of the window, as memories from last night replay in my mind. The buzz on my skin under his touch, his lips on me, his cock inside of me... Jax.

"You tell me now, or I'm calling Lizzy. I just talked to her two days ago, and she said nothing."

"You talked to Lizzy?"

"Don't change the topic!" He bats the air. "Who is it?" He grabs my arm gasping, "Oh please tell me you haven't gone back to dickface."

"God no!"

"Lizzy said he tried to reconnect after Valentine's."

"Yes, but I shut him down. That is never happening again. Be sure of that."

"Praise Jesus! I didn't want to have to kill a man on Easter weekend."

"You're too much. And again, why were you talking to Lizzy?"

"We talk all the time. Mostly about boys and fashion, and recently about you."

"What about me?"

A car blares its horn behind us, urging us along to the exit.

"Oh, fine!" he yells, waving his hand in the air before turning out.

He cranks up the volume on the music as we pull onto the road, but I quickly turn it back down. "Uh-huh buddy. Spill."

He lets out a dramatic sigh, flopping his hands around. "She was just worried about you and told me to help you get some dick this weekend since you haven't had any for a while, but looking at you, I can see she was mistaken. Which never happens."

I reach over and turn the volume back up, and look out of the window. The thinned trees lining the road reveal hints of the wet marsh just behind it. Some trees are starting to bloom and fill in, but it's still pretty spotty. It's nice being home, but I'm definitely missing the guys. I still haven't seen Emmett or Knox, and things between Jax and Callum were left... in a weird place. My stomach tightens just thinking about them. Am I really going to talk to them? Nothing has changed. I would still be picking them over my family. *Lizzy at least knows.*

No. This weekend I'm going to focus on my family, so when I see them next week, I will feel recharged. And hopefully know what in the fuck I'm going to do.

Confident we've moved past the inquisition into my sex life, I look at my brother and turn the music down. "Tell me about you. What's been going on?"

He side-eyes me cautiously.

"Oh stop. I haven't seen you all in several months. Are you still dating Cannon?"

He laughs out loud. "Cannon. God no. We were just messing around. He's not boyfriend material."

"You say that about all the boys you're with."

"Because it's the truth."

"Are you *looking* for boyfriend material?"

"Ehh." He shrugs.

"Didn't realize you were such a man whore."

"Well, someone in the family has to be. Plus, if I always have someone, then mom can't try to set me up on dates."

I pull my face. "She's still doing that."

A sly grin spreads across his face like he knows something, but won't tell me.

"Beckett. What?" I slap his arm out of reflex.

"Nothing."

"Not, nothing. I can tell by the wicked little look on your face you're hiding something from me."

His nose scrunches.

"Beckett. I swear if you don't tell me now!"

"Mom may have invited someone to this weekend's festivities for you to meet," he blurts out, bringing his fingers to his lips like he's nervously biting them.

The blood drains from my face and my hands grow clammy. I absolutely hate being set up, especially when I don't know about it and mom is the worst. Always these strait-laced types who seem to fear their own shadow. All of them from her church, which I don't have a ton against, but she doesn't seem to understand we live in different cities and have different lifestyles. "Who?" I bark out, letting some of my frustration for the situation bleed over onto Beckett.

"I don't know." He changes his voice to a higher octave to imitate our mother, "But she's going to love him. He's so handsome and a lawyer." His hands flop in the air around him like he's a little bird learning how to fly.

I roll my eyes. "Remind me what we're doing again?"

"Tomorrow we have an event hosted by the church for Mrs. Mary Mae and Sunday the church is putting together an Easter egg hunt by the lake for all the kids. Mom volun-told us, so we're hiding eggs Sunday... at like seven in the morning."

"Jesus." I wince. I hate getting up early, especially on the weekend. It should be a rule or something. The weekend is my time!

"Yea, brutal, so you can't be staying up all night banging the lawyer."

I cut my eyes at him.

He laughs. "My department is also bringing a fire truck by for the kids."

"That's fun. Are you still liking it?"

"Being a firefighter? Yes." He laughs like it's a stupid question.

"Mom still worried?"

"Every day. It's been eighteen months."

I pat his arm. "You're her baby boy."

He turns to look at me, face stone cold serious. "I need you to fuck up this weekend so you can take all the attention and give me a break. Then, after you leave, she'll be too worried about you to focus on me for at least several weeks. Try to make it huge to buy me at least a month." He overlaps his hands and rests his chin on them with a Cheshire grin.

I press my fingers together. "I'll think about it."

"If not, I will sabotage."

"You wouldn't."

"I one hundred percent would. I don't think you under-stand the severity of my situation."

"The amazing thing to me is that you're a grown ass man. You can move out of their house and into your own." I explode my hands from my head.

"Don't start that bullshit again. I have a good gig."

"Yea, you do, but you still live with mom and dad. Have you had any guys over? With them there?"

"Seems personal."

"And asking me who I've banged recently, the second my ass touches your seat, isn't?"

He puckers his lips. "Touché."

Happiness bubbles under my skin. I've missed him. This.

This is going to be a good weekend. Hopefully, it will provide clarity on what to do about the guys. Maybe I can somehow bring it up to my parents? Fear grips me. No. What am I going to say? Hey, so I'm dating four men...

Pressing my head against the window, I let the cool feeling calm my nerves as I watch the trees flick by.

Don't think about the guys this weekend. Enjoy the time with my family.

EVERLEE - HIDE YOUR PHONE WHEN YOU'RE GETTING DICK PICS

WE PULL DOWN THE long driveway, which is lined with large Spanish moss covered trees, ending at a white low country cottage house with a large wraparound front porch. The trim around the door and windows is painted black, which contrasts the white beautifully. They moved several years ago to this house, but the manicured landscape and paint still looks new. At first, I was upset because they sold my childhood home, but this is a little smaller and on the lake, which seems to fit them better.

"Are you ready?" Beckett asks, turning the car off and looking at me with an apprehensive gaze.

"I guess." I sigh.

"Mom and dad are going to be so thrilled you're visiting." He raises his voice again. "You know, she just doesn't visit as much as she used to. Breaks my heart."

"Stop. She doesn't say that."

He raises his brows with a smirk.

Smacking his arm playfully, I step out of the car and walk towards the house, focusing on the crunch of gravel under my feet. It's the one thing I can do as my stomach twists with nerves as fear trickles in. It's not like they can sense my sex habits and who I can't get off my mind.

"Don't worry, love. I'll get your bags!" Beckett shouts in a purposefully high-pitched tone, opening the trunk.

"Thank you dahhhling." I say with an accent, throwing my hands in the air.

By the time I get up the three stairs, mom is standing at the doorway with a smile plastered across her face. "You made it!" she says with her southern accent, holding out her arms. She's dressed in a white skirt, yellow gingham shirt and has pinned her light brown wavy hair just behind her ears. It's shorter than the last time I saw her, coming just above her shoulders now.

"I did." I open the screen door and lean in for a hug. Dad is walking down the hall with the newspaper tucked under his arm, wearing a similar outfit to hers. Twinning? Is that what they're doing now? "Hey dad."

"Hey Everlee. Pleasant flight?"

"Yes. Fairly easy. Are you and mom dressing the same on purpose now?" I walk in, letting the door smack shut behind me.

"Nope, all good out here. I don't need you to hold the door," Beckett teases, walking up the stairs. If it wasn't literally one duffel, I'd feel bad.

Dad chuckles. "I can see you and Becks have already started your ribbing." He shakes his head in amusement. "There was an event at the church this afternoon to kick off the weekend. All the couples had to dress alike."

Mom calls over her shoulder. "I hope you're hungry. I've got dinner on the stove."

"Yes. I didn't have a big lunch."

"I'll take your bags to your room, sis."

Wondering what he's up to, I cast a side eye at him. That little fucker better not be snooping. "Thanks, bro," I return with a slight glare in my eye, causing him to throw his head back in a fit of laughter.

"So tell me. Have you met anyone?" Mom asks, pulling my attention.

Well, that didn't last long. Two minutes. That could be a new record. "I'm not sure."

"You aren't sure if you're dating someone?"

"It's complicated."

She chuckles. "Complicated?" Her southern accent is as strong as her condescension.

Beckett said he needed me to fuck up this weekend, so dropping the bomb I've been fucking four men at the same time would definitely do it, but I just got here and don't want to get kicked out yet. "Yes." One word answer. Easy.

"Well, that's great news!" she chimes.

"It is?" I know where this is going, but do her the favor of pretending like Beckett hadn't already spilled the beans.

"I met this guy at our church. His name is Winston, and he's a lawyer." Her voice gets an octave louder with each fact she states. "He's so excited to meet you." Her hands clasp in front of her and the giddy look on her face is the equivalent of a two-year-old stomping his feet back and forth in excitement for a new toy or sugary treat.

My lips pinch in a hard line and I catch my father's gaze, who just shrugs, before he goes back to his crossword puzzle. "You know you don't have to set me up."

"You're old enough to be married and have at least one grandchild for us. Your brother won't be giving us one," she huffs with a touch of disappointment.

Pew, pew, pew! Mom coming in hot and I've just arrived. I need to shut this down, so it doesn't become a thing the entire weekend. "Mom. How do you expect me to go six weeks with no sex after I give birth?"

"Everlee," she reprimands, dropping a spoon on the ground.

"What? That's a long time. Heck, I can hardly go six hours."

"Everlee," Dad chimes in, with that deep fatherly voice to shut it down.

One sure way to get her to drop stuff is to talk about sex. She hates it.

"What did I miss?" Beckett asks, galloping down the stairs.

"Mom's already started with how I'm a disappointment because I'm old enough to be married with at least one child."

"Eesh." He checks his watch. "Ten minutes. That's a record."

"Oh, you two, stop it." She bats the air.

Beckett and I continue to riff off one another. Beckett adds, "I'm sure mom said it's your job since I can't. I mean I would, but being *a gay* doesn't allow that."

"A gay," I cringe. "Shame. You can have my baby card since yours was taken when you came out. But I can't imagine why mom would want you to have a child, anyway. You're almost thirty and still live at home."

"Hey, I resemble that."

I laugh. "Yes, yes, you do *resemble* that."

"Are you two done now?" Mom crosses her arms.

"I don't know." I pucker my lips and stare at her.

She sighs. "Fine. I'm just concerned about you both."

"We know." Beckett walks into the kitchen and grabs some plates out of the cabinet. "You tell us all the time how we should be conforming to the norms of society."

"Not the norms," she defends. "I don't care you're gay."

"Well, when you say it like that..." Beckett chuckles.

Mom's face falls. She and dad had worked hard to get where they are now after Beckett came out to them. They never stopped loving him, but they didn't know how to process everything. It helped when they had several meetings with their pastor and he was very accepting. I can't help but wonder how many meetings they'll need to have with him if they find out about my latest predicament with my guys.

"Is this how y'all are going to be all weekend?"

"Not all weekend." I walk over and wrap my arms around her shoulders from behind.

"I've missed you." She grabs my arms and gives them a light squeeze.

"Thank goodness." I walk over to the fridge to fill the glasses with sweet tea. I add more ice to mine trying to dilute the tea flavored sugar water. Since moving to the north, it had gotten more difficult to drink it when I came home and I didn't want to hear from my mother how much I'd changed.

My phone dings from the other room and I look at my watch.

Callum.

My heart flutters and my cheeks flush.

"Who was that?" Beckett whispers beside me.

"No one."

"Not no one. You got all," he bristles his shoulders to finish his sentence.

"No one," I say more firmly.

He chuckles from his chest. "Oh, now I know it's someone you don't want us to know about." He looks over his shoulder. "Hey mom," he whines in a child's tattle-tale voice, eyes still focused on me.

"You shut your fucking mouth," I seethe, punching him in the shoulder.

"Who is it?" he whispers.

"Did you need something, Becks?"

He looks at me. "No, he was just teasing me," I answer for him.

"Ok, well, it's almost time to eat."

Beckett keeps his eyes on me as we continue our stare off at one another.

I sigh. "Fine. It's a guy I've been talking to."

He shifts closer, butting his shoulder up against mine. "Like talking talking?" His eyes pump up and down quickly, then he backhands my arm. "Oh my God. Is he the one you boinked recently?"

I cut my eyes at him.

"It is." His eyes grow wide with excitement.

I smile. "Please don't say anything."

He zips his lips and throws away the imaginary key. "But we're not done talking about him."

I bobble my head from side to side.

"What did he want?"

"He was just saying he missed me."

"How sweet. When do we get to meet him?"

"Never." I laugh. He thought I was kidding. Unfortunately, I'm not. That's one of the biggest reasons that makes the idea of any future relationship so hard. There would be no family picnics and vacations. No weddings, no grandchildren.

My phone chimes again.

"Now what's he saying?" Beckett tries to lean over my shoulder and read.

"He says I need to tell my brother to stop business minding."

Beckett shrugs and steals a bite of food from the pot on the stove.

My wrist vibrates again. I glance down at my watch and see an image pop up and about choke, pressing the button on the side to click off the message, before nosy rosy sees a dick pic.

Even hundreds of miles away, he makes my stomach clench.

After dinner, I walk upstairs to put my phone on the charger. I needed a reason to text him back in private and to hide my phone from prying eyes. Beckett is almost worse than Lizzy, but at least she knew about my guys.

Everlee: *You can't keep texting me messages like these.*

Callum: *Because it's turning you on?*

Everlee: *Yes, but also because I'm at my parent's house.*

Callum: *Ohh, your parents?*

Callum: *I just wanted to say hi and let you know I was thinking about you.*

Everlee: *Yes. And my brother is all too curious.*

Everlee: *Also, hi and I've been thinking about you all too.*

I don't know why admitted that to him. Probably not the best idea, but nothing about that could be considered the best idea.

Callum: *What are you wearing?*

Everlee: *Callum!*

Callum: *Later then. When you're ready for bed. Also, the guys say hi.*

He sends a winky face emoji.

I can't help but chuckle and roll my eyes, staring at my phone for a few more seconds, wishing time would just freeze so I could stay up here and talk to him- to them- without losing time with my family.

Dominoes crash on the dining room table and I know we're going to be in for a long night of trains.

CALLUM - BOOKS, NOT JUST FOR READING

"Seems quaint," Knox says, looking around the small cottage-like home.

It's not really all that small, with four bedrooms and three bathrooms, with all the standard rooms plus a game loft on the top floor. The rental house's meticulous design considered every detail, including a hot tub on the second-story deck that offered a stunning view of the lake.

It's been a few years since we've been anywhere close to home. I've regretted not coming by more often to visit the woman who undoubtedly saved our lives and gave us the future we have today, but we're always so busy trying to make our dreams a reality.

I know that's just an excuse, but the reality is worse.

Pulling out my phone, I stare at it, willing a text message or a call from one particular person to come through. It's been several hours since Everlee sent her last text and I smile again, rereading it.

Everlee: *Callum!*

A name. One word. But I can still hear her and see her while she typed it. The flush on her skin, the twinkle in her eye, the smile she tried and failed to hide.

My phone rings.

A video chat.

I smile, walking over to shut my door. I don't know why I'm coveting her all to myself. That's not what we do. We share.

Pausing with my hand on the door, I decide to leave it open, walking back over to my bed and climbing in.

"Hey handsome," she says, smiling, her voice light and happy.

"Hey beautiful."

"Where are you?"

"In a rental. Traveling. Are you in your childhood bedroom?" I notice she's also in bed, with her back pressed up against a headboard. Excitement bubbles in my stomach as wild thoughts race through my mind, imagining all we can do.

"Not quite. This is my bedroom, but not the one I grew up in. My parents moved several years ago to this house because it's beside a lake."

"Oh, a lake house. Fancy." I gaze out of the window and imagine we're on the same lake.

"Stop." She smiles.

"So I haven't been able to stop thinking about you since last night."

"I've heard I have that effect on men." She laughs, the look in her eyes betraying the confidence her words hold. There's still a fine crack etched in her confidence that comes through every once in a while.

"Yes, you do."

"What are you wearing?" she asks, a speckling of blush stains her cheeks.

A devilish grin spreads across my face. "I see..." I lift the comforter for show. "Nothing."

"You lie."

Without hesitation, I flip the camera around and show my hardening cock, lazily running my hand over it for good measure. She shifts in bed, undoubtedly squeezing her legs together, and the thought ignites a fever on my skin.

"Fuck," she mumbles out and I can't help but smile. I love her dirty little mouth and how she's so transparent with what she feels and wants.

"What are you wearing?"

"Your t-shirt I stole from you." She smiles coyly, nibbling on her bottom lip as she continues to watch me stroke my cock.

I've never had phone sex before, but excitement is pulsing through me right now at the possibility. The idea of calling the others in here crosses my mind, but the potential inquiries about our location are something I prefer to avoid... for now. I'm not ashamed we met in foster care or the stories that got us there. I just feel it's a conversation which needs to be handled in person.

"Let me see your panties," I command softly.

She flips the camera around and throws the comforter off to show me a pair of sky-blue lace panties.

A groan escapes my lips. "Slip your hand under your panties and touch yourself."

"Callum," she whispers and I remember she's at her parent's house.

I have no idea where her room is in relation to theirs, but suddenly I find myself more aroused and wanting to push her to see how far she'll go. "Now. Everlee," I gently press and she hesitates for a moment. I can't see her face, but I watch her stomach take quick shallow breaths as she weighs all her options and then I hear the two magic words.

"Yes, sir."

The words scrape across her lips in a tantalizing whisper. A promise, causing my hand to pause on my cock as those two words bounce around in my head and cause a tingle to shoot up my spine. The way the words roll off her tongue. The way she said it that very first time at the club without knowing better. I knew it was full of sarcasm, but I turned, eyes on fire. I wanted to punish her for the way she said it and for the effect it had on me. And she saw it too. She read me like a fucking open book.

I look down at my cock and see my arousal glistening on the tip, so I slowly rub my thumb over it as I watch her hand slowly slip inside her panties. A second later, her back arches and a moan escapes.

"That's my good girl."

She moans out my name, causing a pulse to move straight to my cock. The muscles in my legs seize and my stomach tightens. Her moans are going to be the death of me.

"Jax got to watch you make yourself come, but I've not been afforded such a luxury. Tell me, what do you feel like?" I know she's uncomfortable with dirty talk because I see the small glimmer of panic every time she's done it in the past, but I think that's what turns me on the most. She doesn't try to be anything else other than what she is. The way she navigates those awkward feelings is intoxicating. Her resolve to grow and not back down is intoxicating. She... is just intoxicating.

"Wet," she says simply.

I stifle a chuckle, glad she can't see the smile playing on my lips. Not because it's silly, but because I find her innocence so damn cute. I pump my cock harder for her, letting out a low groan. I want to help her get over her fears. Her insecurities. I want to give her the confidence she deserves.

"So wet," she continues, relaxing a little as her fingers continue to move up and down, sliding over her clit.

There she is. My naughty girl coming out of her shell. Each word, each pump of my cock, giving her courage.

"I'm rubbing my finger over my swollen clit, but I wish it was your cock. I want to feel it inside of me, stretching me." She moans out for good measure, "Fuck, Callum. The way it felt inside of me last night... it's all that has been on my mind. The way it stretched me." Her body is waving over the bed, hips thrusting along with her rubs. Taking what she needs.

An uncontrollable moan escapes this time.

Fuck me. When she goes for it, she fucking goes for it and I love it!

She continues. "Before I take you in my pussy, I'd take you in my mouth. I want to swirl my tongue around the tip before you plunge it inside, making me swallow it deep. I want to feel you hit the back of my throat while you fuck my face. Hands wrapped tightly in my hair as you claim me."

"Goddamn Everlee, you're about to make me explode," I say, gripping my cock tighter.

"I wish you did, all over my chest."

"Let me see your breast," I huff out.

I expect her to flip the camera around, but it's being jostled around. Seconds later, she's picking it back up and her breasts and face appear on the screen.

"There she is. My beautiful Everlee. Did you pack any toys?"

She shakes her head. "I would have, if I was staying longer than a few days or known I was going to end up doing this."

"That's ok. I'd rather watch you finger yourself until you come, anyway. Rub your wet fingers over your breast."

Her eyes twinkle in mischief. "Yes, sir."

She dips her fingers off the camera and moments later, she's swiping them past her stomach and around her breast, squeezing them before she pinches her nipple.

"God, I want to wrap my mouth around you. Every delicious part of you."

Her camera falls to the bed and I'm staring at her ceiling and notice her fan rotates slowly, coupled with other noises I can't quite place.

"What are you doing?" I can't fight the smile on my face.

She calls from off camera. "Something. Just be patient." There's an excited hesitation in her voice as anticipation nips away at me.

I hear the flutter of fabric and the heavy thunk of something else in the background. A moment later, the camera is moving again and being propped up on something at the end of her bed.

"You said you wanted to watch." Her head peeks in from the top of the camera, smiling, while her hair dances on the sheets.

"Everlee. What are you doing to me?" My chest tightens.

She climbs onto the bed and lies on her back, with her pussy square in the camera lens, and continues touching herself. A breath escapes my lips as my eyes narrow on the screen, focusing on her delicious looking pussy. God, how I wish I was with her right now with my mouth on it.

Licking it.

Sucking it.

Listening and responding to the way she writhes and moans in ecstasy. Feeling her soft quivers as she's about to come.

I continue to pump my cock harder and faster as I watch her fingers expertly circle her clit before dipping inside, pulsing a few times before she brings them back out again.

"I wish I was with you so I could eat your pussy. Fuck, it looks delicious."

Her back arches, continuing to swirl around on her clit, hints of her juices pooling and seeping out of her, asking to be licked.

"Fuck yourself," I command.

She obeys, pumping two fingers in and out. I can see her biting on her bottom lip, undoubtedly trying to prevent her moans from escaping. She seems to match her thrusts with the pumps of my cock, which tells me she's watching me as much as I'm watching her.

We don't speak as we both silently chase our orgasms. She pulls her fingers out and furiously rubs her clit and whimpers. "I'm getting close Callum."

"Me too."

I watch her take in a deep breath and hold it. Is she practicing breath play? We'd never done that before, but I wonder if that's something she'd be into. I hold my breath too, urging the orgasm along and to stifle the moan when I come.

"Callum," she groans out through heady pants. A second later she's bucking and twisting in the sheets as the orgasm tears through her, followed by a loud crash, a string of curse words, and then the camera tumbles to the ground.

A rush of pleasure courses through me, causing my muscles to tense and a shiver to run down my back as I release onto my chest.

She scrambles off the bed with a soft banging, and then I hear a knock on her door.

I hold my breath, like they can hear me through the phone and then slowly release, hovering my finger over the end call button in case a face appears that's not Everlee's.

"Who is it?" she asks in a controlled, singsong voice.

"Everything ok?" a man's voice asks.

"Yea. All good," she sputters quickly. Too quickly?

My heart is pounding a hole out of my chest as I listen with bated breath.

I can barely hear the squeak of a door handle as it turns, followed by a large thunk and a bang. Images of Everlee leaping across the floor like a baseball player sliding for home as she slams the door shut filter through my mind and I can't help but chuckle.

"I'm all good," she repeats. "I had some books fall."

I hear soft whispers, but can't make out what he's saying.

"No. Not that. It happened while I was changing, so I'm half naked."

"Gross," he blurts.

"Yea. See you tomorrow morning," she huffs.

"Mom says to wear a nice dress and we need to leave here at ten."

Her brother.

She sighs. "Fine."

"You may want to be careful... with the bookshelves." His words are laced with innuendo.

"Shut it!" she snaps back.

"Just saying."

"Good night, Beckett."

She pads across the floor and a moment later the camera is being swung around to her beautiful face, tinged with pink.

"Should I be jealous?" I tease.

"That was my brother." She stares at me for a moment, her pupils dilating briefly.

"What are you thinking about?"

"How much I miss you. How much I missed you. How stupid I was for leaving to begin with."

"Are you free Tuesday night?"

She nods.

"Good. Because the boys are eager to see you. They weren't too happy when Jax and I told them we saw you."

"You saw me?" she teases, pumping her eyebrows.

"Yes. We saw all of your delicious body riding my cock and sucking Jax off."

Her skin flushes, and she quickly looks across the room like she's expecting someone to walk in.

My cheeks are hurting from smiling so much. "I can't wait until Tuesday."

"Me either," she yawns.

"I'll let you get some rest. I need to work on a few things before I call it a night."

"Night, Callum."

"Night, love."

After I press the end button, I stare at my phone for a second before I roll out of bed. I'm glad I claimed a bedroom with an attached bathroom, so I don't have to pad through the halls with come running down my chest.

Tomorrow we'll see Mrs. Mary and I'll be here in the moment with her and not think about Everlee. I laugh because I know it's a lie. She's always on my mind.

A drug.
An addiction I can't shake.

EVERLEE – SURPRISE DATES

We're in the car at three after ten. Mom only played with my hair three times at the breakfast table, tucking pieces here and there, so I look perfect for the lawyer. I tried telling her several times I didn't need to be set up, but she wasn't having it and I gave up. I'll go to this event, meet her lawyer, put on a good show and then come up with a reason it won't work out.

"So tell me again what we're doing." I peek out of the front windshield as we drive down the road. I don't mind riding in the backseat, but I like to see where we're going. Unless Callum's mouth is between my legs. Then I definitely don't care.

"Miss Mary Mae at our church is turning eighty-six, so we're holding a little party for her."

"A party?"

"Yes. Years ago, when she lived several towns over, she used to run a foster home. She eventually became too old to manage it and the home got shut down. She was devastated because she loved that job with all of her heart. The children were her priority and without her, who knows what would have happened to them? We came together as a community and raised some funds so we could open a community center in honor of her. She's given so much to this area, so we wanted to give back. We're going to present her with a framed picture of the new center at lunch and then dance and celebrate the afternoon away. And then tomorrow the church is hosting an Easter egg hunt for the children. It's going to be such a fantastic weekend!" she says, clasping her hands together. "We've got all these fun plans and I've got my babies under one roof."

"We're not babies, mother," I tease her.

"Maybe they'll be one in the family after this weekend," Beckett chimes in. "What's the lawyer's name again?"

I cast an evil glare at him and he just shrugs.

"Yes! Hopefully!" my mother says, turning around to look at us, completely beaming. "And his name is Winston."

I pinch my lips together. "Right. And Winston is going to be there today?"

Winston. I cringe at the name. Nothing wrong with the name Winston per se, it just seems like the kind of name for a real strait-laced guy that uses an abacus, has a pocket protector, and still has the original Nokia brick phone.

"Yes, of course. He's the one who oversaw the whole thing and gathered all the funds and really made this happen. Without him, I don't know if this would have been possible."

I sigh and cut my eyes at Beckett, who is chuckling. With him being gay, mom never tries to set him up on dates. Perhaps she would once I'm married off, but who knows? Although I vaguely remember Beckett telling me of one time she tried to set him up, but it was a huge miss and they had some enormous blow up fight.

We pull onto the gravel driveway and follow it around the church, down a hill to a large open green space that ends at a lake. I don't remember it being this large last time I was here.

"This looks a lot bigger with all the trees gone." I will talk about anything to get us off Winston, even if it's the pollination cycles of trees.

"Yes. Lots of space for parties and events. Like weddings."

I slowly turn my head to look at Beckett, who is having silent convulsions in the seat, trying to hold his laughter in.

Mom points out of the car. "See, they have a nice large tent set up over there for lunch and dancing after the ceremony and kayaks and canoes to go on the water. This is quite the hang out in the summer. Well, when there aren't weddings, which really is all the time since it's such a nice large space."

"Hint received mother," I drone.

"What hint?" she asks, surely playing coy before she climbs out of the car and stomps over to her girlfriend with her arms open wide.

Dad turns around and looks at me, his eyes soft. "She means well," he says, trying to defend her.

"I know. But it's exhausting having her try to set me up all the time. We like different types of men." She likes strait-laced lawyers and I love four tattooed sex gods who own a nightclub.

Oh God. Did I just think of love? No. No. No love. Like. I like four sex gods who own a nightclub.

Fuck!

"Well, at least meet the guy. He's nice and really excited to meet you. Your mother has been talking about you and showing pictures to him for months now."

"Geez, are you serious?"

He pats my knee, then climbs out of the car without speaking another word.

I hurriedly turn to Beckett. "Don't you dare leave my side today!"

"Ev. What fun would that be? I'd rather watch you squirm from afar."

"You're an ass, you know that?"

"I like ass? What did you say?"

"You heard me! You better not. I can't do this Becks." I'm almost pleading, willing to get on my hands and knees in front of him to convince him.

"Fine. I'll be stuck to you like glue."

My eyes narrow at him, waiting for the other shoe to drop, but he doesn't speak, and climbs out of the car. I feel like there is a big but there or something unspoken in his words, which I will probably regret finding out later, but for now I will take it at face value.

"You can do this Everlee. One weekend. Two days," I mumble to myself.

When I finally decide to step out of the car, I find mom dragging a man over who's wearing a light brown jacket with matching pants. He's smiling that sort of awkward smile when a crazy woman is dragging you across the lawn to meet her all to uninterested daughter.

I glance at Beckett, who looks up and sees the scene unfolding and smiles.

"Beckett," I whisper quickly, trying to draw him over to me.

His brow furrows, like he can't hear me and is trying to make out my words.

"Beckett," I whisper again when I notice he's not moving. I try not to stamp my foot like a petulant child.

He waves his hand. "You'll be fine. I'll be right back. I need to go check on the fire truck."

"You-" I whisper shout just as mom is coming to a stop in front of me.

"Everything ok, Everlee? You look flustered."

"Everything's great, mom. Beckett went to go check on the fire truck."

"Ok then." She nods, not listening to a single word I say. Her eyes are as huge as her smile. "This is Winston. Winston, this is my daughter, Everlee."

"Hi," I say awkwardly, waving my hand.

Winston isn't ugly, but he didn't compare to my guys. He had boyish good looks with a head of brown hair trimmed short with brown eyes and a few freckles on his face. Judging by his sideburns line, I'd venture to say he just got his hair cut, and that makes me feel a little bad. Did he get it cut for me?

"Well, I'm going to let you two chat and get to know one another." She wiggles her fingers in the air like she's playing an air piano.

"I doubt there's anything I could tell him you haven't already," I retort sarcastically.

"Thanks, Mrs. McKinley."

"Oh, you stop that. You can call me Donna, or mom," she jokes, walking away. "Ta-ta." She flips her hand in the air over her shoulder without a care in the world.

"Jesus. I'm sorry about her."

He chuckles. "It's fine. It's sweet. She talks about you all the time."

"I wish she would talk less," I mumble.

"Look. It's awkward being forced to meet me, and if you don't want to hang out, it's totally ok."

"No. It's fine. We can. I was just a little blindsided, that's all. According to my brother, you've had months to prepare for this meeting. I've had less than twenty-four hours."

"Eesh. My mom used to set me up on dates, too. So I get it."

"How did you get her to stop?" I laugh.

"Oh. She passed away almost two years ago."

"Fuck. I'm sorry." Insert foot in mouth.

He chuckles awkwardly. "No. It's my fault. I kind of left it open."

"Well, I'm sorry about your mother."

"We knew it was coming. She had cancer for years, so it was only a matter of time. It was incurable, so in some ways I'm glad she's moved on to a better place because she was in so much pain. But I miss her. Fortunately," he pulls his face, "Or maybe not so fortunate, I see a lot of her in the women at church. They have sort of taken to mothering me." He tilts his head to the side. "With or without my knowing." He laughs again. "In fact, after Christmas they set me up on a date, but didn't tell me. Imagine my surprise when I walked into a party only to find there was no party and just this woman sitting at a table waiting for me." He slaps his forehead. "I had no idea it was a date, so I showed up late and the poor girl had been waiting there for over an hour."

"Oh, my," I grimace.

"Yea. After that, I had a talk with the ladies and told them no more surprises. I should have been more specific," he says, nodding at me.

"Well, at least we can talk about our mutual irritation at being set up. They will think we're getting along splendidly and then we can tell them distance and what not are a factor and it won't work out."

"Sounds good." He looks at the lake. "So, tell me about yourself."

Winston and I talk for close to an hour by the lake when a bell rings in the distance.

"I guess that's our sign." He chuckles.

If it was a different time and I lived here, I could see myself wanting to go out on at least one date with him. He's good looking and easy to talk to, but he just isn't my guys.

Everyone is filtering to the tent to take their seats, with most stopping to pay their respects to an older woman in a wheelchair with a plaid blanket thrown across her lap. She has bright white hair which has been curled up, and a dusting of light pink on her cheeks, wearing a bright green knitted top with a pearl necklace. She is the epitome of class and sophistication, but looks like a woman you don't want to cross.

After saying a quick hello to her, I take a seat at a round table in the middle of the room. Not too close, but not too far from the front. There are several extra tables in the back no one is sitting at, so it'd be pretty obvious and awkward if I chose one of those. On the way to the tent, Winston told me he'd come find me after he said a few words and introduced some special guests.

"You two seem to hit it off," Beckett says, leaning over my shoulder from the table behind me.

"Shut your mouth, asshole. You left me," I fire back, not turning to look at him.

His hands grip my shoulders. "I've been keeping an eye on you. You haven't seemed miserable enough, so I didn't intervene. Could it be true love?"

That gets me to turn and look at him so he can feel the lasers shooting out of my eyes. He clasps his hands together under his chin and twists his neck, batting his long lashes like a fairytale princess.

Without thinking, I whip my cloth napkin at him, causing a loud pop. He retreats, but not before I get a scornful glare from mommy dearest and several other curious sets of eyes. I smile meekly and turn to the front as they're about to start.

"Mrs. Mary Mae," Winston announces. "You've been such a pillar of this community for so many years and a backbone to this church. Tomorrow is your thirty-ninth birthday." The crowd chuckles. "So we wanted to present you with something."

My dad carries out a framed object covered in thin velvet fabric while my mom is at the front table snapping pictures with her and dad's vintage camera like her life depends on it. I've tried to get her on digital, but she likes to take her pictures to get developed. I don't get it because nine times out of ten, half of them don't turn out and she doesn't know until days later.

"Before we let you open your gift, we wanted to talk about what you have accomplished. Years ago, in a town just down the road, you had a home for children where you took care of and mentored over thirty young boys and girls during your time." Winston pauses, allowing everyone to clap.

"Truly amazing work. God's work." A few people in the crowd shout, praise Jesus, and hold their hands in the air.

"Today, we are gifting you a plaque, which will be affixed to a brand new, fully funded, community center for at risk youth which we have named the Mary Mae center. Here, children will be able to get food at any time of the day. It will be a safe haven where they can get free tutoring or play sports."

Tears well up in her eyes with her hands clasped shakily over her mouth.

"And we thought you would like to see a few of the lives you've changed over the years, and I believe a few of them have some words for you," Winston says before walking off the makeshift stage to sit beside me.

With that, a line of men and women file out from behind the tent, each pausing to bend down and say a few words to Mary Mae.

"You did good." I lean over and pat Winston's hand, and then feel it.

The pull.

Something in the room changed and when I look up, I freeze.

EVERLEE - DON'T LET YOUR GUYS SEE YOU ON ANOTHER DATE

I SEE THOSE ELECTRIC blue eyes staring at me from the makeshift stage and my heart literally stops beating in my chest.

Callum.

What is he doing here?

And Jax, and Emmett, and Knox.

Knox looks the same, but Emmett.

Fuck me sideways and call me Santa, because shit. I think I just spritzed in my panties.

He has a beard now and looks like a mountain man. Like a sexy mountain man that has chopped wood all day instead of creating delicious cuisine. Damn! I'd like to pop his suspenders.

I shake my head to clear away all the dirty thoughts that are currently bombarding me like water drops under a waterfall- a waterfall that is currently gushing between my legs.

I realize I'm frozen in my seat with my hand still on Winston's, and Callum's eyes locked on mine. At some point, before this very second, I must have leaned back to escape this nightmare of my world's colliding, because the legs of my chair buckle and I fall out of the seat, crashing to the floor.

Staring at the ground, I let out a string of curse words, no doubt making the ladies around me clutch their pearls. I take a moment before I stand up, trying to regain my composure and process what's going on. Callum looked just as surprised to see me as I was to see him, so they didn't come for me. But what then? For Mrs. Mary Mae?

Someone taps the microphone, pulling me back to the present, like a loud whoosh of air sucking me out of a vacuum. Beckett, through his fits of laughter, squats down and grabs my hand to help me up. Thankfully, only a few sets of eyes are still on me, four of them being my guys.

"Hubba hubba," Beckett mumbles as he walks back to his chair. He is drooling... over my guys. My guys!

Jax takes the microphone from Callum, looking beautiful as ever in his dark blue suit with a white button up underneath. His pinched brow glances at me before settling on Mrs. Mary. "Mama Mary. We wanted to come and wish you the happiest of birthdays. We don't get to see you as much as we'd like, but we think about you all the time. Your love and support gave each of us up here a life that we wouldn't have had without you. We are grateful and humbled to share this weekend with you."

"Was he in the navy? Hello captain, my captain," Beckett moans from over my shoulder.

"SEALs," I answer without thinking and then try to play it off. "Probably. Seems like the type."

Definitely a SEAL. I remember the frog tattoo on his chest, over his heart. My thoughts drift back to the time in their hot tub and then afterwards in their bedroom. Fucking Niagara Falls near my lady bits right now!

"Do you need a fan?" Winston asks. "You seem a little flush."

"No. I'm ok." I swallow and lift the water to my bone-dry mouth.

I thought it odd they had so many empty tables in the room when we first sat down, but now it makes sense. They had surprise guests coming and I don't think anyone is more surprised than me. How close had we been growing up? Several towns apart? What are the odds? Wait until Lizzy hears-

"May we sit here?" A voice booms behind me with a gentle touch on my shoulder that sends a jolt of electricity through me.

I look up and see Callum standing there and my breath leaves my body. Traitorous bitch. Mouth hanging open like a fucking fish, all I can do is nod. But not like a normal nod, like a jerk, that leaves the other party questioning if you are actually nodding yes or having some sort of neck spasm and need medical attention.

Thankfully, Winston chimes in. "Yes, yes, of course. Anyone who got to grow up with Mrs. Mary Mae is always welcome." He fans his arm out to the table like a model on a game show.

Callum takes the seat to my right, with the others sitting to his right. I look at each of them, still unable to remember how to use my tongue. Or my mouth. And apparently my eyelids, because the way my balls- eyeballs!- are burning, I haven't blinked.

Callum and the others were foster siblings? Except Jax, who is his actual brother. No wonder they are so close. How didn't I know this about them? I guess to be fair, most of the times I was with them ended up in extraordinary fucking sessions. But that's what it was before. Just sex. Only I got attached and stupidly left. But not again. We planned on a meeting in a few days to talk about that. It hadn't worked with them and Sophie years ago, but I'm different. We're different.

Suddenly, I remember when I first met Sophie at the Valentine's gala. She was the celebrity chef they had brought in for a cooking demonstration. She had seen us before the event and made a mention of Callum always supporting events with children and I never thought to ask him more about it. Would he have told me then? Would he have told me now?

The table is quiet as the guys stare at Winston and me. Jax is clenching his hand in and out of a fist, Emmett is biting on his bottom lip, Knox... he just looks confused and happy, and Callum. The anger emanating from him is almost palpable. His jaw continues to clench and unclench, repeatedly.

How can I tell them it's not what they're thinking, without it coming out awkwardly? Why would a girl who just met four random guys say, 'hey, I'm not on a date with this guy right here, even though you just saw me holding his hand. It's not what you think.' Because that wouldn't be awkward or seem out of place.

It was getting increasingly awkward and unsettling to just stare at them, so I decide to speak up. "Hi. I'm Everlee," I say, playing the game, introducing myself to the guys who know me better than I know myself. Who knows how I feel. How I taste. Who knows when I'm about to orgasm based on the way my pussy quivers.

But this is the game, because no one can know our secret.

"Knox," he says, holding out his hand. As I reach out, he firmly clasps my hand and tenderly presses his lips against the top of it, making me inhale sharply. His eyes roll back briefly, and I can almost hear him thinking about how much he misses the taste of me.

"Emmett," he says, reaching for my hand. He gently cups it in his paws, letting his pinky brush the inside of my wrist, causing me to freeze. There are so many emotions and thoughts flittering through my mind right now.

"Jax," he says simply, followed by Callum. No touching, no kisses. Nothing. They are pissed.

Nervously, I rest my hands on my lap, fiddling with the bottom edge of the tablecloth as my mind still tries to process what in the hell is going on.

"I'm Winston."

Callum looks at him and nods. "Yes, you're the individual who helped set all of this up." His tone is cool, but polite.

"It was a team effort," Winston cheers with a smile beaming across his face.

If a storm cloud suddenly appeared in the center of the table, it wouldn't surprise me. Between the dark and brooding on my right and Winston's bright and cheery on my left, coupled with all the turmoil I feel inside... like I said. I would not be surprised.

"Things are always better when there's a team," Jax chortles, causing me to choke on air.

"Sorry." I run my fingers over my mouth, embarrassed by my reaction.

Winston rests his hand on mine and the entire table tenses and stares at us. A heat shoots up my spine as I see the guys predatorial looks focus on Winston, like an unsuspecting hyena bouncing into the middle of a lion's feed. With my other hand hidden beneath the table, I cautiously run my fingers along Callum's leg, careful not to attract any attention.

"Looks like I have to go back up to say a few words. Excuse me." Winston quickly shuttles off and I immediately lean forward, taking the opportunity. "It's not what it looks like."

"Hey Ali," Knox says. "I've missed you."

"I've missed you all, too. What are you–"

Someone sits to my left, filling the seat where Winston had just been, causing the hairs on my arm to stand.

Great.

My mother.

"You seem to be having a great time on your date."

Fuckin' aye!

The men bristle in their seats, but I fight the urge to look at them.

"Mom. I've already told you. I'm not looking for anyone."

"Well, sometimes love comes along unexpectedly in places you wouldn't expect to find it."

I want to say something sarcastic about what she just said with the whole unexpectedly unexpected, but I just want her to leave so I don't engage and simply say, "Ok."

"I can't wait for later."

"Later?" I panic.

"Baby, this party is just getting started." She shimmies her shoulders. "There will be dancing and cake and..." she claps her hands quickly to finish her sentence, before scurrying off.

What does that mean? What is clapping code for? I need to know now!

Once she's gone, I look back at the guys.

"Date?" Jax repeats with his brow lifting before I can even get a word out.

"My mom. She set it up. I didn't know."

Callum's lips pinch in a disapproving hard line.

"I'm back. What did I miss?" Winston asks, interrupting us.

It takes everything I have not to lose my shit. I just need two minutes to explain to my guys what's going on.

"Nothing much," Jax says coolly.

The men are all sorts of manly, protective, caveman sexy right now. It's written all over their faces. They don't like the fact I'm on a date with Winston and it's driving them crazy. Hell. Driving me crazy.

My phone dings, so I look at my watch. Lizzy.

Lizzy: *Bitch. What is going on?*

"Excuse me." I quickly push back from the table and they all tense.

"Is everything ok?" they all ask in unison, then look at one another. I'm sure it's very confusing for Winston to have men I just met be concerned about me.

My eyes scan over all of them, landing on Winston. "Yes."

Sneaking out of the back of the tent, I stroll alongside the lakes. Its calm waves lap against the shore, a juxtaposition for the turmoil boiling inside of me.

Finding her name in my contacts, I quickly press the call button, glancing back at the tent.

"What's going on, hooker?"

"Did Beckett text you?"

"Beckett? No. Why?"

"Because, as always, your timing is perfect."

"What happened? Are your parents asking about me? Miss me?"

"Callum and the guys showed up," I blurt.

"Shut the front door!"

"Yes, and they're sitting at the table with my date and me."

She bursts out in laughter. Fits of laughter. Laughter so loud and hard that she'll likely have a hernia when she's done. "You're shitting me."

"I wish."

"Shut the fuck up. Your date?"

"Mother dearest set me up. A lawyer."

"Fancy. What kind?"

"Focus Lizzy! The guys are here! Here, here! With my family here!"

"How do they look?"

"Hot as sin."

"No. Obviously that. I mean with Winston."

"Oh." I peek back at the tent and they seem to be talking about something. "Well, he's still alive, so that's a good sign." I roll my eyes. "It's especially fun when Winston grabs my hand in front of them."

"Shut the fuck up! To be a fly on that wall. How long do you have to stay?"

"Apparently, the whole freaking afternoon."

"Any place you could sneak away for a quick fivesome with the boys?"

I choke out a laugh. "We're at a church and you want me to sneak away with four men and have sexy time?"

"What better place to cry out 'Oh God' than on the cock of a man at church? Or four dicky dicks in your case."

"You're going to hell."

"Most likely."

"Remind me why you couldn't come?"

"Personal question Ev. And I come. Quite regularly, though probably not as much as you."

"Lizzy!"

"I can see we have serious, flustered Everlee right now. Not jokey joke, Everlee. I couldn't come because of a holiday called Easter."

"Right. You're going to your dads."

"I'm so excited," she says deadpan.

"You should totally ditch and come hang out with your BFF."

"I'd love to see you."

"Oh, not me. I was talking about my brother. What the hell? Trying to tag team me?"

"I thought that's what you liked," she snipes back, then chuckles. "We've been through this before. You're my hoe and I have to look out for your pussy."

"Jesus," I cringe, saying the name here. I, too, am going to hell. At this point, via the bullet train.

I know I'm going to hell because even thinking of the words bullet train conjures up dildos, dicks, and anal plugs... not an actual fucking train.

She bursts out laughing. "Gotta go hooker. Stay safe and use protection. Or don't and let one of those handsome four knock you up. Can't go wrong with any of them."

"Lizzy."

"What? Kidding... kind of."

"Bye."

"Bye boo."

When I get back to the table, Beckett is putting his phone back in his lap, chuckling. Every bone in my body tells me it's Lizzy.

Looking over his shoulder, I see a picture before his phone flicks off. "What was that?" I whisper. I don't miss the fact Callum tenses as I lean over Beckett. He's looking at Winston, but his focus is on me.

Beckett smiles. "Lizzy told me to take a picture of your table."

I shake my head, trying to snatch his phone, but he laughs, holding it out of my reach.

"Beckett. Will you stop? You're being immature."

His face is inches from mine. "Immature? You're the one acting funny here. What did you say to Lizzy that made her want me to take a picture? Did you tell her about all the insanely hot men at your table?"

Callum's lips pull up slightly, and his shoulders relax. Had he already not fucked me in every hole I had, I'd be embarrassed. "Beckett. I just want to see the picture."

His eyes narrow.

"I won't take your phone." I put my hands behind my back.

His phone dings with another message from Lizzy.

Lizzy: *Any of those will do.*

"What does she mean?"

"Those deliciously desirable men you're sitting with."

"What about them?"

"She said any of them will do for you."

I roll my eyes and sit down.

"Everything ok?" Winston asks.

"Yes. My brother is being a jerk," I say, mostly for the guys. I can't have them thinking I'm a hussy for any other men but them.

The guys all look over my shoulder at Beckett. This is so weird to have everyone in the same place, but separate.

Everyone finishes speaking at the microphone and my dad gets on stage and directs the crowds to some food. I don't stand immediately, hoping Winston will, so I can have some time with the guys to smooth things over, but no one moves.

I should play the lottery, because all of my bad luck is pouring out in droves here, so there can't be any left.

After one of the front tables sits back down, I stand, followed by everyone else. Fuck. Is this some sort of thing? Does Winston feel threatened by the guys? We aren't even on an actual date. Does he feel like he's protecting me or something?

I walk over to the tables with the food and pick a side and, of course, Winston follows, right on my heels. Callum and Emmett are across from me, while Knox and Jax are behind Winston. They tower over him. He's not a short man, but they are tall and just command any space they're in.

"Did you boys play football?" Winston laughs awkwardly.

"No," they respond simply.

I hand the tongs for the fruit salad to Callum, whose fingers brush along mine. My stomach clenches as wave after wave courses through my body. I just want to run away, to escape, and have them all. I missed them with every fiber of my being.

"Food looks good," Winston chimes and I can't help but look at Emmett. "Did your mom make the potato salad?"

"I don't know."

"She usually makes it for most of our church functions."

Emmett winks at me and I can't help but smile.

We continue down the table, choosing between hotdogs, hamburgers, pasta salads, and chips. I grab one of the already poured drinks at the end of the buffet line and head back to the table.

Callum gets there just before me.

"Winston seems... cheery," Callum teases.

"Shut up." I glare at him playfully.

"He could give you a pleasant life," his tone drops.

I gaze at him, trying to decipher if he's still teasing me or not.

"I don't want nice. I want dirty and sexy. I want you all."

"We can definitely do that." He brushes a piece of hair behind my ear, letting his fingers glide down my neck.

"Hey. Getting handsy with my date there?" Winston chuckles, walking up in that awkwardly passive aggressive tone.

"He was helping me. I didn't want to eat my hair," I say, holding up my hotdog.

"Such a gentleman. It shouldn't surprise me coming from Mary Mae's house." He takes a quick bite, then looks back up. "Say. Are all of you still close? You know, after leaving Mary Mae's?"

They look at each other and nod, and I can't help but chuckle. I try to hide it with my hotdog, but Knox calls me out.

"Something funny, Everlee?"

It's so weird to hear him use my name since I'm fairly certain he's only ever called me Ali.

"Nothing at all." I glare at him and see him smile as he takes a bite of food. Callum's leg brushes along mine under the table and I don't move. I enjoy feeling him there. It's all I can get right now, so I'll take it.

My eyes catch Knox's, so I slowly take the hotdog in my mouth, trying to be as covertly seductive as possible. Knox's eyes bore onto my mouth around the hotdog, lips parted. When I have him where I want him, I bite down. Knox's knee hits the underside of the table, and I smile in evil satisfaction. This time I'm able to hide it with my napkin.

"Everything ok, Knox?" Emmett asks.

Knox watch's me for a second then nods.

"This hotdog is so good," I say, moaning just a little at the end. The guy's eyes slowly turn to me.

"I'm more of a hamburger guy myself. Love the layers, the patties, the juice." Jax holds up his hamburger. "Plus, this is a really nice bun. Is it toasted?"

Is hamburger codeword for pussy or am I just that horny? "I've never had a toasted bun with a hamburger before," I say awkwardly, now completely botching any sexy talk as I watch him take another bite. If I'm keeping track, I just said I've never had anal with a woman before. While true, it's not what I was trying to say. Or the other, very real, possibility is that I'm making up all the code words, and they were really just talking about a bun. "Maybe I should try a toasted bun with my hotdog?"

What the fuck am I doing? Seriously. What the fuck? Toast my hotdog bun?

"Get this woman another hotdog!" Winston yells, thumbing over his shoulder, laughing and completely missing all the innuendos that are flying around. Or maybe I am. Maybe this is all in my head and Jax really does like toasted buns on his hamburgers?

The rest of lunch passes in a similar fashion. Little comments or questions being asked that elicit some sort of double meaning response. We feed off each other. All of us are eager to be anywhere else but here and we do a poor job of hiding it. We can't help but tease or flirt, and poor Winston is sitting here watching it. He tries to take part a few times, but there's a whole other level to the conversation he isn't even aware of.

After lunch, my mother jumps on the microphone and asks for all the guys to help get the tables off the dance floor while the ladies wrap up all the leftover food.

A sudden touch on my shoulder jolts me, and I instinctively spin around, assuming it's one of my guys, only to discover it's Beckett. "What's going on?"

"What do you mean?" I spit out quickly.

"Well, shit. I was just trying to have a simple conversation, but the guilt laced in your question now has me curious."

"Guilt? What would I have to feel guilty for?"

He thinks about it for a minute. "Maybe that you haven't been able to stop looking at those men at your table and they can't stop looking at you. Poor Winston."

"No. I'm not looking at them a lot. We were all having a conversation with everyone, including Winston."

"Ok. I'm just saying if you want one of the others, then go for it. They are hot as fuck and look all dark and delicious. You need to find out if any of them are gay. Hook a brother up."

"They aren't."

His brow furrows. "How do you know?" Before I can come up with a reason, he continues, "Are you trying to be stingy mcstingy pants?"

"And cock block you, dear brother? Never." I pat his chest.

"All I'm saying is that you can't have them all."

"Can't I?" I retort without thinking.

He gasps, "You little hoe bag."

"I learn from you."

"Touché. I'd do them all at the same time if they'd let me."

"Are you going to find someone to settle down with?" I need to change the topic.

His lip snarl. "Eww no. Where's the fun in that?"

The music starts behind us.

"Care to dance?" He holds out his hand, clearly wanting to change the topic.

"I'd love to," I say after sweeping my eyes around the tent. My guys are with Mrs. Mary Mae, and Winston is talking to an attractive woman by the tent entrance. He catches my eye and panics, but I wave my hand and point at the girl, giving a thumbs up. We aren't going anywhere and we both know that. I don't want to fill up his entire weekend when he can possibly find someone else.

Beckett and I dance like crazy children to the upbeat song, hands flailing in the air, with our hips shaking. He spins me a couple times, then brings me back in and we continue to dance. I've missed him. This.

"You should come visit me sometime. I miss you." I catch him off guard.

"Are you ok? Are you sick?"

"No, why?" I laugh.

"Because you aren't the sentimental type."

"I'm just enjoying my time with you. Asshole."

"There we go. That's better."

The song changes to a slower song and Beckett and I look at one another.

"Well, this just got awkward." He laughs.

We start walking back to the seats around the border, when I feel a hand on my arm. Turning, I find Emmett.

"Would you care to dance with me?" he asks with a twinkle in his eye.

"Yes." I wave off Beckett, whose eyes grow wide. I mouth for him to stop, trying to downplay it.

Emmett moves to wrap his arm around me, but pulls back and puts his hand on my hip instead. For people who just supposedly met, we can't seem too comfortable with each other. I place my hand in his and we move back and forth, a respectful distance apart.

"You look nice," he whispers.

"So do you. The beard is new."

He smiles. "Do you like?"

"I do. I want to run my fingers through it."

"There will be time."

"Promises, promises," I tease.

"Most definitely." He leans forward, so his cheek is barely touching mine. "I can't wait to taste you and have your sweet juices all over it."

"Emmett," I pant, my heart beat thumping in my ears.

He pulls back some. "That's not all that changed."

I study him curiously. "What else?"

His lips pinch in a hard line. "I don't want to tell you. I want you to find out on your own."

I smile. "Can I see it?"

"Right now? No."

As I suck my bottom lip into my mouth, my eyes pulse wide, a mixture of excitement and anticipation coursing through me.

"Don't do that, Trouble. You'll make me suck it back out and we're in public." His low hum resonates through my body, sending a wave of desire that tingles my nipples.

Glancing around the floor, I find Jax dancing with Mrs. Mary Mae, and Callum right behind her, ready to catch her if her legs get tired. It's so interesting to see them with her, so loving, so gentle. I can't help but wonder what their story is. How did each of them end up with her?

When the song ends, I realize during the course of it, Emmett and I had edged closer together, our chests touching, with his hand on my lower back.

Nerves coursing through me, I quickly glance around the room to see if anyone noticed, and land on Beckett, who is holding up a fire extinguisher in the back corner. My brows pinch together, curious about what he's doing, and he points at Emmett and me and then fans himself. I roll my eyes.

"Your brother is funny."

"Don't encourage him."

"It's nice to see you here. Like this." He smirks, pausing for a beat, then says, "But I'd rather see you tonight with nothing on."

A flush sweeps across my cheeks.

"Samesies," I hear whispered behind me and turn to see Jax sweeping by to sit at the table.

Body on fire and heart pounding through my chest, I follow Emmett back to our seats and sit down. "Are you staying here?"

"And miss out on the festivities for tomorrow? Mrs. Mary says we're expected to be here," Jax answers. "And we rented a house about fifteen minutes from here. It's on the lake and has some amazing views."

"You're on a lake?" I ask hesitantly.

"Yea. Why?"

"My parents live on a lake about fifteen minutes from here."

Jax smiles a ruthless smile. "It's not a very big lake."

"No, it's not." A sort of nervous excitement flows through me. Could they really have rented a house close to my parents? There's no way. Right? I mean, there aren't a ton of rental homes in the area, so that definitely improved the odds.

Oh no! What if they are right beside them? I mean there's a good amount of space between houses, but next to, maybe too close.

Winston jumps up on stage and thanks everyone for coming out and celebrating the wonderful Mrs. Mary Mae and reminds us all to be here at seven in the morning to hide eggs for the children. He also reminds us about all the competitive activities planned for tomorrow, so we can come prepared.

We get in the car and my mom turns around and starts asking what happened with Winston. She's in a kerfuffle because she saw him with another woman. I let her down softly, telling her it won't work out with us, and then she immediately starts talking about Emmett and how he doesn't look like my type.

I want to bark back and tell her we aren't the same person. That her type and my type are very different. Drastically different. But I don't. I don't want to ruin the weekend, so I just cross my hands in my lap and look out of the window. I smile to myself as I imagine her expression in the event she ever finds out about all of them. That makes me happy. Her sheer terror and mortification.

EVERLEE - NEVER COMPLAIN ABOUT HAVING ONLY ONE ORGASM... IF YOU WANT TO WALK AGAIN

<hr>

After dinner, I tell everyone I'm going to take a walk by the lake for a while to talk to Lizzy. Beckett tries to come with, but I shut that down. I'm on a mission to find my guys and I don't need Beckett hanging around twat blocking me.

Through texts with Callum before dinner, we determine we're on the same lake, rather, oversized pond. I get to the water's edge and pull out my phone, about to call them, when I look to my left and see a large three-story balcony house with glass paneled walls several houses away. There is a shirtless, tattooed figure on the second-floor balcony stretching his arms towards the air. They're far enough away that I can't be certain, but I have a gut feeling. The closer I get, the more my stomach twists.

This weekend was supposed to be quiet. I was supposed to focus on myself and figure out what I want and need from them before our meeting. But I don't care what it *should* have been. I'm over the moon they're here.

When I get closer to the house, I recognize Knox, who sees me walking up and waves me around to the front. When I get there, he throws the front door open and runs out, lifting me into his arms. Instinctively, I wrap my legs around his waist as he presses his lips to mine. His kiss is soft, tender, but with an underlying passion.

He pulls away, staring at me for a minute, then carries me inside.

"I missed you too," I whisper, still wrapped around him.

"Look what I found wandering around outside," Knox announces to the house, carrying me into the kitchen. It's much smaller than theirs, with a table for six tucked to the left, in front of a bay window overlooking the lake. Across from it, and to my right, is the kitchen and small island with seating for four. And there, in the space, are all the guys, standing shirtless, wearing a pair of joggers low on their hips, with that delicious v pointing to my happy place.

Fuck me. I think I'm drooling.

"Do you all not own shirts?" I pant, trying to catch my breath.

I stare at them, greedily drinking them in. They are my home.

The feeling that washes over me the instant I'm standing in front of them almost brings tears to my eyes. I know in this moment I'd do or say anything, lie to whoever, to be with them. Lizzy knows, but everyone else... I will lie to until my last breath.

"You ok, Trouble?" Emmett asks.

Nodding, I say, "I just missed you all." I continue quickly so I don't get too emotional. "You want to make me a drink? Shot first, then old-fashioned. I haven't been able to recreate them quite like you."

Walking around the island, Emmett surprises me by wrapping his arm around me, gently tilting me backward as he leans in and kisses me. When he stands me up, a wave of dizziness washes over me.

Jax walks over, followed by Callum, so they're all around me.

"You should have never left us, Everlee," Jax growls lowly, causing the hairs on my arm to stand.

"I was a fucking idiot."

Jax smiles, taking another step forward, and rubs the pad of his thumb across my bottom lip. "I'm going to love punishing that mouth of yours." He grabs under my chin and pushes me backwards, pressing me against the wall. He brings his lips close to mine and waits for me to chase his kiss before he backs away. His nose runs up my neck, blowing a warm breath on my skin, inhaling my scent, causing goosebumps to erupt across my body. He is teasing me.

"Ooh. Jax is in beast mode." Knox jumps up and down, excited.

I try not to laugh, because I don't want to ruin the moment, but I can't hold it back. I'm so turned on and so happy right now.

Jax exhales and puts his forehead to mine. "He's an idiot." He cracks a smile before he presses his lips to mine. His tongue pushes its way in, and I let out a moan as I nearly melt into a puddle on the floor.

He reaches under my dress and brushes his hand over my panties. A whimper escapes as my legs buckle slightly. He leans down, pressing his lips to my ear. "I can't wait until your pussy is wrapped around my cock."

"Samesies," I whisper back.

He chuckles, removing his hand from under my dress, grabbing the hem and pulling it over my head. "Clear the table, boys." He lifts me with ease.

I squeal in delight, wrapping my arms around his neck, and hear a crashing of wooden bowls and silverware hit the ground behind me. He lays me on the table and pulls my panties off, tossing them on the floor.

All the boys turn their eyes towards me, their hungry expressions impossible to ignore. God, I fucking love them and the way they make me feel!

Jax runs his finger down my chest, across my navel, to the inside of the thigh, causing me to suck in a breath. "A few days ago, we gave you what you wanted... but you should have been punished."

I take in a deep breath, watching the boys take a step closer, their hardening cocks pressing against their pants.

Jax runs his finger along the inside of my leg all the way down to my foot, causing me to squirm. "Jax," I pant.

"No, no, no, no, no." He continues sliding his finger up the inside of my other leg, brushing over the outside of my pussy.

I move my hips to meet his finger, but he pulls away. I'm so hot right now, so ready to be touched, licked, and fucked, that I'm close to losing my mind.

"How should we punish her?" Jax asks.

"Well, there's the obvious," Emmett says.

I cut my eyes at him, not sure what the obvious means.

Jax looks at me. "Do you want to be spanked?"

I've never been spanked before and I don't know how I feel about it. It just seems so... childish. I shake my head slowly, full of uncertainty.

"No?" He tilts his head to the side. "Or cupid no?"

Cupid. My safe word. They remembered.

I look at each of them and just say, "No." My chest tightens with excitement.

"That's our good girl," Callum says, walking over and grabbing my leg. In one swift motion, Callum and Jax pull me off the table and flip me around so my feet are on the ground and my chest is on the table.

"You have been a bad girl, though," Callum says, causing me to whimper.

I feel his hand lightly brush over my skin and without warning he slaps my ass hard, but the brush of his lips on my spine quickly mutes the sting, while his other finger presses against my clit. My scream turns to a moan.

Hashtag newkinkunlocked. A sexier version of the Mortal Kombat theme song plays in the background of my mind while my Madame Kink avatar cheers at the new level I've gained. Purchase of whips, chains, handcuffs and a black leather one piece now available. But wait, there's more. That sneaky little bastard gift with purchase is there, too. A ball gag!

"You're so wet." He presses his finger in and pulls it back out again. "I can't wait to taste you and have you ride my face."

He steps away and Jax walks up. His fingers inch slowly down my spine, over my ass, and then brush along my wet folds. He rubs my clit, circling, causing my hips to gyrate and move on their own, and then without warning I feel a slap on my other cheek. The burn is a little more intense. He grabs both of my hips and pulls me back into him, so I feel his cock pressed at my entrance. When I move into it, he steps back. "You're being punished right now."

"I think you all are just torturing yourself, too. So who's winning here?" I mumble with my cheek against the table.

"We're winning, love. We're winning," Jax states matter-of-factly.

A second later, I feel a heat between my legs, followed by the wet tongue and flowing beard of Emmett. His tongue slowly glides along my entrance from my clit to uncomfortably close to my asshole, making me clinch. He chuckles as he moves back down for another swipe before pressing his tongue in.

My knees get weak and a moan escapes.

"We're punishing her right now," Callum reminds.

Emmett's hands grab around my hips, and he pulls me to his face. If this is punishment, then I'll never be a good girl again. He eagerly laps and sucks on my clit, like he's making up for the last two months in these two minutes.

I'm moaning now in pants.

"Emmett! Don't you make her come!" Jax warns, but he doesn't stop.

I'm so close. My chest lifts off the table and, just as I'm about to crest, he stops.

I collapse back down, catching my breath. "You asshole," I murmur out.

"That was too fucking close," Callum reprimands.

"Maybe. But she tastes divine, and I missed her."

I look over my shoulder and watch him wipe his hands through his beard as Knox walks up. He is the cinnamon roll, the sweet one, of the group. I don't feel like edging or slapping my ass is in his cards, but curiosity has me excited.

He brushes my hair to the side and I feel his cock pressed against my entrance as he leans over my back and plants kisses along the nape of my neck. Soft, delicate. He moves to the left side and gently takes my ear in his mouth and starts nibbling. My body slowly grinds along Knox's cock as I sigh out, relishing in the feel of his hard length between my legs. He releases my ear and kisses along the inside of my neck, across my shoulder and down my spine, stopping at my lower back, where he gently sucks on the skin.

This fucker.

He's aiming for my erogenous zones. Of course he would. I didn't pick up on it at first, but now... that's exactly what he's doing. He moves over each ass cheek, kissing where Jax and Callum smacked, before he works his way to the inside of my ankle, the back of my knee, and the inside of my thigh. By the time he's done, I'm a writhing, wet mess.

He backs away, and there's a silence hanging in the air. As I rise to my feet, my eyes are drawn to the boys, their naked forms standing confident and unashamed.

They all laugh when I glare at them.

"I'm sorry. I won't leave again."

"We know," Callum says matter-of-factly. "But we aren't done punishing you. You aren't allowed to come yet."

The need is there and I'm so close. My eyes narrow at him, a clear challenge, so I slowly rub my hand down my stomach, inching closer to my pussy. The need to have them inside of me is all-consuming, so I decide to turn the tables. They can want to punish me, but will they want to fuck me more?

"Don't you dare," Callum threatens, stepping forward.

"Don't do this?" I slip my hand between my legs and let out a moan. "Oh, I'm very wet." My other hand travels up to my breast.

Their eyes are wild. I love when they watch me touch myself. The feeling of power I have. I never knew exhibitionism would unlock something so primal inside of me.

Callum takes another step forward, eyes set, so I stop, holding my hands up so he doesn't make me. "I want to come, and I will, with or without you."

They all let out a low chuckle, almost daring me.

Glancing over my shoulder, I find a quick path out of here, and my heartbeat quickens. Time for a little cat and mouse, I smile.

"Everlee," Jax threatens softly, almost like he can read my mind.

Smiling, I blow them a kiss before running out of the room.

The men all yell various expletives as Jax shouts commands, telling them each where to go.

Fortunately, this house is a similar layout to my parents. I probably could have found a place to hide quickly, but I'm laughing too much. Trying to be as silent as possible, I run up the stairs and duck into the first bedroom, leaving the door open. I've always had this crazy idea, almost like reverse psychology, that if one leaves the door open, then the person looking for you wouldn't go into that room. It's probably silly, but I don't care.

I jump on the bed and lay along the headboard, slipping under the covers. My other bright idea is to pretend to be a pillow. The floor groans ominously in the hall as someone stalks down it slowly, causing me to freeze in place, holding my breath.

With a slight creak, the door inches open further, and my heartbeat quickens, its rhythm reverberating in my ears. A second later, the door closes and footsteps move down the hall. I let out my breath, but a second later feel the bed is moving.

Fuck!

They're crawling towards me and drag the cover back slowly. I pinch my eyes shut, because obliviously if you can't see them, they can't see you!

"Ali," Knox huffs, sliding his fingers up my leg. "I can still see you."

I open my eyes, smiling at him, and he motions for me to scoot forward so he can pull the pillows off the bed and slide behind me. "We can't hide here very well if the pillows are in the way."

"Sardines?"

"We never got to play a second round last time," he whispers against my temple.

I blush, remembering that night. The night I had all four of them at the same time.

His lips press against the base of my neck while his fingers make swirls on my stomach. "I don't want to lose you again," he admits almost too quietly for me to hear.

"I'm not going anywhere," I say, looking over my shoulder at him.

His hand travels up to my cheek, and he drags me towards him. His kiss is soft, but passionate. It's different from the others. It's sweet. After a moment, I roll my body so my chest is pressed against his and I throw my leg over his.

He pulls away from our kiss. "You know the rules. No orgasms with less than three people."

"Rules are meant to be broken," I whisper against his lips, eager to feel his cock against my pussy. "Plus, no one is going to orgasm right now." I smile before leaning in to take his lips again.

His hand travels around to my back, pressing our bodies together, deepening our kiss and connection. I reach my hand down and guide his cock to my pussy and position his head right at my entrance. Our breaths synchronize, releasing a puff of air as he enters me with excruciating slowness. A tingle shoots up my spine, through my fingers and back to my core as he slides in, stretching me. We thrust slowly, meeting in the middle, focusing on the kiss, but relishing in the feel of our sex. Knox differs from the others, softer. Damn, I missed him.

"If we aren't careful, they're going to find us," Knox whispers against my lips.

I roll over on top of him, still under the lip of the comforter. "Let them." With hands pressed firmly on his chest, and back hunched over, I rock my hips, concentrating on the feel of me wrapped tight around his shaft.

The door creaks open and I freeze, lowering back down on Knox's chest, both of us chuckling softly.

"I wonder where they could be?" Emmett questions, like you would a child. "Are they behind this chair? Nope. Are they behind the curtain?" He moves across the room. "Nope." He walks over to the edge of the bed and Knox and I hold our breath, hearts racing, eyes darting back and forth, waiting to be found with smiles spread across our face.

"Are they..." the covers fly back and the cool air of the room stings my skin.

"Get under here!" I motion, laughing.

He climbs on the bed and lies beside Knox, against the headboard, and covers us back up. Knox rolls us over, since he's still inside of me, so I'm in the middle of a Knox and Emmett sandwich. My favorite kind.

"Such a good hiding space. Totally couldn't find you," Emmett teases, placing a soft kiss on my shoulder.

In a synchronized motion, I twist my neck, press my lips to Emmett's, and feel Knox's thrusts resume.

"We have three people," I moan against Emmett's lips as his hand travels to my breast, rubbing my nipples between his fingers.

"We *do* have three people," Knox echoes, thrusting a little harder.

Emmett's hand continues to travel down, so he's rubbing over my clit slowly, matching the speed of Knox. Between the clitoral stimulation and Knox filling me, it won't be long before I come.

My hand grips Knox's head as he thrusts in. This moment is hard to describe. It feels like we're in a bubble, just enjoying the feeling and the connection of each other. It's not like this with Jax and Callum. While there's always that feeling of connection with them, this is softer, more pure. Jax and Callum are pure sex and passion. With them I feel like a wild beast who can never have enough, with Emmett and Knox... I don't know. It's like I also can't get enough, but for a different reason.

A second later, the covers are being thrown off us and Emmett, Knox, and I freeze. Jax is standing at our heads, while Callum is at our feet.

"In my room?" Jax groans. "My head goes up here," he whines, throwing his arm out towards the headboard.

"Oh, Everlee." Callum chuckles with a smile on his face.

"Care to join?" I offer.

He looks at me and smiles. "I'll watch for now."

I look at Jax. "I'll watch for now as well," he says, stroking his cock.

I look at it, right there in front of my face, staring at me like a glow worm looking for a hole. Does that make sense? No, no it does not, but I can't help it. I want it. I shake my head slowly, sucking on my bottom lip.

He chuckles. "You want me to feed you my cock?"

I nod.

I look over my shoulder at Emmett. "Pick a hole and fuck me like you missed me."

"Goddamn, Trouble."

"I think I just came a little," Knox jokes.

"Jax?" Emmett asks, clearly relaying a request with just his name.

"Yep," he answers Emmett's unasked question, bending down to the drawer at his right and pulls out a container of lube.

"Do you always travel with lube?" I tease.

Jax winks, but doesn't answer.

The cap clicks open, and I feel the cool gel spreading along my backside. A moment later, Emmett's finger is pressing in, prepping me, and the feeling shoots tingles through my body. Before these men, I never realized how much of an ass girl I am. Emmett lines up a minute later and presses his head against my opening, pausing while he slowly moves through the tight ring of muscle. Knox stops allowing me to adjust.

Emmett's right hand grips my hip tightly as he lets out a sigh. "Fuck, you feel so tight."

"I've been working my ass out for you." I laugh, but stop when I feel it clench around him.

He slowly pulses in and out, each time moving deeper and faster.

"What is that?" I ask, feeling something different.

"What is what?"

"On your dick," I blurt.

He pulls my hair behind my shoulder. "I got a Prince Albert piercing."

"A who?"

He chuckles. "I pierced the tip of my cock."

He gently pushes it inside and I don't know if it's because I'm so focused on it, but my entire body shudders in ecstasy. It feels... amazing. Like it's hitting on hidden spots of love.

After a few more thrusts, Knox starts. God, I missed this feeling. Pleasure washes over me, beginning at my toes and gradually moving up my body until it settles in my breasts. As I piston my hips between them, I become lost in the intense sensations and the electrifying contact that ignites every one of my sensitive parts. There is a part of me that wants to rock faster, but another part of me resists, wanting this to never end.

When I look up, Jax is standing before me, gently stroking his cock, while Callum sits in the room's corner, quietly observing us. He winks at me and a second later I grab Jax's shaft and pull him towards me, then realize the angle I'm at is going to kill my neck, so I hold up my finger.

"We need to rotate," I dictate.

"Yes ma'am," Emmett replies.

I sink all the way onto Knox, while Emmett and I roll as one on top of Knox. Emmett could have pulled out, but where's the fun in that?

Knox smiles and rubs my cheek. "All good, Ali?"

"Great."

His hands fall to my hips as he guides me up and down, while Emmett pumps harder. My back arches as a sigh escapes. "Y'all feel so fucking good."

"Bring you back to the south for one day and you're saying y'all," Jax laughs.

"Shut the fuck up and give me your cock," I demand, looking up at him through my lashes.

"As you wish." He grabs the back of my head and guides me to his hard length. I wrap my hand around it and began pumping, as I suck the head in, twirling my tongue around the tip. "Are you teasing me, Squirt?"

I hum around the head of his cock and open my mouth wider.

He presses in and lets out a puff of air. "I love to watch you take our cocks." His pace picks up as he matches Emmett's thrusts. He hits the back of my throat, bringing tears to my eyes, but I love it. Knox and Emmett are moving faster and faster while a faint thwap thwap thwap echoes from the corner of the room where Callum is pounding his hand along his cock and hitting the top of his thighs. The room is pure sex. Hot, wet, and fantastic.

My insides spool up as they continue to pound into me. Lust, need, want, crackling on my skin like a live wire hot to the touch. My body takes over, rocking back on Emmett and Knox, taking what it wants. What it needs. I'm so close and don't want to lose it again, so I drop my hand from Jax's cock and circle my clit. A second later, the top of my hand is burning from a pop. Emmett just smacked my hand!

Emmett takes over. "I got you, Trouble."

As tingles pulse through my body, I can't help but moan out. Yes. Yes, he did have me. Fuck, he knows what to do.

"She likes that," Knox says. "She's getting close."

"I know how to please our girl," Emmett coos.

"Squirt, you got to hold up. I can't come before you," he says through muted grunts. I can tell he's straining to hold on, and it makes me only want to go harder and make him come before me.

"Emmett. Fuck. She's..." Jax pants. "Hurry up!"

I can't help but smile around him.

Emmett swirls his cock around in my ass as he thrusts, and it hits new spots I've never felt before, while his finger continues to expertly move around my clit.

"Hey Jax, you may want to come before she does," Callum warns.

I hold my thumb up and they all laugh.

"Ok Ev." He grabs my head, his hands cupping around my ears like earmuffs as he takes over control, fucking my face. Drool slips down my chin as he relentlessly pounds into me. "Here I..." He lets out a low groan as his warm saltiness hits the back of my throat. I swallow him down, gulp after gulp, before he pulls out, rubbing the pad of his thumb along my bottom lip.

"God. I love..." he pauses. "The way you suck cock."

I look up at him and can't help but wonder if he's telling the truth or if he was going to say something else entirely.

Knox chimes in. "I especially love when she sucks it right over my head, so I get tea bagged over and over again."

"Shut the fuck up, Knox. You love my balls on your forehead."

I laugh and am surprised when both the boys moan.

"I love when you laugh with my cock buried deep in you," Emmett says.

"I love to laugh with them buried deep in me. Now shut up and fuck me."

"You're never leaving us again, Ali," Knox says, pulsing his hips up into me.

"Yes!" I lift my head up and press back into Emmett.

"Give her what she wants, Emmett, or I will," Callum commands.

He drops his hand from my clit and grabs my hips, pulling me into him. He reaches new depths and I cry out in ecstasy as my insides slowly clamp down. I'm... so... close.

I scream out as my orgasm pulses through me. It feels like it's ripping me apart from the inside as my hands grip the sheets, holding on for dear life. Knox and Emmett both come two thrusts later, their cocks quivering inside of me. I ride the orgasm, rather let it ride me, because it's almost too much.

"Thank fuck you came because I was about to fucking explode," Knox sighs.

Emmett pulls out and I sit back on Knox and look at him with my hands on his chest. "You are a beautiful man," I murmur.

"Can you say it louder so they all hear you?"

"Your dick is in her, so it doesn't count," Jax retorts, sitting on the edge of the bed, tucking his leg under him. "How do you feel?"

"I only had one orgasm, but I guess I can't complain." With a shrug, I glance at the wall to conceal the smile on my face.

Knox mumbles something as he starts to scramble, but before I know what's happening, I'm being lifted off Knox and thrown onto the bed.

Jax's knee presses into the mattress between my legs, his hands on either side of me as he leans over, his face inches from mine. "That was the wrong thing to say, princess."

I narrow my eyes at him. "Princess. That's new. How about queen?" I snap back.

Jax's lips curve into a smile. "I'm going to make you come, followed by Emmett, then Callum, and then Knox, and then maybe me again. We're going to make you come so much you won't be able to walk home, because your legs will be nothing more than limp noodles." He bends down and takes my breast in his mouth, swirling his tongue around it, before sucking just hard enough to send prickles to my throbbing pussy. He peppers kisses down my chest, stomach, and lands on my clit, holding nothing back.

"Shit Jax," I mumble, grabbing on to his hair for dear life.

EVERLEE – SEXHAUSTED

- -

As I CLIMB OUT of the shower, the scent of my shampoo lingers in the steam-filled bathroom. Padding across the floor, I wipe by hand across the fogged mirror and look at myself, cheeks flush but not from the shower. I wrap the towel around my hair, squeezing as much of the excess water out before I head to my bedroom. It's been several hours and my legs still feel like jello and unfortunately, my entire family noticed when I got back, wobbling into the house like a newborn deer. My mother just assumed I'd gone on a longer than average run around the lake which I went with, because telling her I just spent hours getting railed by four delicious man gods covered in tats who gave me seven glorious orgasms probably wouldn't have gone over well.

I collapse on my bed the first chance I get and have to force myself to roll over when I hear my phone ding.

Lizzy: *Hey! Call me!*

I sigh and video call her, knowing if I don't, she'll blow up my phone or worse, send Beckett to check on me.

No, thank you.

"Hey Queen!" she chirps, way too perky when my face pops up.

"Hey boo," I mumble. "Why didn't you just call me?"

"What's wrong with you?" She pauses, then her eyes grow wide as she looks at me through the screen, her head swiveling like it's examining a piece of art. "You were with them? Oooh girl, you're sexhausted!"

"Sexhausted?"

Her brow furrows and her lips twist like I'd asked a stupid question. "It's where you're exhausted from having too much sex."

"Of course it is. Where do you come up with these terms?"

She throws her head back, laughing. "How did you get time with them? You didn't tell your parents, did you? Beckett?"

"No! No. No. No. Could you imagine?"

"They're open minded."

"They're getting there. First a gay son and then a poly daughter." I laugh.

"Nothing wrong with either."

"One hundred percent agree. But..." I roll over to lie on my stomach and prop the phone against the headboard because my arm is getting tired. "We'll see where this goes first."

She shrugs. "I was just calling to check in on how your day was going."

"It was good. We went to that party and then I went on a walk and realized they're renting the house a few down from my parents."

"What are the odds?" She beams.

I shake my head.

"Have you decided what you're going to do?"

"I'm seeing this through. I can't leave them again. When I left, it felt like a piece of me was missing. When I saw Callum at the club, it was like everything clicked... and then Jax...

and then with them here. In some ways, it's like a day hasn't gone by without seeing them, but in other ways, it does. While I hated leaving them, it showed me... and perhaps even us, what we don't want to live without. It showed us what we're fighting for."

"I feel you should write a song," she says, wiping an invisible tear from her eye.

"Shut up."

"I know what you mean, though. Not exactly... but I get it."

"How's Tony?"

"He's fantastic!"

"You had your dinner tonight at Bo's, right?"

"We did."

"How was the food, and why am I having to pull answers out of you?"

She's beaming and slowly raises her hand onto the screen to show a beautiful teardrop engagement ring on it.

"What?! Wow! Congrats!" They've only been dating for what? Not even six months, but I guess you know when you know.

"It's so beautiful!" she squeals, holding her hand to her chest.

"I'm so happy for you! Tell me all the details! Did you have any idea?"

"No idea. You know, I thought he was going to do it on Valentine's Day, so I didn't even think about Easter. Emmett apparently hooked us up, though. He got us a private table in the kitchen so we could see everything being made and just before our dessert came out, Tony stands up, walks over and gets down on one knee. I squealed so loud the manager ran over thinking something was wrong."

I laugh.

"It was amazing."

"So, when's your date?"

She laughs. "We just got engaged!"

I stare at her in disbelief, knowing that's not an excuse she can use.

"Fine. I have several in mind that I want to run by him. I have to figure out if we want a winter wedding or a summer wedding." She quickly adds, "Next summer, of course."

"Of course." I smile, half believing her.

"When do you get back?"

"We have Easter events all day tomorrow. My flight is at like nine in the evening, I think."

"What time are the boy's flights?"

"I don't know."

"Let me know if you need me to pick you up from the airport."

"Thanks, boo."

"Now if you'll excuse you me, I'm about to go get sexhausted from riding that dicky dick. I had to tell you first, of course. Chicks before dicks and what not."

I'm still laughing when I plug my phone on the charger. Before I make it back to the bed, my phone dings again.

I walk back over to look at it, thinking it's Lizzy, but see Callum's name pop up.

Callum: *The boys and I wanted to wish you good night.*

Everlee: *Good night. Tell Emmett thanks for what he did for Lizzy tonight.*

Bubbles appear, then disappear.

I sigh, waiting, and then a moment later I'm getting another video chat.

A smile is already plastered on my face when I answer the call. All four guys are standing there looking hot as fuck. I want so badly to be in the middle of them right now, with their arms wrapped around me, not houses apart.

"Hey queen."

My cheeks hurt from smiling so much.

Emmett leans forward. "So? What happened?"

"Tony proposed to Lizzy. She said the table you set up for them in the kitchen was absolutely amazing and she was really appreciative."

"I had an idea when Tony called for the reservation. He was very particular and had that nervous quiver in his voice."

"She's probably excited?" Knox asks.

"Over the moon. But this is something she's always wanted from the time we were young." I ignore the weary smile on Jax and Callum's face as they study me, trying to get my feelings on this. "I'm thrilled for her. She's trying to figure out if she wants a winter or a next summer wedding."

"Well, if Bo's can help in any way," Emmett plugs.

I laugh. "I'm sure she'd love to use Bo's for something or everything. Engagement party, rehearsal dinner, reception... maybe all the above." A yawn escapes, catching me off guard. "You boys wore me out."

"You asked for it," Jax says coolly, without an ounce of remorse.

I narrow my eyes at him, then remember to ask, "Oh. Are you all flying back tomorrow?"

"We are."

"What time is your flight?"

"Whenever we want."

I laugh. "Because you have your own plane?" I tease, then stop laughing when they don't correct me. "No, the fuck you don't."

"It's not ours, per se. But a buddy let us borrow it." Jax smiles.

"Want a ride back?" Emmett asks.

"On your private jet? No thanks. I have to keep it classy back in coach, specifically one row in front of the bathroom."

"Sounds delightful." Knox smiles.

"Yes. I would love a ride back! Just need to figure out how to coordinate with my family. My flight leaves tomorrow night at nine, but I think we'll be done in the early afternoon tomorrow. The nine o'clock flight was the next flight after the two o'clock." I yawn again. "I need to get some rest. Tomorrow is going to be a big day and I need to get prepared for all the activities."

"Activities?" they ask, intrigued.

"Competitive Easter egg hunting. We hide eggs for the kids in the morning... and then we split up in teams after lunch for the adults."

"Competitive Easter egg hunting?"

"It can get pretty intense. One year we had to have Beckett's fire house get someone out of a tree. They climbed up to hide an egg, but got too scared to climb back down. And then tomorrow will also be canoe races, egg run, egg toss, and some others."

Jax is rubbing his arms, causing the muscles to flex. My teeth scrape over my bottom lip as I drink him up. Drink them all up.

"Sounds like we need to get some rest, boys," Knox says, clapping. "Tomorrow's going to be a big day."

"You don't need to come. Beckett and I have the record for the longest egg toss and I don't need you all ruining it." I laugh.

"Oh, we're definitely coming." Jax winks, causing a heat to race through me.

"See you tomorrow, Trouble."

"Sweet dreams," Knox offers.

EVERLEE - FFFF FUCK, NOT DDD DUCK.

WE'RE WALKING ON THE field leading down to the lake at six before seven. I feel like a zombie. A zombie who's been thoroughly fucked the night before, but still a zombie. The air is cool and damp and the lake has a layer of fog hovering above it, giving it that beautiful, eerie look.

"This is way too early," I groan.

"Well, if you hadn't gone on that... run." Beckett peers over his shoulder at me. "Which one did you... I mean, where all did you run?"

"What?"

He nods looking at the group of four guys who just walked up looking bright eyed and bushy tailed and oh so fuckable. I feel bad being at a church with all the dirty thoughts that are racing through my mind. They're all wearing a mixture of khakis, dark blue, or light blue pants with a collared shirt and light jacket.

"I don't know what you're talking about."

"I'm not stupid. Who was it? The one with the beard? He's dreamy, but the others... the one with the dark hair looks like he'd be a good time."

Jax. If only he knew...

"Will you stop?"

"Hell, the way they're looking at you, I'd think it was all four."

I look around, trying to find Winston. I've never wanted to hide eggs so badly before.

Beckett slaps my arm. "You dirty whore."

"Ow." I grab my arm. "What was that for?"

"All of them?"

"I didn't say that. Why would you assume?"

His face drops. "But you don't deny it either, and you know them! How do you know them?"

I shake my head incredulously.

"I will get it from you or from Lizzy." He pops his hip out with a boatload of sass.

"Reign the sass in queen. I already have Lizzy and she's more than enough."

He raises his brows and doesn't move, so I grab his arm and pull him to the side and he squeals, garnering several glances from others and especially the guys. I can feel their eyes penetrating into me, which is a lot less comfortable than their cocks. "Will you stop?"

"Tell me, tell me. Oh God, it would be a dream come true to have them all." He's biting his bottom lip with his hands tucked by his mouth, like a rabbit eating an invisible carrot.

"Stop. We're at a church function, for God's sake."

"I heard once that God's favorite word was come."

"Fuck Beckett!" I slap his chest. "You're going to hell!"

"I'll save you a spot." He grabs his stomach, laughing. "So?"

"Yes, I know them. But don't say anything or make it a big deal, please. They own a nightclub near Lizzy's house."

"A night.... Club? Like a sexy club?"

"No. A dance club you perv."

"Not a perv. Why don't you want anyone knowing that you all know each other?"

I shrug. "I just feel like it would lead to a lot of questions I can't and don't want to answer right now."

Beckett studies me for a second. "So which one?"

I stare at him. He's about as bad as Lizzy. In fact, he is the male version of her. Wildly inappropriate, but can sniff out bullshit better than anyone. He's also my best friend, but in a familial sense. He and Lizzy are equal. The three of us had gotten into a lot of trouble around the house growing up. Lizzy and me more than him, because he was the baby, so his little bitch ass used us as scapegoats. Just a bat of the eye or a quiver of the bottom lip and suddenly we were a horrible influence on that darling angel. He's a few years younger than us, so we weren't in school together a ton. One year in highschool and that was enough.

That was the year he came out to Lizzy and I. His ninth-grade year. He got a lot of shit for it at school, but we shut it down and I don't think anyone messed with him again. If they did, he didn't say. After we graduated, Lizzy would occasionally swing by and have lunch with him, just to be seen.

His foot taps impatiently as I struggle with which one to tell him. My go to is Callum, because that's what I'm used to, but Emmett's the one I danced with most yesterday, so that would make the most sense. "Emmett. The one with the beard."

"Yes, queen."

My heart flutters. Lizzy and Beckett rarely call me queen, but since the guys called me queen and took me on the O-Train repeatedly last night, the word does something to me now. Like my body has been conditioned like one of Pavlov's dogs to orgasm with the word.

I look over Beckett's shoulder and see the guys walking over to us, and my heart races.

Beckett glances over his shoulder, sees them, and looks at me. "Oh my God, they're coming over here... how do I look?" he asks in a shrilly voice, sweeping his hand through his hair.

I punch him in the arm. "Please don't embarrass yourself or me."

"Everlee," Callum says, walking up with a hint of a smile curling on his lips and his hand tucked in his pocket.

Wet. Fucking. Dream.

"Hi." Beckett waves quickly, his cheeks blushing.

"Beckett, this is Jax, Callum, Emmett and Knox." I point to each one as I say their name. "Guys, this is my impossible brother, Beckett."

"Nice to meet you," they all say softly. I can tell by the looks on their faces they're wondering how much I told him.

"I told him we all knew each other because of the club you have down the way from Lizzy."

"And that you took her to pound town last night."

"Jesus, Beckett." I slap his arm so hard my hand stings.

"She only admitted to Emmett."

"Only admitted?" Callum asks curiously.

"He thinks–"

"Everlee! Beckett!" our mother calls out, waving us over to a large bin of eggs.

"We've been beckoned," Beckett says.

As we start to walk over, I feel a hand on my elbow. Turning, I find Callum. Before he can I ask, I tell him, "I didn't say much. He has a nose like Lizzy, so he knows I slept with Emmett, even though he thinks it was all of you because of the way you look at me."

"The way we look at you?" He smiles and looks up as we reach the back of the group huddled around the bin of Easter eggs.

Winston speaks, "I want to thank you all for coming out this morning. The kids will be here in about forty-five minutes, so we need to hide all these eggs before then." He pats the bin, which probably has close to one thousand eggs in it, and chuckles. "We'll have varying degrees of difficulty and send the kids out in waves by age. Kids younger than five will go out first, so those eggs can be on the grass... then we'll send out the older kids every couple minutes later. We can hide some around, but don't get too close to the lake or too far into the woods. Stay on the green." He claps.

Excitedly, some, more than others, we all move forward to grab a basket and fill it with eggs. I try to ignore the brush of Callum's arm against mine, or Jax's leg touching mine as we dip our baskets into the bin.

A palpable tension lingers in the air, making every breath feel heavy. Want, need, desire, lust, fear, all dance around me. Like everywhere I move or they move, I'm aware. It's like bands stretch and pull me all over the field as I naturally gravitate to where one of them is, just wanting to be near them, but knowing I have to keep my distance.

The next two hours pass quickly. We had hidden all the eggs, and the kids stormed the field. I'm standing on the mulch near the lake, watching the chaos unfold in front of me, while also acting as a guard for the children. Several times, I catch glimpses of the guys, with their guard down, playing with the kids. Knox is army crawling on the ground with a little boy and girl, around the age of five or six. Another little girl has taken a liking to Callum, who is lifting his arm while she dangles, his face full of joy and laughter. Emmett has a small hoard of older kids around him as they scout the hillside looking for eggs and Jax... He's sitting on a log talking to a boy who has tears in his eyes. My heart feels like it's going to burst out of my chest.

These guys, full of their dirty mouths and tatted bodies, are so gentle with these kids. They genuinely look like they're having a good time. Occasionally, they talk to Mrs. Mary Mae, pushing her here or there at her command. The love and adoration they have for that woman... it's like a completely different side to them.

"Fuck."

"That's a bad word."

Nearly jumping out of my skin, I look down to find a little girl looking up at me. She's probably six or seven years old, wearing a pink gingham dress with a flower sewn on the front.

I must have completely zoned out, watching and thinking about the guys, because I had no idea there was a kid around me.

"Duck? I thought I saw a duck flying by."

"You said fuck."

My body does some sort of weird wave shake thing as I panic and drop to my knees. "No. No. That's not what I said. I said duck. Like quack, quack." I flap my arms around.

"You said fuck. Not duck. Ffff not ddd," she holds out the letter sound of each making the difference *very* distinguishable.

I pinch my lips in a hardline. "You shouldn't say the word that starts with an f."

"Neither should you. You have a potty mouth."

"Not the first time I've heard that," I mumble.

The girl puts her hands on her hips.

"Can I help you with something?"

"No. I just wanted to look at the water."

"Ok. Well, sit on your bottom here. I don't want you accidentally falling in. And don't go past the green."

"The grass?" she asks with a sassy tone.

"Yes. The grass."

"You ok over here?" Callum walks over.

I smile at him, but before I can say anything, the girl looks up and says, "She has a potty mouth."

He chuckles and squats down beside the girl. "You know. I say the same thing."

The girl's eyes grow wide, and she covers her mouth, giggling.

"Har har har." I smile.

Callum looks at the little girl. "I think they're about to count up all the Easter eggs to see who won."

"I didn't win. I only have three eggs."

Callum leans over, peaking in her basket. "I count over three."

"I'm seven. I know how to count to three."

Callum chuckles and places a handful of eggs in her basket. "Looks like you have more."

She smiles. "Thanks Mr. Callum."

"You're welcome, Bianca."

She runs off with her basket in hand towards the group. I look up and see Knox at the center of it all, like a grown child. It's amazing to me how naturally they fit in and how fantastic they are with the children. I'd seen it before with Callum when we were ice skating. All the kids bustling around like wild animals being let out of their cages and he never got irritated or impatient. Always laughing and understanding. He'd even caught a girl that was skating beside us and stopped her from falling.

Watching them all, I can't help but wonder how they feel about kids. Do they want them? Looking at them here today, they seem to like kids and would be fantastic parents. But again, that begs the question. How? I'd have to get some books on poly relationships with children.

When the egg count ends, the counselors and teachers shuffle the kids up the field, where they have other activities planned for them. Now the adult fun starts and first up is the egg toss.

I find Beckett talking to a guy by the fire truck and whistle to get his attention. He sees what's going on and pats the guy on the arm and runs over to meet me. My gaze lingers on the guy by the fire truck, and I can't help but wonder if there is something between them. He hasn't mentioned anything, but there's a prickle on my skin and a feeling in my gut.

A small crowd has formed and there ends up being twenty groups. They decide to run it in two sets of ten. Beckett and I are in the first round, while my guys are in the second. The best two teams from each round will then go into the final.

I look at Beckett, pointing my fingers between my eyes and his. "You got this?"

"Totally." He squats like an outfielder and claps his hands.

"Don't drop the egg," Jax chides softly.

"Already scared of us?" Beckett snaps back playfully.

"Hardly." Jax rolls his eyes with a glimmer of humor.

"We'll see," Beckett says, walking to the other side of the field.

I give Jax a 'ha-ha-ha' glance and take my spot.

My mother takes to the microphone. "You're starting five feet apart and will move back in five-foot increments until two groups remain. If your egg falls, but does not break, you get one more chance. If it falls and breaks, you're out. You'll wait for our mark each time, before you throw."

I clap my hands together a few times. "Let's go!"

When I glance to the sides, Jax winks at me, causing my stomach to bubble. I refuse to let him get in my head!!

"Go!" my mother shouts.

Beckett tosses the egg and I catch it, swinging my arms gracefully behind me. It probably isn't needed at this distance, but it's a good warmup for when we get further apart.

We go back and forth for several rounds, eliminating all the groups but two others. One is Winston and the girl he was talking to yesterday, and the other is a couple I've never met. We just need to survive one more group to get into the finals. At the twenty-foot mark, Beckett launches the egg deep. I back up three steps and catch the egg, quickly cradling it towards the ground. When I open my hand and see that it's intact, I let out a sigh of relief. I thought for sure it was going to crack in my hand.

"Sorry!" he yells across the field.

I look to my right and see the firefighter guy Beckett was talking to earlier is chatting with Emmett, while keeping his eyes glued on Beckett. My gut churns again, telling me if they aren't dating, there is definitely something there.

Maybe they're interested in one another? I need to dig around once we're done with this round.

Suddenly, a loud crack echoes from my left, breaking my trance. The unknown team's egg breaks all over the woman, causing her to laugh and toss her hands in the air.

"Next teams up," my mother commands, without waiting.

As Jax and Knox pass, I tease, "Don't drop the egg."

"Oh, darling. We're coming for you." Jax smiles, high-fiving Knox. Emmett and Callum make some snide comment under their breath, garnering a chuckle from Knox.

My mother goes over the rules again and the game starts. The first throw eliminates two groups and the second throw, another three. I thought this was going to be a quick round, but I was wrong, since the other teams make it back to the twenty-foot line. The guys are good, but really... should I've expected anything different?

The eggs are released. Jax catches his, followed by Emmett rolling on the ground to catch his. The other three teams either drop their egg or don't swing back enough and the egg explodes on them.

"Looks like we have our four teams," my mother announces, and I shake my head in disbelief.

I look down the row. It's my guys, Beckett and me, and Winston and his date.

Beckett says something to Knox, causing Knox to throw his head back in laughter.

"Trying to sabotage us?" Jax asks me.

"Would never dream of it," I retort.

"Watch your back, Squirt."

A flush colors my cheeks, and I narrow my gaze at him, looking around quickly. "I'd rather you watch my back while I'm fucking you."

His head snaps in my direction, his eyes on fire.

"Jax. Get your head in the game!" Knox calls out, casting daggers at me.

"Yes Jax. Get your head in the game," I tease.

"Oh, I'm going to get my head in something. You're going to pay for this later."

"I hope so."

He's shaking his head when I step back to my spot.

Beckett is watching me with an intense gaze, so I just shrug my shoulders and smile at him.

The egg toss starts on the ten-foot line and we get back to the twenty-foot line, before Winston and his partner miss. How did we end up here? I'm at a family event with my guys. Sure, my parents don't know them or even know that I know them, but if I daydream long enough, I imagine this is what it could feel like. Like the Gods are trying to show me I can have it all.

We're thirty feet apart, which is the furthest Beckett and I have ever been. The underhand toss is probably not going to work this time, so he baseball throws it. A risky move, but it's our only option. The guys try the underhand approach, but I don't have enough time to see if it works, because an egg is being hurtled at me.

Beckett releases a little too fast and crooked. Not paying attention, I run into Jax, tripping over his foot. He wraps his arm around me so I don't fall and catches the egg with his other hand out of reflex. Unfortunately, because he's focused on me, the egg cracks in his hand and drips onto my chest. Our eyes lock for a moment until we realize where we are and he stands me back up and uses his finger to scoop a large piece of yolk off my chest.

Beckett is over a moment later with a towel. "Thank God the fire department is here," he huffs, tossing the towel in my face. A very brotherly thing to do.

"Why?" I ask, a little dazed.

"That stare between you two. Fire," he sings. "Even made my pants wet."

I whip the towel at him, ignoring his other comments. "What kind of throw was that?"

"Admittedly, not my best."

"Ya think?"

When the guys walk over to us, Beckett swings his arm around Emmett's neck. "Congrats." He gives a slight nod to Callum before he drags his arm off Emmett.

"I thought you were going to take him out sooner," Emmett says to Beckett, pointing at Jax.

"I had to make it look accidental," he replies, laughing.

"You didn't," I growl.

"Only teasing," Emmett winks. "But that *was* a pretty epic finish."

"We didn't win," I pout.

"It's ok. We can let someone else win every once in a while. This just means y'all have to come back next year." Beckett shimmies his shoulders.

I look from him to the guys, but before they can answer, my mother walks over with the microphone.

"A little post egg toss bantering," she jokes awkwardly. "Congrats to our new winners..." She looks at them, waiting for their names.

"Callum and Emmett." Callum smiles.

"Callum and Emmett," she echoes, handing them the coveted golden egg. They grab it and thrust it into the air.

"Can't wait to see you here next year to defend your title." She smiles and looks at me. I can't decipher what her look means. Was she happy because someone finally defeated Beckett and me, or had she seen the way we looked at one another? Perhaps she saw Emmett today with the children and the big man with a beard melted her little heart?

"We have lunch now, then the competitive Easter egg hunt, followed by boat races. Teams of three."

I walk over to the food table and Beckett rushes up behind me, resting his chin on my shoulder while we walk. "Ooh. Who are you going to choose for your team? So many good options."

"Are you picking the handsome little firefighter you were talking to earlier?"

"Stop. We're talking about you right now, not me."

"I'm totally fine switching." I smile.

"Sharing?" He pries playfully.
"Firefighter?"

EVERLEE - WET. NOT JUST FOR YOUR PUSSY.

Mrs. Mary Mae grabbed Emmett's attention during the competitive Easter egg hunt and is now asking all sorts of questions about Bo's, so he told us he'd sit out of the boat race. Beckett called dibs on Will, his new friend, and Knox to be in his boat, so I get Jax and Callum.

As we're walking to the water's edge, Callum asks, "Not as many people in this one?"

"They're scared of getting wet."

A low chuckle sounds in his chest. "But you aren't?"

"I enjoy getting wet."

"I enjoy making you wet."

"That makes two of us."

"I can't wait until we're back home."

"What happens then?"

"We're never letting you leave again," he whispers coolly, but his words send a heat pulsing through my body. He brushes his hand across my back, then distances himself from me, listening to the instructions.

Home. Tonight. Ideas race through my mind about the plane ride, and then the car ride to their house. I've never done it on an airplane before, but somehow I don't think the mile high club would have the same ring if it's in a private jet versus the cramped bathroom of a passenger plane.

A whistle blows and I shake my head, clearing it. I didn't hear the instructions, but assume it's the same as every other year.

"Ev, over here!" Jax calls out.

"Yea, Ev," Beckett chimes from the boat beside ours.

"Careful, or I'll dump your ass in the water," I threaten playfully.

"Not with me in the boat!" Knox defends.

"Definitely with you in the boat, princess," Jax retorts.

"Well, I *did* leave my crown at home, just in case," Knox shoots back, climbing into the boat.

"Why do I feel like we're going to get wet?" Will asks the group, resting his chin on the paddle.

"They have to catch us first." Beckett rubs his back affectionately.

When I catch Beckett's eye, I pump my brows. He tilts his head to the side and gives me a look that's a cross between fuck off and so what, causing me to chuckle as I climb in. There are some questions being asked, but we aren't listening. We're in our own world of sexual tension and forbidden romances to pay attention. All we care about is the next verbal jab and how not to get flipped over, because the looks being thrown around right now yell that's exactly what's going to happen.

"I want to caution everyone that the water will be cold..." I say.

"Evy baby. Is that fear I hear?" Knox twirls the paddle on his lap.

"Evy baby?" Beckett looks over his shoulder. "Am I not here with you? Are Will and I chopped liver?"

I glare at Beckett, then shift my gaze to Knox. "Of course not, Knoxxy baby. It was simply a warning for when we dump your ass."

Everyone chuckles.

"I think it best if we start down there." Callum points to the opposite end of the shore.

I agree, so Jax and Callum lift the boat with ease and carry it over their head while I simply walk beside them.

My mother sees us and chuckles. "Everlee and Beckett are so competitive. Always looking for the advantage on how to beat each other."

I chuckle, but she has no idea what's about to go down. We aren't racing around any buoy. We're racing to take each other down.

Callum climbs in first, followed by me, then Jax in the back. I look down at the few other boats and see Beckett with a huge smile on his face. He's as excited as I am. Will turns around to say something to him and I see Beckett place his hand on his shoulder, and Will put his hand on Beckett's. Ooh, they like each other. I wish I was closer so I could taunt him, like he's been taunting me, but the eyebrow pumping and winks will have to do for now.

Jax leans forward on my right side, sliding his left hand around my hip. "You ready to take them down?"

"Ready and excited would be an understatement." I laugh.

The horn blows, and Jax pushes us off the edge of the lake. We paddle, at first, very clunky, until I pause a beat to get in sync with Callum. I glance to my left and see Beckett's boat, just a tip behind us.

"Let's go!" I pull the paddle through the water.

We get in sync, leaning forward, pulling back. One... two... one... two.

We're ahead, and I hear Beckett yelling commands and Knox laughing like a wild hyena. His joy is infectious.

After a few more minutes, Callum dictates. "Left side."

I continue to paddle, while Callum and Jax switch sides. Our canoe starts slowly turning left around the large red and white buoy. By the time we turn, we're coming up on Beckett and Knox's boat in the opposite direction. I stick my tongue out and Beckett takes his paddle and reaches out, knocking mine down and tries to pull it. I, of course, don't let go and reflexively try to pull back. Before I know what's happening, I'm in the water, swimming back up to the top to get air, along with Callum, Jax, Knox, Beckett, and Will.

We're all doggy paddling, wiping the hair out of our face when Beckett chuckles and says, "Well, that didn't go exactly as planned."

"What did you think was going to happen?" I splash water on his face, irritated.

"You could have let go!" he retorts, splashing back.

I look at the guys. "I'm sorry about my idiot brother."

Callum, Knox, and Jax only look mildly irritated, thankfully.

"Let's get back in the boat," Jax says.

"Do you all need help?" A man from another boat asks, rowing up to us.

"No. We're all good." Jax swims around me. "Knox, help me. Beckett, you and Will are going to bring your boat over once we're in."

I rub my hand over Jax's ass, causing his head to snap in my direction. He returns the gesture, running his hand over my panties with a wild gleam in his eye.

"You ready?" Knox asks.

"Yea." He gives an affectionate pinch on my backside before he moves to the boat.

They count to three and at the same time kick with ease out of the water, on opposite sides of the boat. Their pants are glued to their legs and I let out a moan, as I trace the fabric up to find no seam line. They aren't wearing underwear. Fuck me! They look divine.

"Everlee, are you ok in the water for a little longer?" Jax asks.

"Yea." I move over to Callum.

"You aren't going to ask about me?" Callum jokes.

I splash Callum with a little water. "Obviously, I'm more important."

"Obviously," Callum says, dunking me under the water, laughing.

I pop up a moment later, looking like some sort of wild sea creature with my hair covering my face. "Ass." I splash him again, this time with more oomph.

"I know." He sweeps his arm through the water and hooks it around me.

I pat him on the chest and his hand moves to cover mine. Beckett smiles with a big 'I told you so' look on his face. I roll my eyes and shake my head.

Ten minutes later, we're all in the boats heading back to shore. I hadn't noticed how cold it was when we were in the water, but moving on top of it now, I'm shivering and my teeth are chattering. Fortunately, the guys don't need my help rowing, so I can scoot up close to Callum.

"What happened?" my mother asks with that look of equal parts shock and embarrassment.

"Your s-s-son thought it would be f-f-funny to take my paddle and tipped b-b-both boats over," I mumble through chattering teeth.

"What?" Beckett throws his hands in the air, trying to act innocent.

"That may have worked when you were a kid, but you're an adult now, Beckett!" our mother scolds. She turns towards the rest of our little group and apologizes profusely.

The guys are nice and tell her everything is fine, passing on all the things she offers as a way to make up for it.

I glance at my watch. "Mom. I'm going to head back to the house and get this lake water off me and get in some warm clothes before I head to the airport."

"Leaving so soon?" She frowns.

"It was close to time before Beckett dumped us."

She looks at my brother. "Can you manage taking her to the airport without causing trouble?"

He shrugs.

"Beckett!" She swats at his arm, then stops. "Wait. How are you getting back to the house?"

"Callum said he could drop us off," I offer quickly.

"He doesn't have to do that. I can get your father-"

"It's really no problem, ma'am." Callum steps forward.

"You can fit all these people in your car?"

"It has a third row."

"Fancy." She smiles, with a flush hitting her cheeks.

I lean across the space and give my mother a hug. "Thanks for this weekend."

"Call me when you get home."

"I will," I whisper.

Her hand cups my cheek. "It was great seeing you. I wish we could have spent more time together, but it was so crazy with Mrs. Mary's event and what not."

"It's ok. I'll come visit soon, or you all can come up and visit."

"On a plane?"

My brows raise. "Or you can drive." I chuckle.

"We'll see." She half smiles.

She never really travels outside of her little town and hates planes with a passion. My father and I have tried to explain they are safe, but you can't convince that woman of anything. She's stubborn and set in her ways.

"Go find your father before you leave. I think he's over by the food table. Can't get him away from there," she grumbles. "And get warm. Your lips are turning blue."

"I'll go say bye to him really quick, then meet you at the car," I say to Callum.

"We're going to grab Emmett and say goodbye to Mrs. Mary and then I'll drive around to the front to pick you up." Callum winks before walking off.

I find my father over by the food tent and give him a quick hug goodbye. I have to explain why I'm standing in front of him with chattering teeth and blue lips. He chuckles and mentions he'd heard the commotion in the water and knew it had to be us two. He wishes me a safe flight home and gives me one more hug. I scurry across the lawn, arms wrapped tightly around me, feeling like a freaking ice cube. I have to figure out how to pay Beckett back.

EVERLEE - WHEN YOU'RE AN ICE CUBE, FUCK THE RULES!

By THE TIME I get to the front of the church, Callum is pulling around the circle. The back door swings open and Emmett climbs out, holding his arm towards me, inviting me in.

As I approach, his jovial expression fades away, and worry takes its place.

"Fuck, Trouble. What have you done?"

I look up at him and try to smile, but find it difficult since my jaws ache from the chattering. "Beckett."

"Take your dress off!" he commands.

My eyes grow wide with surprise, but my shivering body does not afford me the flush that usually accompanies such commands.

He looks over my shoulder. "There's no one out here." He pulls me towards him, and turns us so I'm between him and the seats, blocking the view from anyone else who could walk by, and bends down to pull my dress off, throwing it on the floorboard before pushing me inside. "You're going to get hypothermia." His words are short and filled with panic.

I climb in and see Beckett and Will are in the third row and Jax is in the second row, casting a disapproving glance.

Emmett climbs in and shuts the door. He pulls his shirt off and I hear either Will or Beckett gasp in the backseat, but ignore them. Emmett hands me his shirt. "Come here." He lifts me onto his lap. "Straddle me."

I catch Beckett's eye this time and the look on his face is screaming 'I fucking told you so' with his one brow lifted. I quickly glance at Jax, and he rolls his eyes. He's clearly uncomfortable with the public displays of affection in front of Beckett and Will, but knows I need to get warm.

I press my chest against Emmett's and his skin feels like fire. He wraps his shirt around my back and then wraps his arms around me, holding me tightly. I lay my cheek on his shoulder and look at Jax, who reaches out and rubs the back of his finger across my cheek affectionately.

"We need to get her warmed up. She's like an icebox," Emmett groans.

"Just take her to your place and Will and I will walk back to my parent's house."

I can tell Jax wants to say something, to correct him, but it's no use. Beckett has a pretty good idea of what's going on, even if he isn't certain.

"After we all shower, we'll swing by and pick up her stuff and take her to the airport with us," Jax concedes.

"You have the same flight?"

"They have a jet," I brag.

"Of course they do," Beckett huffs with a note of jealousy.

"It's a buddy's," Jax corrects.

My shivering has slowed to random bursts of shakes, as Emmett's body heat helps to warm me up. He runs his hand over my head. "Are you ok, Trouble?"

I hum, and he laughs, placing a kiss on my head.

The rest of the car ride is quiet. When we get back to the guy's rental, Emmett wraps his shirt around me and carries me to the house. Fortunately, his shirt is long enough to cover my underwear so I'm not flashing everyone.

"I'll see you soon." Beckett winks and I flip him off. He throws his head back in a fit of laughter as he and Will walk arm in arm towards the walking trail that surrounds the lake. "How convenient they were so close." He calls over his shoulder, not turning around.

Callum opens the door and runs inside, saying something about starting the shower. When Emmett drops me in the bathroom, I frown because it's small- very small, compared to his and the group shower in the voyeur room. I want all the guys with me, but they won't fit.

Callum nods his head. "Go on. We'll see you when you're done."

"Four of us need to take showers, and there are only two bathrooms in the house," I say, assuming it's like my parents.

"Three in this house," he intones.

I hold my hand out to him.

He looks over his shoulder at Emmett, who holds his hands up. "I'm going to finish packing us up. I may run over to Ev's house and get her luggage."

"You don't have to do that." I smile at him.

"I'm not doing it to be nice." He steps forward, wrapping his arm around me, pulling me towards him. "I'm doing it because I don't want to wait longer than I have to, to fuck you." He takes my mouth in a hard and passionate kiss, then pulls away like nothing's happened and pokes the tip of my nose. "Now go take a shower and make it quick." He turns me around and smacks my ass before he walks out of the bathroom, shutting the door.

Callum strips out of his clothes, and I take a deep breath.

"You heard the man. We need to be quick." I wrap my arms around him and squeeze his butt.

"I think you're talking about something else completely."

"Does it matter?" I slip out of my underwear and let my bra fall to the floor.

His teeth scrape over his bottom lip as he drinks in the sight of me, his cock hardening. "You're so fucking beautiful."

I pull the curtain back and climb into the shower, quickly running the water through my hair to wash away as much of the chill as possible.

"Let me," he commands in a low and sultry voice.

The door opens and my heart bursts with excitement. "Hello?"

"Don't mind me," Emmett says. "Just grabbing a few things." The door closes a second later.

Callum reaches beside me, his chest brushing over mine as he grabs the shampoo. Even him pouring shampoo in his hand is hot as fuck. Everything moves in slow motion with a Marvin Gaye song playing in the background. He turns me around and presses his chest to my back and glides his cock between my thighs as his hands work into my hair.

My head bobbles back as a moan escapes.

"Oh baby, don't do that."

"It feels so good, though." I reach down to rub the underside of his cock, lifting it so I can rock my pussy over it.

His breath stutters.

"You feel so good," I moan again, rocking my hips more, pulling his cock up so it lightly brushes over my clit.

His fingers dig into my scalp each time his cock slides along my pussy.

I turn around to rinse the soap out of my hair and when I tilt my head back, his mouth clamps around my breast while his fingers press into me. Another moan escapes as my body clenches around him. It feels like butterflies are exploding in my stomach.

"I'm sorry," he mumbles lightly against my hot skin.

"For what?" I ask, confused.

"For the way I'm about to fuck you." He lifts me out of the shower and bends me over the sink and plunges into me without hesitation.

"Fuck, Callum."

His hands clamp to my hips as he pounds into me hard and fast, causing my ass to jiggle and my boobs to flop wildly around. This is raw and pure animalistic need.

"All day." He pants through thrusts. "I've seen you... walking around in that... dress. God!" He continues to thrust harder and faster, if that were even possible. "And all I wanted to do was... rip it off of you and make you come." His thrusts slow only a little as his hand moves to my clit and he rubs. "I wanted to fuck you in front of... everyone. I wanted them to know you are... mine." He pulls out and flips me around, sitting me on the edge of the sink, throwing my legs over his shoulders. "I wanted them to know you are ours." He dives in, his tongue moving quickly with pinpoint precision. His goal is to make me come in the quickest way possible and I'm so fucking close. Between him, his cock, his tongue, and his words. I grab onto the back of his head and hold him to my pussy while he eats like it's his last fucking meal.

"Shit, Callum," I whimper out as he sucks on my clit.

He stops and stands up, pulling my hips to the edge of the counter while he presses into me again. "I want to feel you come around my cock," he says, using both of his hands to push the hair away from my face before he presses his lips to mine. His tongue thrusts in, mimicking his cock in my throbbing pussy. His kiss is wet and needy, and I want to give him everything.

The faster he pulses, the faster I feel my orgasm coming. Because of his height, his cock is angled in such a way that it rubs on all the right places inside of me, making me wild with desire.

"Harder Callum." I grab his back, pulling my body just a little closer to him. He lifts my legs, so I wrap them around his waist. A second later, he's carrying me across the hall to the bedroom. He kneels onto the bed, his cock never leaving me as he continues to thrust. He grabs my legs and pulls them in front of him and up his chest, so the bottoms of my feet are pointed at the ceiling. This angle allows him in deeper as he pushes up on his knees. I moan out as pleasure and pain rip inside of me.

"Are you ok?" he asks, pausing.

"Yes. Yes. Don't stop." There's pain, but the pleasure is... fuck, he is deep.

He thrusts his hips, as one hand holds my legs to his chest and the other circles my clit. That's all I needed. The one touch. I explode, crying out in ecstasy, feeling the inside of my pussy pulse around him.

He lets out a low groan as his eyes roll into the back of his head. "I love to feel you around me. Your pulsing pussy squeezing on my cock." He grunts out with two more thrusts, then stops, pressing his cock in deep. His breath shudders as he collapses on me, my legs falling to the side, completely useless.

"So much for the shower." I laugh.

"We'll give you a bath when we get home." He winks, then brushes a kiss across my nose before he pulls out and climbs off the bed.

I watch him walk to the door, then call after him. "I hate to see you go, but I love to watch you walk away."

He casts a side glance over his shoulder and winks as he walks back into the bathroom to shut the water off.

I lay on the bed and wait for a second before I feel the warm ooze pool. I leap from the bed like a ninja, and sumo wrestler walk across the hall into the bathroom, then dart to the toilet.

"What in the hell are you doing?" I hear asked from the hall.

"I didn't want your come leaking all over the place, so I ninjaed myself into the bathroom."

"Is that what you call it?"

"Yes." I start peeing. This should be awkward for me, but it feels so natural. "You probably didn't even see me because I moved so quick."

He takes the small towel in his hand and rubs it in his hair. "I was getting you a towel. They didn't have any in here, so I had to go to the other bathroom. When I got back in the hall, I saw..." he shakes his head, chuckling. "You." He struggles for the words to describe me.

I stand up, wiping several times. "You have a lot of come."

He throws the towel at my face and walks away.

I'm still laughing when I walk back into his room a moment later. "I have nothing to wear."

"What you're wearing is fine." He zips up his suitcase.

"I'm naked," I retort.

"I see no problem with that." He sets his suitcase on the floor.

I tilt my head to the side. "So you won't mind everyone at the airport seeing me naked?"

His eyes narrow into thin slits as he stomps across the room in two steps. He uses his two fingers to lift my chin. "You're our little bunny and no one else's. If another man sees your naked body, I will cut his eyes out and serve them to him on a fucking platter."

A puff of air escapes as a wave of passion and desire pulse through me.

"Is it safe to approach?" Emmett asks from down the hall.

We slowly turn our heads to look at him, and Callum drops his hand. "All good. I was just reminding her who she belongs to."

Pressing my hand against his chest, I push him away. "I don't belong to anyone but me." I walk down the hall, but not before Callum reaches out and slaps my ass.

"You can belong to you, but that ass is mine."

"Nope. It's mine," Emmett says, grabbing it. When I try to reach for my clothes, he holds them just out of reach with a mischievous grin. "I dried them for you while you were... showering. Or whatever you were doing." He smirks.

I grab under his chin and stand on my tippy toes to give him a kiss. "Thank you."

I slip on my underwear, bra, and dress in the middle of the hall and pause for a second. Never in a million years would I have ever thought I'd be in a relationship with four men at the same time. I'm still getting used to the idea of this lifestyle and occasionally it catches me off guard. But damn, is it great!

I follow Emmett and Callum downstairs. "Your brother just dropped off your suitcase, so we can leave whenever you're ready," Emmett calls over his shoulder.

"Nice shower?" Jax asks, walking through the room, letting his hand glide from one side of my waist to the other.

"It was great."

My phone dings.

Beckett.

I roll my eyes before I even open his message, because I know it's going to be some smart-ass comment.

Beckett: *Have a safe flight.*

Everlee: *That's it?*

Beckett: *I love you?? When did you get so needy and sentimental?*

Beckett: *I would have thought those boys took care of that.*

Everlee: *There it is. I was waiting for some smart-ass comment.*

Beckett: *Glad I could oblige.*

Everlee: *How's Will?*

Beckett: *What do you mean?*

Everlee: *Seems like you two were cozy in the back.*

Beckett: *You mean when you were straddling Emmett while making eyes at Jax?*

Everlee: *Because your stupid ass almost gave me hypothermia.*

Beckett: *Hypothermia, schmipopermia.*

Everlee: *Bye.*

Everlee: *And love you too.*

Beckett: *Use protection.*

Everlee: *You too!*

Beckett: *Everlee!*

Everlee: *You and Will need to come see me sometime.*

Everlee: *And bye for real this time.*

Everlee: *We're headed to the airport.*

"Everything ok?" Emmett asks.

"Yes. Beckett being Beckett."

"Him and Will seemed to be getting along."

"That's what I said, but he won't admit they're dating or anything more than buddies."

"He seems to have his theories about us."

"Well, it didn't help you undressed her, then had her straddle you in the car," Callum says, walking back in.

"Please. He already knew or had his thoughts, and she was a fucking ice cube. Sorry, not sorry. She's more important than keeping this secret."

I pat him on the chest. "Aww, boo boo." I feel a brief pang of guilt using Lizzy's name on him, but what he says gives me all the feels. I look over at Callum. "He's the male version of Lizzy."

"Shit."

"Yea. Plus, he doesn't care. I can have him sign an NDA or something if you want."

Callum looks at Jax, who shrugs. "We'll wait and see what happens."

"With?" I ask hesitantly, nervous of the answer. Is that a we'll see what happens with our relationship?

I must have a certain look on my face, because seconds later, all four guys are shoulder to shoulder surrounding me. I turn in a circle, looking at them, confused, but also smiling.

Jax grabs under my chin. "Not with you. You are ours."

Callum spins me around, so I'm facing him. "You're never leaving us again."

Knox grabs me. "And if you even think about leaving–"

Emmett spins me around, so I'm facing him. "We'll burn down the world to find you."

Knox spins me back around to face him, my head woozy from the spinning and their words. "But not in a creepy way." He smiles, before he boops me on the nose, playfully.

Jax huffs, and Knox defends, "What? It sounded a little creepy." He imitates in a deep robotic, caveman-like voice. "You shall not leave. We will burn world to find you."

My insides get all oooey gooey. "Let's go home."

EVERLEE – DON'T TRY TO DISCONNECT A VIDEO CHAT WHEN YOU'RE TWO DICKS DEEP

••

WE'RE AT A PRIVATE hangar at the airport thirty minutes later and tucked inside is a small jet. Well, not small, but smaller than the planes I'm used to riding on.

The door opens and the steps flip down and standing at the top is a man dressed in a gray suit.

Brady.

He sees me and smiles. "Ms. Everlee. This is an unexpected surprise," he says when I get to the top of the stairs.

"Hello Brady. I would have to agree with you." I chuckle.

Brady is a multifaceted man, with a captivating aura of mystery surrounding him. He knows how to wear a suit, is as muscular as all the boys, and has a military-isk presence about him. Perhaps he served with Jax in the SEALs? It would make sense, but why act as chauffeur to them and now, apparently, a pilot?

As I walk down the spacious, dark hardwood aisle, the lacquered surface gently reflects the lights above. On the left are two sets of cream colored, leather seats facing one another with a table in the middle and on the right is a long couch and further down the aisle, behind it, is another set of individual seats.

Six seats.

And a couch.

Settling into one of the chairs by the couch, I secure my seatbelt, then close my eyes and lean back, trying to focus on the supple leather beneath my fingertips.

"Everything ok?" Emmett asks, letting his hand glide over my head.

"Yes. Excited to get back home." And a little nervous. I was supposed to use this weekend to decompress without the guys to figure things out, but that obviously didn't happen. We had planned to meet Tuesday night to talk about our future, but now I don't know if that's still happening. I don't want to dampen the weekend, but there are things we still need to discuss. I know I don't want to go anywhere, and I think they want the same, but what does that mean?

The sound of someone sitting down catches my attention, causing me to open my eyes.

Knox.

"Hey Ali."

"Hey Knox." I feel my stomach tighten.

Jesus, get a hold of yourself, Everlee.

Brady closes the door and moves to the cockpit, closing that door as well. Moments later, we pull out of the hangar and my hands grip the armrest. I'm not usually scared of flying, so I don't know what's going on.

"You ok?" Knox notices, nodding towards my hands.

"Oh. Yea." I pull my hands off the armrest and clasp them in my lap.

"Ok." He eyes me cautiously.

I look out of the window and see us lining up, ready to take off. Brady chimes over the speaker and lets us know we'll be home in about an hour and a half. I glance at my watch. A solid two hours earlier and right at dinnertime.

Dinnertime? Why am I thinking about dinnertime? Once we're up in the air, I look around at the guys and they are quietly sitting in their seats, looking out of the window or flipping through their phone. The air feels... weird. Or is it me? Had I expected we were going to have a high-altitude orgy? What are they thinking about? They've said they don't want me going anywhere, but that's when we were in our bubble away from home and now we're going back.

I hear Jax behind me. "Brady, turn these cameras off."

"Yes, sir."

A flutter tingles in my stomach as I sit up in my seat, my pulse racing.

My seatbelt unbuckles and I turn to my side to see Jax has reached around to unclip it.

"What are you doing?" I ask breathlessly.

"I feel you pulling away. Like you're getting nervous. Second guessing this," he says slowly as he stands up and walks around in front of me, pushing the table against the wall and hooking it in place. He falls to his knees, kneeling between my legs, hands clasped on my thighs.

My breath hitches in my throat. All I can do is shake my head, because his words, his movements, suck the air from my lungs.

"So you aren't second guessing?"

Jax's fingers slowly, painfully, inch up my leg. "Have you ever been fucked on a plane?"

"No," my voice peeps out.

"Would you like to?"

I bite my bottom lip, nodding.

Knox sits back in his seat watching Jax and me, and I don't know what turns me on more. The anticipation of what's about to happen with Jax or the knowledge that

Knox and the others are about to watch me. If you would have asked me before if I was an exhibitionist, I would have emphatically said no. God no. Not even. Ewww. I don't want others watching me. But now. With them...

Fucking show me the money. You get a pussy view. You get a pussy view. You all get pussy views!!! The way their eyes watch me causes a heat to stir inside of me. It's intoxicating. Powerful.

He lifts my dress slowly, exposing my panties.

He runs his nose up the inside of my leg, from my knee to my pussy, and takes in a deep breath. I fight the cringe that my body wants to do. That the self-conscious me would have done. Instead, I run my fingers through his hair and just hold him there for a second, taking what I can get from him.

Emmett and Callum move to the couch, the bulges in their pants giving away their excitement.

My breasts swell, pressing hard against the fabric of my bra, at the same time my stomach twist into knots.

"I love the smell of your pussy."

"Thanks?" I don't know what in the hell to say. I laugh awkwardly. Seriously, what the fuck is wrong with me?

He hooks his fingers in the top of my panties and pulls them down slowly, tossing them to the ground. He reaches around the back of me and pulls my hips closer to the edge of the seat and lets out a low hum as he gently kisses the inside of my knee.

"Take your dress off, Everlee. I want to see your breasts," Callum commands.

I look at him, my head in a daze, and smile. "Yes, sir."

He swallows hard, the fire blazing in his eyes. "Good girl."

I slip my dress over my head and, with my hands clasped on the back of my bra, I look at the guys. "I want you all to take your pants off and stroke yourself so I can watch you while you watch me fuck Jax's face."

"Goddamn," Emmett moans.

Callum just continues to stare at me, uncertain of this shift in power, so I level my gaze at him. "Now," I whimper out, sounding a lot weaker than intended, because Jax just ran his tongue up my pussy. My intention was to give a command, but my voice betrayed me and sounded like a desperate puppy calling out for its mother's teat.

My eyes catch Jax's and he's staring up at me like he knew exactly what he was doing.

"Asshole," I tease.

"I'll play with that later." He winks before settling between my legs, pulsing his tongue in and out before sucking on my clit.

"Fuck," I moan through clenched teeth, running my hands through his hair.

"Language, Everlee," Callum says, freeing his hard cock from his pants and slowly stroking himself. That's a beautiful fucking man, with a goddamn glorious dick, and his tattoos. So many, but so fucking hot.

My gaze flips to Emmett who's stroking himself with his piercing gleaming at the head of his cock. I can't help but wonder what it would feel like in my mouth, then realize I'm biting my bottom lip.

"You taste so sweet," Jax says, running his tongue up again.

I rip my bra off and toss it at Knox, who pumps his cock up and down, slowly. He chuckles, grabbing it off his face, and sets it on the ground.

My hands explore my breasts, applying pressure and gently tweaking my nipples, as I fantasize about their hands on me while Jax continues to lick and suck. As I'm getting closer to the edge, my moans become more frequent, echoing through the air. I'm aware of the dangers of expressing my needs openly, as the guys take delight in teasing and prolonging my pleasure. I hate-love it, because while they're a huge twat tease, the orgasm is always one hundred times better because of it. I believe this is why they say good things come to those who wait - the anticipation builds up and makes the outcome even more satisfying. Because damn.

"Don't stop," I plead, grabbing the back of his head and holding him to me. My legs are on his shoulders and I'm at his mercy. My stomach is clenching, my pussy is quivering. I tilt my head back, pushing my pussy closer to his face. He's not stopping and I'm too fucking happy. He presses three fingers in and the fullness of me stretching around him with his tongue lapping hungrily over my clit causes my body to explode.

My ass slides to the very edge of the chair, while my hands grip onto the back of his head, while I ride his face and my orgasm. A groan so deep inside comes out that I'm certain Brady is going to chime on the intercom asking if we'd hit a flock of bison or something.

A flock of bison? What the fuck, Everlee?

"Fuck Jax." I try to push him away because it's too much. He's too much. My clit is hypersensitive right now, and he's like a wild animal starved. He continues lapping and sucking all of my sweet juices. I let out another moan and press my hands to his forehead, pushing him away. "Fuck me, Jax. Now!" I need to feel his cock inside of me.

He stands up and rips his pants off and points at Emmett and Callum, who leap off the couch and to the side. They grab under the lip of the couch and pull out and it flattens into a small bed, probably the size of a full.

Miracle Jet. That's what this is. Although miracle jet sounds like the name of some superb lube. I chuckle at myself, proud of my little joke.

My phone rings. Yelling *'hooker pickup the phone'*, *'hooker pickup the phone'*. When did she change the ringtone on my phone? I'm going to kill her. Is this why she's been texting most of the weekend?

I grab my phone and try to shut the ringer off at the same time Jax pulls me from the seat and bends me over the edge of the makeshift bed and plunges into me without warning. I jerk forward some, taken by surprise as he fills the depths of me, causing my phone to tumble out of my hand onto the bed.

"Fuck Everlee. You're so wet." He lifts my hips up as he pounds into me repeatedly. I try to press my hands to the bed, to push up some, but I'm too weak and the angle he's at, is hitting spots I never knew existed. I'm already chasing another orgasm.

"Your asshole is begging to be played with," Emmett cries.

Turning my head to look at him, I smile. "I kind of want you in my pussy, though... with Jax," I peep out. Though my voice was light and innocent sounding, nothing about my request was.

Emmett looks at Jax, who steps over my leg so it's between his, making room for Emmett on my left. Jax pulls out for a second while Emmett presses in. I feel the cool sting of Emmett's cock ring on my hot, wet pussy and shiver in excitement. He thrusts a few times, coating his cock in my slickness, his breath shallow.

I love the feel of him inside of me.

He pulls out and rubs his fingers around my opening, stretching me a little, prepping me. They line their cocks up together and press in slowly, barely getting past their head before they stop, allowing me to adjust around them. They pull out and thrust back in, taking their time.

My back arches as a rippling sensation sweeps through my body. My hands ball into fists as I try to restrain myself from slamming back onto them because I know I'm not ready yet. Well, I am, but my little puss puss isn't.

They press in again. "Oh my God," I moan, repositioning myself. "Y'all feel so good."

"Samesies," Jax says, causing me to chuckle.

"Fuck Everlee. You can't do that," Emmett spits out, voice strained.

I rock my body back, slowly, letting them press in fully until I feel the sting in my pussy telling me it's too much. I lean forward and press back again, taking control as their hands rake over my body.

"You're a goddess, taking those cocks." Callum smiles.

"I want you all," I whimper.

"You'll have us all, just not now."

I pout before pressing back on to the guys, moving faster. My body is spooling up again with the pressure and Emmett's ring taking me to new heights.

'*Hooker, pickup the phone. Hooker, pickup the phone.*'

"Damn it, Lizzy," I chuckle, quickly pressing the button to shut the phone off.

A moan escapes as I rock back faster. Emmett and Jax each place a hand on my hips as they rock in unison. Claiming my pussy.

"This feels fucking fantastic," Jax moans.

"Mmhmm," Emmett responds.

"So good," Lizzy murmurs seductively.

We all freeze. What the hell?

I grab my phone and flip it over to see Lizzy's eyeball and face pressed against it. "You sick fuck. Next time, decline the call!" she growls. "I mean, I appreciate the sentiment." She looks around the phone like she's trying to look over my shoulder. "But that's a kink I'm not into. I mean, maybe I could be if given a heads up or something. How many do you have right now? Two? Three? Fo-"

"Shut up Lizzy!" I disconnect the phone, stare at it for a second to make sure it's off, then throw it on the floor and drop my head down. I'm so mortified right now. Nothing like being two dicks deep with an accidental video chat from your BFF.

"She has like a sexth sense or something. It's amazing," Knox says in awe.

"Sexth?" I mumble, looking up to smile at him.

"It's fucking weird, is what it is," Jax says deadpan, causing me to chuckle and then pause.

Both Emmett and Jax huff at the same time. I forgot my laughing causes the muscles in my pussy to contract around them, only further intensifying the feeling inside.

The intercom chimes with Brady warning us we're about thirty minutes from landing.

This is a calamity of errors. Is God trying to clam-jam me because I'm fucking several guys at the same time on Easter Sunday? Is he smiting me?

I rock back and forth, moving faster and faster, trying to erase the last several minutes from existence. I growl softly, letting my body take over. Letting it take what it wants, what it needs. "Yes. Yes. More."

"Are you close, Trouble? Between Jax's cock and your pussy, I'm about to fucking unload."

"Yes. I'm close," I pant out.

"Let me help you," Emmett coos. A second later, I feel a pressure at my ass and I moan out. "Do you want it?" he asks.

"Yes, please." The sex beast inside of me growls out.

A wetness slicks over my backside just before he presses a finger in. My back arches and as a tingle shoots through my body up to my head, around my breast and nipples down to my core. It's like an orgasm without the feeling of tightening and waves. Like my body is trying to sneak and pretend it didn't just have one because she's a greedy little bitch and wants more.

Jax's fingers work down my spine while Emmett's presses into my ass and their cocks slam into me, punching my wet pussy. The sound of our sex fills the cabin. "God, this feels so good." I pant as they continue to thrust into me, and I onto them. A moment later, I explode. I try to suppress my scream, not wanting to startle Brady, but fuck. I can't control myself as pleasure seeps out of every pore.

Emmett removes his finger and grabs my hips. They're sliding into me one after the other, not in sync like before, so their dicks rub against one another, not for me, but for them. My pussy is just the conduit for them. Fuck, it's so hot. It's like I can feel their cocks rubbing along one another inside of me, feel Emmett's ring as he strokes along Jax's cock. I bury my face in the couch, because my body is spooling up again. This isn't possible. This is too fast.

"Oh my…" I'm panting. The thoughts of their cocks rubbing against one another are driving me absolutely insane with lust and desire. We're out of control and I feel it hit again. I slam back into them hard. I want to feel them deep inside of me. I shudder and feel Jax's hand on my back, holding me down.

"That's right. Take our cocks like a good girl," Jax calls and then grunts.

I yell out a string of words as I come again, at the same time, I feel Jax and Emmett come. They thrust a few more times, then pull out and we all collapse. I don't have far to go because I'm already laying down, but they fall on either side of me rolling to their backs. Their cocks in the air, my ass in the air. Cocks and buns in the air.

The plane shakes as it hits a bit of turbulence and I grab Jax's arm. He rolls onto his side and looks at me. "Are you ok?"

"Well fucked, but too weak to move. Which one of you will carry me around?"

Emmett snakes his arm around my waist and pulls me into him. "I got you, boo."

Brady chimes in. "Looks like there's a little more turbulence up ahead. Please take your seats and buckle up."

I groan. "I'm leaking come and need to go to the bathroom."

Emmett stands up and grabs my arm, walking me towards the door in the back. "Are you ok?"

I reach up to cup his cheek. "I am. Thank you."

Stepping into the bathroom, I fall onto the toilet, a combination of weak legs and another shake of the plane. Before I pee, I let their come ooze out of me. I ignore the little sting, because she's been fucked pretty good, so it's to be expected. Plus, it was my fault near the end, because my body went a little crazy. When I pushed back the last time, I knew it would hurt because I was lost in the frenzy of it all.

I wash my hands, then throw water on my face, giving myself the once over.

When I walk back out, Callum is standing by the door with my clothes in his hand. "You can sit in this chair." He points to his right, so I sit in the chair and finish getting dressed and grab my phone, which someone had set on the table. I don't want to flip it over, but the anticipation is killing me. I have to see what craziness Lizzy messaged, because there's no way she's not going to text something.

Regretting it almost immediately, I flip it over, read the quick text and roll my eyes.

EVERLEE - LO SIENTO DOUCHECANOE

BRADY PULLS OUT OF the airport parking lot close to an hour later.

"Can Brady take me home?"

The air in the car shifts.

Chuckling, I say, "I'm not running away. I just..."

"What time are you coming over, then?" Callum asks.

My eyes widen. "I love sex, but I don't know if she can handle anymore tonight." I point down below.

"No. Not for that."

I look at him, confused.

"We want to take care of you and just hold you. We've fucked you over these last several days and haven't really had the opportunity to take care of you afterwards like we should."

"It's not your fault." They couldn't help their rental wasn't equipped with a tub built for a small football team.

His hand brushes through my hair. "That doesn't change the fact we want to do it and you deserve it." He presses, "What time?"

"I need to eat dinner."

"Emmett will cook you something."

I smile. "You're going to have all the answers, aren't you?"

He nods. "Rule one."

I press my hand to his chest. "I thought we were past all the rules."

"Never. If we were, then what would you have left to break?" He stares at me, waiting for an answer.

"Give me an hour after you drop me off."

"We'll have Brady drop us, then come back and get you."

"He doesn't need to do that."

He puts his hand on mine, and I can tell there's no use arguing with him.

"Fine."

"Good girl," he says playfully, without the usual sexual innuendo, running his finger along my jaw.

Even though he's only teasing and not using his dom voice, those two words still send a tickle up my spine. "Thank you, sir." I wink back.

We pull up to the front of my building twenty minutes later. Callum looks at his watch. "Brady will be here around seven thirty."

"That's not an hour," I say slyly.

"Come when you want." He boops the end of my nose. "I know you will, anyway."

I lean forward and give them each a quick kiss before I jump out of the car. "See you in a little while, darlings. Ta-ta!" I wave over my shoulder and grab my bag from Brady.

"See you in a bit, Ms. Everlee."

"Thank you, Brady."

It isn't until I'm inside the building that Brady pulls away and I inhale a deep breath.

I'm home.

We're home.

The weekend hadn't fully gone as planned, and I didn't get anytime to figure out what I wanted to do, but really what is there to figure out? I'm not going to be stupid enough to leave them again, but the questions still linger. How are we going to do this? I'm still terrified of getting hurt, but... I think that's more of a fear that exists because of dickface. I don't want anyone to hurt me like that again, but I also can't live in fear and not put myself out there, because I'd miss out on everything else. All the wonderful things out there.

I let that fear win before. It won't win again.

When I get to my floor, I see a heap of clothes bundled near my door. What in the world?

When I get closer, the clothes move and then stand up.

I gasp, shock taking my breath. "What are you doing here?" I snap.

"Ev," Dickface pleads. "I had to see you."

"You could have called," I say, unlocking my door, but keep my hand on the handle.

"You wouldn't have picked up. Can we talk?"

"No, we can't."

"Please?"

"No! N.O. I can't understand why it's so hard for you to understand."

"I miss you."

"You really seemed like it when I saw you at your birthday party. Is that what this is all about? You saw me, and want to weasel your way back in?"

"No. Not exactly."

"I don't have time for this. I have plans tonight." As I push my door open, a new feeling smacks me in the face. It feels so different in my apartment now. With everything that's happened over the weekend... it just feels lighter.

"With him?"

"Who?" I spin around, head smacking back into reality.

"The man from the club."

"It doesn't matter who I have plans with. It's not you. And it's none of your business." I start to shut the door, but his hand smacks against it, holding it open. "Rich," I caution, eyes set into a glowering stare.

"Just give me five minutes. That's all I want and then if you say-"

"When I say."

"If you say leave, I will."

"And you won't ever come back again?"

"Never," he quickly answers with an upbeat tone.

He thinks he's still talking to the old Everlee. The one he could manipulate and guilt trip into anything he wanted. The one who always forgave him because she believed all the garbage he spewed because she was terrified of being alone. The one who he convinced if it wasn't for him, no one would like her or love her. The one who thought he was it, her rock.

Sucks for him, because she died when the relationship died. This Everlee is strong and knows her worth thanks to the four men she's going to see later tonight. This Everlee doesn't need a man's validation to feel worth because she knows she's worthy without it.

"Fine. You have five minutes. I'm setting a timer and when it goes off, you will leave or I will throw you out."

He chuckles.

"I'm not kidding," I return with a cool glance.

"Ev. Don't be like that," he coos, trying to work his charm.

Lo siento douchecanoe. It won't work.

I hold up my hand and use my other to set the timer. "You have five minutes."

"Ev." He tilts his head to the side, trying to be cute.

"You're wasting time."

He huffs. "I wanted to start off and say I'm so sorry. I'm sorry for the way I treated you during our relationship and after."

My brows rise, but I say nothing. Did he expect me to take that and fall to my knees and forgive him?

He continues, "I know I don't deserve you, but I can't picture a life without you in it. You were. Are! My everything. And I was such an idiot for letting you go."

"You didn't let me go. I left after I found out you were sleeping with three other women."

"Yes. I was broken. I needed something that you weren't giving me in our relationship."

"So it's my fault you fucked other people?"

"No. Jesus. Fuck! Stop twisting my words!" he yells, then catches himself. "I'm sorry. I've been going to therapy to help deal with my problems. Mine. Not yours."

"That's great."

"See. I'm trying to change. For you."

"You should never try to change who you are for another person. I learned that the hard way. You need to change for yourself and only yourself."

"I mean, I am. I'm changing for me, but to also show you I *can* change. I should have treated you so much better. You were my world, and I completely stepped all over you and didn't treat you the way you deserved."

He pauses like he's waiting for me to correct him and tell him he didn't step all over me and treated me great, but I'm not here to make him feel better about how shitty of a person he is.

"I haven't been with anyone since Valentine's."

My head snaps back in shock.

"Well, not in a relationship."

That makes more sense.

"See. I'm being honest."

"Congratulations?"

"Stop." He laughs like I'm teasing him.

I'm not.

I glance at my phone. "Just under two minutes left."

"Ev. What can I do to make you forgive me and give me another chance?"

"There is nothing you can do. There is nothing left to forgive. I don't hate you. I'm not mad at you. I have moved on from you because I don't care about you anymore. You mean nothing to me. I can see you in the street, or hell, waiting for me in front of my apartment door." I hold out my hands in front of me. "And not care." I grab his wrist and look into his eyes. "I hope you hear me when I say this. We are never getting back together. There is nothing you can say or do that will change my mind. I'm glad you're getting the help you need because I want to see you happy, but it won't be with me." My timer dings.

He looks at my phone and his face falls. "Ev."

"It's time for you to go."

"Come on, Ev."

"Let's go." I push him towards the door.

"I hope you don't think the club owner will give you anything better than what I can. You don't think *he's* going to cheat on you when those half-naked girls are throwing themselves at him?" He laughs condescendingly.

"Fortunately, who I spend my time with, or date, or fuck, is absolutely none of your concern."

"If you kick me out, then we are done. When he cheats on you and breaks your heart, I won't be there to take you in and pick up the pieces."

"At your next therapy session or whatever you're doing to help with all your problems, ask them if they can teach you how to take no for an answer and not lash out like a petulant child when you don't get what you want. You're a narcissist. Ask about that too, and learn empathy."

"Ev," he pleads in the hall, his reactions giving me whiplash.

"Thank you for stopping by and having this talk with me. I'm glad you're getting the help you need. I truly mean that."

"You don't want to do this!" he yells, pressing his hand on the door. I can see panic in his eyes and hear the fear laced in his words as he realizes he no longer has an ounce of control over me. I'm stronger and it's thanks to my four men.

"But I do Rich. I really do." I start closing the door. "Goodnight and goodbye." When the lock clicks, I stand there for a moment, letting my pulse slow down. I hear him hit the wall in the hall and mumble something, so I roll my body over and peek through the peephole and watch him leave a moment later.

I let out a sigh.

I've done it.

EVERLEE - A WHOLE NEW LEVEL OF THE SHOCKER...

I DIG IN MY purse and grab my phone out to video chat with Lizzy.

She picks up on the third ring with her hands over her eyes. "Moan if there's a skin flute in a hole right now. I'd say vagina, but I know you've been exploring lately. Call you fucking Dora."

"Skin flute?" I ask, ignoring the latter part of her soliloquy.

She peeks through her fingers.

"No peen in sight."

She sighs. "Why did you pick up the phone while you were getting boinked? I knew these guys were bringing out the kink in you, but seriously? We need to draw some lines... in the sand, of course, so I can mark them out and redraw if needed." She throws her head back, laughing.

"You're still too much."

"Probably, but I don't care. Weeds out the weak ones."

"What's up? Why did you call earlier?"

"I forgot. Something about seeing you bent over getting fucked really cleans out the ol' memory banks. So how many? I mean, just asking for a friend... and by friend, I mean me. I'm the friend I'm asking for."

"I'm not telling you."

"So, more than one? Damn girl. I mean I'd love to see it... like maybe snap a side profile pic or something next time, because I've been doodling the logistics and diagrams of how you get so many Long Dong Silvers inside of you and it looks like a three-year-old learning how to draw a square. Lines everywhere and nothing is touching."

"Oh my god. I'm not taking a picture for you. I'll explain it to you, but not right now."

She pumps her eyebrows. "You look happy." She changes the topic.

"I am." I smile, falling into my seat. "I have my men back."

"That you left."

"Yes. Stop reminding me. I was an idiot. Lesson learned. Never happening again. Although the reasons I left are still very valid and need answering. But we plan on doing that tomorrow night."

"So you're home tonight? I can swing by?"

"No. Brady is on his way to get me. I'm going over there."

"Damn girl. You spent all weekend with them. You gotta spread out the fuckings. Gotta keep it tight and not all loosy goosy down there. Speaking of... how did that go?" She screams out a slur of sounds. "Oh! That's why I was calling you. Beckett. He totally knows and called me asking for info. I played dumb, but..." she points her finger at me.

"Yea. I figured he did. The dumbass flipped our canoe in the races today and dumped us all- well all, except Emmett, into the water. By the time I got to their car, I was a freaking ice cube. Emmett made me strip and then straddle him. After he took his shirt off."

Lizzy fans herself. "I think you just made me moist and Tony isn't here. Shame on you!"

"Stop." I laugh. "That's on the list to talk about. I don't think Beckett will say anything... but it's one of those things... I don't know." I frown.

"That's tough." She puckers her lips, and the line goes silent for a moment as we stare at one another.

"Oh, so...."

"Do tell." She sits up in her seat, rubbing her hands together.

"When the guys dropped me off, I got up to my door and saw Rich sitting there."

"What?" She grabs the phone and pulls it close to her face. "Tell me you didn't let his little stankass in."

"I did."

"Everlee!" she scolds.

"No." I smile. "It's all good. I stood my ground, and he's done coming around."

"So you say."

"No. I really think he is this time. We had a pleasant talk."

"Pleasant talk? Do you realize who you're talking about? He wouldn't know what a pleasant talk was if there was a big ass billboard posted right in front of him. He's an asshole. A narcissistic asshole."

"You're right. And that is what I told him."

"You did?"

"Yep." I smile. "He tried to tell me he was going to therapy and realized he didn't treat me like he should have blah blah blah and that he's really changed."

"Bullshit," she fake sneezes.

"I told him I was thrilled for him, but this would not be a thing. We were done. I wished him a good life."

"You did?"

"Yes. That's how I know I'm over him. I feel nothing Liz. Like not an ounce of anger or hate. I'm one hundred percent apathetic towards him. He's no different from Joe-Smo down the street."

"Well, I'll be..." she says in a southern twang.

"I feel great."

"He just took it? Like said ok and left?"

"Not exactly. He lashed out when he realized he couldn't manipulate me anymore. Said the club owner I was seeing was going to cheat on me because the girls at the club just throw themselves at the owners and he wouldn't be there to pick up the pieces. He even smacked the wall outside of my door when he left."

"I'm so proud of you."

"I thought you would be. That's why I called you. I really have come a long way, and it's thanks to you and also the guys. They've showed me what I deserve."

"Yasss Queen."

An alert pops up on my phone.

"Brady is here, and I haven't done anything yet. I need to change out of my clothes. Lunch Tuesday?"

"Can't. How about tomorrow?"

I think about it for a second. Mondays are usually tough, but I have to see her. "Yea, that works."

"Love you, sis."

"Love you, too."

"Hey," she says in a serious tone, catching me off guard. "Think about the picture thing. Nothing too graphic, but something that shows enough detail."

"Shut the fuck up."

"You know, I've been seeing STFUATTDLAGG floating around a lot on those smutty social media groups. I'm going to throw one out. STFUATODLAGG."

My lips flattened into a hard line. "I see what you did there. The why choose version?"

"Pew, pew, pew," she says, shooting her fingers like guns at me. "You shouldn't limit it to just one dick."

"I really do love you."

"I know. Unfortunately, I don't have four dicks. Or even one." Her eyes grow wide for a second. "Oh, my god. Do you think they have a double dick strap on? Fuck, what about a triple dick strap on? Two for the pink, one for the stink."

"Shocker," I say deadpan.

She bursts out laughing. "I see what you did there and I approve." Her brows fall into a more serious and inquisitive stare. "Although I think that saying was referring to fingers and not one-eyed wonder worms."

"We're done. I can't with you and your cock slang."

"But seriously. I wonder if they have straps on like that."

"Bye."

"You're right. I'll do some searching tonight. Obviously incognito mode. I don't need anyone thinking I'm the kinky fucker in this relationship."

I hang up the phone and lean my head against the back of the couch for a second, taking a breath. I just need to relax, but know the boys are waiting to see me. And I'm fairly certain if I don't show up tonight, they'd come get me.

I stand up and walk into the bedroom to change my clothes over in my suitcase before I walk downstairs.

EVERLEE-HOT TUBS AND HISTORY

I WALK INTO THE house and sit my bag by the back door and hear the men talking in the kitchen. "Hello?" I announce in a singsong voice, leaning forward into the space. Why do people do that? You aren't leaning around, or into, anything. I shake my head, trying to reel my random thoughts and nerves back in. This is my first time back here since I ran away and it all looks the exact same, almost like no time has passed.

Knox runs out and slides to a stop in front of me.

"Hey love." He slips his arm around me and tilts me back into a kiss.

When he pops us back up, I look at him, trying to figure out why he's in such a good mood.

"What's going on?"

"Nothing." He grabs my hand and walks me into the kitchen with an extra bounce in his step.

"You seem to be in a fantastic mood."

"I'm just happy you're here."

"Hey!" they all shout, just before Emmett slides me an old-fashioned across the bar.

Grabbing the glass in my hand, I eye them all curiously. "What's going on?"

They get quiet and look at Emmett who's at the stove, flipping over what looks like steaks in a pan.

"Emmett?"

He scoops the sauce over the steaks, then looks at me.

"Bo La Vie was just named Best New Restaurant."

"That's so exciting!" I squeal.

"Very! This is the first step to getting a Michelin rating."

"Michelin. If anyone can do it, you can!" I walk around the counter to wrap my arms around him. "I'm so proud of you."

"Thank you." He kisses my forehead, then continues spooning some sort of reduction over the steaks.

"How was your house?" Jax asks, rubbing his biceps. Between the scents of what Emmett's cooking and the muscles on display, I'm nearly panting.

"Fine," I say cautiously, tilting my head to the side. I take a sip of my drink and let the crisp, cool burn of the bourbon slide down my throat. "These are marvelous."

"They are," Jax says, grabbing my hand and pulling me over towards him and kissing my temple. I can't tell if he's just relishing in Emmett's happiness or if he's searching for the truth about what happened at my house. Does he know about Rich and he's testing to see if I'm going to tell him? But if he knows, then how?

"So... I had a visitor."

"At your apartment?"

I nod. "Rich was there."

"Why?" Jax asks, pushing me away a little to look at me. "Are you ok?"

"Yea. I'm great. He saw me Thursday at the club, so he came around again trying to worm his way back in. Unfortunately for him, I've moved on."

"You have?" he asks softly, pulling me towards him again, shoulders relaxing.

"Yea. I found." I pause as he places a gentle kiss on my neck. "These guys."

"Tell me more," he murmurs with his lips against my neck, his fingers brushing the skin just above my pants.

"They're... ok." I'm getting turned on and this was not the plan for tonight. I'd have them all and deal with the consequences of an achy pussy later, but damn, my little girly girl needs a break.

"Only ok?" He gently bites then sucks my fevered skin into his mouth, as his tongue swipes over the surface causing me to moan.

"Well..." I sigh, as my eyes roll into the back of my head.

"We said no sex tonight," Callum reminds.

Jax sighs and pulls away. "I know. I'm just teasing."

"Clit tease." I rub my hand on the inside of his thigh.

"It's time to eat, anyway," Emmett says, pulling a dish out of the oven.

Jax looks down at my hips and pumps his eyebrows.

"Stop!" I playfully smack his arm.

He laughs, rubbing his bulging biceps as he stands up. "What can I help with, dearest Emmett?" he asks, strolling over to the counter.

"You can pick a bottle of wine and grab some glasses."

"Ev, you want to help?"

Callum chuckles. "I think she'll do better staying up here instead of down in the cellar with you."

"Next time." I wink.

He pats the doorframe and takes off. I realize I have no idea where he's going and, based on Callum's comment, he's going downstairs. There's really so much about them and this house I don't know about. But that's going to change.

I grab the plates Emmett's preparing and take them over to the table. Jax is up a few minutes later and we're toasting the future Michelin star chef and enjoying a delicious dinner. I'm over the moon happy and realize this is the first normal thing we've ever done together. All of us just sitting around a table eating food and joking, nothing sexual about it. Just enjoying each other's company. Is this what it will be like?

I have to force them to let me wash the dishes after dinner, because I needed to contribute somehow. After the last dish is dried and placed back on the shelf, Knox swoops me into his arms and carries me upstairs to the roof.

"No sex," he says, looking at me. "So keep your hands to yourself." He winks.

My cheeks flush.

A moment later, I'm standing stripped down on their roof. I don't know of a time ever in my life where I have felt this comfortable being completely naked in front of someone. Hell, in front of four deliciously hot as fuck someone's. I've always been self-conscious, even after a year and a half with Rich. Although, that could be because he would occasionally comment if I looked bloated or would suggest I needed to hit the gym after patting my belly or ass. Near the end, I guess it was because I was fairly certain he was cheating on me, and figured it was because I wasn't good enough, or thin enough, or pretty enough. But these guys... they appreciate me for who I am, curves and all. A warmness bubbles inside of me... I'm falling for them and fast, and the thought terrifies me.

Callum and Jax are already sitting inside the hot tub with a stemless glass of wine perched on the deck beside them, with three other glasses poured around the outside. Knox is climbing in a moment later, as Emmett walks through the door.

"Come on in," Jax offers, walking across the hot tub, holding his hand out.

I grab it and step in, letting the hot water bite against my skin, looking around awkwardly.

Jax chuckles. "We won't bite. Unless you ask." He pumps his brows, then sits back down.

"We aren't trying to trick you," Callum adds, noticing my awkwardness. "We really just want to take care of you, since we didn't get the chance to do that all weekend."

"You don't have to." I skim my hand across the top of the water. I'm not used to having this kind of attention shown on me. Sure, this isn't the first time I've been in the hot tub with them, but it's usually sexually charged and I know what the result is going to be. Usually several orgasms. But this… this is uncharted territory. This is open-ended.

"We know," he says, picking up my foot and rubbing his thumbs across it. He hits a spot, and a moan escapes my lips as my head falls back. "But we like to." He laughs.

We're all in the hot tub enjoying the bubbles, heat, and soft jams of Teddy Swims when Callum releases my foot. "Your family seems nice."

I open my eyes and look at him. "They're great, but can be a little much at times."

He chuckles. "Your mom really wanted you with Winston."

I shrug, cringing at the memory of them walking in and seeing me on a date with him.

"He's a nice guy," Callum repeats his words from this weekend.

"I don't want him," I huff.

"What do you want?" Jax asks and I feel the air get heavy.

I look around at each of them, their eyes fixed on me. Is this what we're doing? Are we having this talk right now? Well, no time like the present to rip the Band-Aid off, I suppose. "I want you all. I've always wanted you all. Even when I left, I wanted you all. I didn't want to get hurt and thought you didn't want me." They all sit forward and start to speak, but I hold my hand up. "I know. I get why you have the rules, and I was just trying to follow them. At least that's what I tried to convince myself."

I don't realize until I'm done speaking that Emmett is running his hands through my hair.

Jax starts, "We have rules to protect everyone and to protect us. We know you've talked with Sophie quite a bit during these last two months. She wouldn't divulge the details, however, she shared the gist of what your concerns are which mirror ours. As you know, Sophie was the first and only serious relationship we had and the reason for the rules. We got hurt, she got hurt. In the end, we knew what happened was what needed to happen, but when you left us..."

"I'm sorry."

"We know," Callum says. "Look. Tonight isn't for talking about our future. We'll talk about that Tuesday. We just wanted you to know we aren't going anywhere and will make this work. We want you to think about what that really means, though, because we can't be hurt again and we don't want you to get hurt, either. Family, kids, lifestyle. Just think about it. There are things I just don't know if you can have with us."

I nod.

A moment later, Emmett wraps his arm around me and pulls me into him, so I lean on his chest and my feet prop on Knox. We sit like this for who knows how long, just relishing in the music. In the connectedness. I've never heard of this artist before and it's a shame because his voice is... silky, gravelly, perfection.

"I know we're not having sex tonight, but next time we are..." I point to the speaker.

"Yea? You like you some Teddy Swims?" Jax asks.

"Love." I laugh.

"Did you talk to Lizzy... after, you know?" Knox asks.

I smile. "Yes. She said she wanted a picture of... you know... so she could figure out how it works."

Their eyes grow large and I laugh, "But don't worry. I shut it down."

"She's a strange bird." Jax chuckles.

"That she is. But she's mine."

"You've known her a long time?" Knox asks.

"Since grade school." I smile, remembering the day she walked into the classroom for the first time. Hair poofed on her head, books clutched to her chest, wearing a jean dress with rainbow zigzag knee-high socks. I should have known then she was going to be a force to be reckoned with. "What about you all?" The question had been weighing on me all weekend, but I didn't know how to ask or even how to start the conversation. Now seemed like the best opportunity, since they cracked the door open.

They all look at one another, then Emmett speaks as he mindlessly twirls his fingers through my hair. "We've known each other for quite some time. I was first at the foster home, getting there when I was four. My dad apparently wasn't in the picture and mom died in a car crash. I have this scar here to remind me." He points to a white line on his arm that was about two inches. "Next came Jax and Callum."

I look at them.

"Similar story," Callum says. "Dad was gone and mom liked drugs, more than she liked us. She overdosed on heroin when I was nine and Jax was seven."

"And then our precious Knox joined our little crew."

Knox adds, "Mom left when I was a baby and dad got arrested for murder. Although, I still think it was a bogus charge. He was at a bar one night and some man was beating on a woman, so my dad stepped in to break it up and when he threw the guy backwards, the man stumbled over his drunken feet and hit his head on the edge of the bar."

"Have you seen him?"

Knox shakes his head. "He got out and when I went to the prison, he'd left a note for me. Said it was better this way if he wasn't in my life. So I enlisted in the military with Jax and never looked back." He takes a large gulp of wine and sits the empty glass back down. It's obvious he still has problems with the way his father left things, even if he doesn't want to admit it.

"I went to business school," Callum continues.

"And I went to culinary school," Emmett adds.

"But you all had Mrs. Mary Mae." I smile.

"We call her Mrs. Mary and she is wonderful," Emmett says, his fingers dancing up and down my arm.

"Strict as shit, though." Knox laughs. "Military was a cake walk because of her."

"Only because you were unruly!" Jax waves his fist in the air. The way he says unruly makes me think that was a word they heard often growing up.

Callum adds with a serious undertone. "If it wasn't for her though, who knows where we'd be. She definitely saved us."

They all agree and silence fills the air again.

The bubbles shut off a few seconds later, followed by a yawn.

Emmett pats my arm. "Let's get you to bed."

I sit up, and everyone looks at me. "What's wrong?" Callum asks.

"Where do I sleep? There are four of you and one of me."

"Where do you want to sleep?"

"No. You can't do that. You can't make me choose between you all. This can't work if I have to choose."

Callum steps forward and grabs my hands. "We'll figure it out. Tonight, we'll sleep in the voyeur room, so we can all sleep with you and so you don't have to choose."

I nod. "So I'm weird and want to take a quick shower before I go to bed."

"That's fine, we will too."

Fucking hell. What are the chances they'll use the showers in their bedrooms?

EVERLEE - I'M A FUCKING SEX GODDESS TREE!

Zero.

Zero chance in hell, they use their showers.

I'm standing in the middle of the row of rainfall shower-heads along the back wall of the enormous bathroom with two men on each side of me. All cocks and muscles and tattoos and cocks and water and cocks.

Fuck! Get ahold of yourself, Everlee.

Clit teases! The whole lot of them.

Are they teasing me? Testing me? Trying to toy with my clit strings to see if I'll give in and demand them to ravage me? I want to. Fuckin' aye, I want to. But if they *are* testing me, the other part of me, the more or less sensible part—not sure which, at the moment, doesn't want to give in.

I look to my left and see Jax standing with his hands brushing through his hair while the water cuts through his muscles, then dribbles down to the drain beneath him.

"You're moaning," he says without even looking at me.

A flush passes over my body from embarrassment.

"Why did you stop her?" Knox whines.

I turn around to look at him behind me as soap bubbles slide down... down... goddamn. I feel like I'm in a zoo, rather an aquarium, where I'm surrounded by venomous snakes I'm not allowed to touch. But that doesn't matter because I want to pick all of them up and fit them inside little hand knitted sweaters and take them home.

A second later, a body presses up behind me as hands slip around and slowly take the soapy loofa from my hand. "Let me help you," Jax murmurs beside my ear, causing goosebumps to form on my perfectly smooth skin.

Come here, little snaky snake. I have a beautiful sweater I've knitted for you.

The loofa and his hand circle around my breasts slowly, gliding easily around the soap bubbles. "We're going to take care of you. Is that ok?" I hesitate long enough for him to continue. "No penis sex."

"No penii?" I don't know if it's a confirmation or a whine.

"No," he whispers as his fingers travel down. "We're going to clean every inch of you, though." His words cause my head to lull backwards onto his shoulder.

"Mmhmm."

Mother's ass! Bring the lot of those venomous fuckers home! Knitted sweaters and all.

One set of hands strokes up my left leg, while another set does the same on my right leg. I want to open my eyes to see, but I also don't care. My heart is thrashing against my chest, my core is clenching, and my pussy is pulsating. She knows what's coming, and it's her. She's going to be coming.

Jax lifts my head off his shoulder and continues sucking and kissing the skin on my neck, while another mouth starts on the other side. After a second, I recognize it as Callum's.

"We're going to make you come," Callum whispers against my skin, his hand kneading my breast. "A lot."

"You're going to beg us to stop," Jax continues, then grabs under my chin and turns me to face him, his eyes penetrating into mine. "But we're not going to."

I shudder out a breath before his mouth crashes onto mine and his tongue pulses in. A whimper escapes as I kiss him back. Kiss him so hard, I forget about everything and everyone else. My head is spinning like I'm on a merry-go-round.

"My turn," Callum says, curling his fingers under my chin and pulling me towards him. "And we will stop," he kisses the corners of my lips. "If we hear the word cupid." He kisses the other corner. "But I pray you don't say it." He breathes out, his lips finding mine. His kiss is equally as hot and tantalizing as Jax's.

One thing about Callum is he has rules. Guardrails. And he always makes sure I know they are there and I'm safe. And does it in such a way that makes it sexy. Not like a tax auditor coming in with a calculator, pen, and pocket protector, listing out all the rules.

The water is still falling on us and if I close my eyes, I can imagine I'm in one of those romantic movies where they're outside and have just professed their love for one another and start kissing passionately, just as the rain pours and they pull away laughing, but don't care. Only I'm inside, under a rainfall showerhead, and they've just professed their intense desire to make me orgasm repeatedly.

So, similar.

Knox and Emmett kiss and lightly nibble up opposite legs. Emmett pauses behind my knee and Knox pauses on the inside of my thigh. I know I'm so wet, slick like a greased pig. Not completely the image I want in my head, but damn it. I'm about to hump the air like a bunny. It is Easter after all, I chuckle to myself.

Jax and Callum each take to a breast, sucking and biting, licking and grabbing while Knox continues kissing up my leg, pausing when he gets to the top. I look down at him briefly and see him suck his bottom lip in, letting his teeth slowly scrape over it as his hands grab the sides of my hips. His tongue slowly licks up, and I hear him groan in appreciation as he realizes just how wet I am. And not from the water. He readjusts and hungrily laps, causing my legs to buckle slightly before I regain control. I grab onto both Jax and Callum's head and hold them there as Knox sucks on my clit.

"Oh, God," I plead, wanting more.

"Tell me if you want me to stop," Emmett says.

A second later, I feel him kissing my ass cheek, while his fingers grip onto the other. My breath hitches in my throat with a combination of worry and excitement at what he's going to do next.

"Use your words, Everlee," Callum commands softly, taking my breast in his mouth again.

"Ok."

"Do you want me to stop?"

I hesitate for a moment. "No," I whisper. And a dirty, excited wave passes over me.

His finger swipes over my hole while Knox continues to suck and lick my pussy. A second later, I feel something else at my forbidden entrance. Something I'd never felt before, nor ever thought I'd feel. Emmett's tongue.

Holy fuck! I feel my breath pick up and then feel a gurgle in my stomach.

Oh shit! Fuck! Fuck! Don't you dare fucking fart! Hold that bitch in! Batten down the hatches!

The rumble stops and my mild heart attack passes. I hesitate for a moment, scared to move. Scared to test the waters, but my head gets swept away in all the sensations. Here I am, standing like a fucking sex goddess tree while they all lick, flick, and suck on me.

"Oh my God!" I pant as my legs grow weaker. "I can't stand."

They don't stop.

"I'm going to come," I whine out as a warning, but they don't see it that way. They take it as incentive, to push on harder, faster. Knox slips in two fingers and pulses them in and out, while his tongue continues to suck on my clit. Jax and Callum suck and knead, lick and pinch. And Emmett. No words. I'm feeling things I'd never felt before. His finger is now sliding in and out, pressing on areas that shoot straight to my clit.

"Ohhh!" I scream out, rising on my tiptoes. "Fuccccccck-kk. Shit. Ass. Helllaman. Damn." I wrap my arms around Callum and Jax's heads and squeeze like a vice, holding myself up while my legs give out.

"I got her." Jax sweeps my legs out from under me.

I'm panting, my head is still reeling. My body is still clenching. That is by far the most intense orgasm I've ever had. It's like two orgasms meeting in the middle and shooting out of my mouth in a string of words.

I let my body fall back in Jax's arms and he chuckles, laying me on the bed.

"We're not done." He plants a kiss on my nose and starts working his way down, letting the stubble from his beard brush over my chest as he inches further and further down.

My pussy has stopped pulsating, but as soon as his tongue laps up the middle I feel this... feeling. It's like she's fallen to her knees and is begging for a reprieve. I don't want to stop, but I have to. The pleasure is too much.

Knox and Callum lay on the bed beside me and start kissing on my neck and breasts.

"I can't... too much," I pant. "Cupid," I sigh out.

Instantly, they pull away and I lay there like a pile of flesh jelly, too weak to move.

Emmett walks in the room a minute later and asks if I'm ok.

"I think we broke her." Knox pokes my cheek softly.

"It's late, anyway."

I roll over, "No. No, no, no. You haven't... you know." I motion for ejaculate. I don't want to give them blue balls, especially after that orgasm. Number one, greatest of all time. Like the kind of orgasm you'd expect Kayne to interrupt... at least he let me finish.

"We'll be fine. We already told you that tonight isn't about us." Jax brushes my hair back and plants a soft kiss on my forehead that tells me not to argue.

I want to fight. Need to fight. But I'm beyond exhausted and in that post orgasm coma.

I roll onto my side and throw my leg over Knox. I feel him plant a light kiss on my temple before the darkness carries me away.

EVERLEE - DON'T SAY BUNDLE OF NERVES

"WHAT THE FUCK?" LIZZY slams her hands on the table and looks at me.

"Quiet." I try to shush her in the very crowded restaurant. It's really my fault for meeting her in public places when I give her the lowdown on what's going on.

"You can orgasm from your butt?"

My face forms into what I suspect is a cross between what a clown and a mime look like when acting surprised. "Apparently. When I tell you it was the most intense orgasm I've ever had, it was like..." I try to come up with words, but end up just shaking my head a bunch of times looking like a bobble-head doll on the dash of a car.

"Well, he is a chef."

"What?" I ask, confused, missing the connection.

"He likes to toss that salad," she says in a deep voice before throwing her head back, laughing so hard.

"Fucking help me." I slam my hand to my face, trying to hide it from anyone who could have heard her and also from shame that I missed the salad connection.

"Sorry. Continue. I can tell you're in that nerdy girl mode where you researched all day to share this stuff with me, and I'm ruining it. Please tell me how I may too, make an o face from butt play."

"So yes, I did search it up this morning and there's another spot in your ass," I clarify. "Like the g-spot, but it's called the a-spot."

"For ass? Let me hit that ass spot," she says in a deep voice, pointing her finger down, like she's rapping, then quickly corrects, "Sorry." She zips her lips and throws away the imaginary key.

"Why do I bother telling you these things, or even being seen with you in public?"

She scrunches her nose. "What? Fine. Fine. I'm serious now." She wipes her hand over her face like that's going to fix her. "But it is kind of your fault. You're literally teeing them up for me."

I shake my head, laughing, and then smile, knowing that the next surprise will leave her completely speechless. I've been teeing them up and while she could humiliate me; I don't care. She's my bitch and I love her with all I have. "Your clit has legs," I say simply, then sit back and wait. I'd equate it to taking the pin out of a grenade and dropping it to see what happens.

"Shut the fuck up!" She spits her food out. "That bitch better not get up and walk away. I like her just where she is."

Smiling, I continue, "That reaches to the ass, where they culminate into a..." I start speaking slower because I know this next part is her favorite.

She picks up on what I'm doing and shakes her head. "Don't say it. Don't you dare say it."

"Bundle..."

"Everlee. Don't."

"Of…"

"I'll leave!" she threatens, palms pressed to the table.

"Nerves."

She throws her arms in the air, making a show of standing up. "Son of a bitch! You said it. I told you not to say it. Bundle of nerves? Really? You know I hate that." She clenches and shakes like she's been doused in cold water.

"I thought it was only when reading it in books." I deepened my voice and speak with a French accent, "He pressed gently on her bundle of nerves, sending her into a spiraling climax, while her bountiful breast bounced beautifully."

She starts dry heaving at the table.

"You're being dramatic."

"I know." She smiles, taking another bite of food.

"So some ass play." She sighs. "You think Tony would go for it?"

"Ass him." A smile spreads across my face.

"Ass him? You're proud of yourself for that, aren't you?"

"So proud."

My phone dings.

"Is it them?"

I glance at it quickly. "No."

"Work?"

"No. So last night they were all about me, right? So I may have reached out to all my smutty social media groups and told them what happened, and asked for recs on one girl servicing four guys, but not through penii sex. Something deeper I guess."

"Are you about to try some more sexual origami shit?"

I laugh. "No. Just trying to figure it out. I have two hands and one mouth."

"This is why I say you should never fuck more than three guys at a time."

"Is that what you say?"

"Well, I've said it… once. Just now. But what are you? A fucking time keeper?" She scribbles in her hand. "Let me note when I exactly said this... date. Time." She holds her finger in the air. "Wind speed."

"Shut up." I glance through my phone. "One person said, one in each hand and two in the mouth."

"Isn't that like a saying or something? A cock in each hand is worth two in the mouth?"

"You mean a bird in the hand is worth two in the bush?"

"Tomato tomato."

I don't know why I tell her that, because she's a visual person and of course she opens her mouth wide like she's imagining taking two dicks at once. In the middle of a restaurant.

"You better do some mouth yoga," she says, dropping her hands, proud of her assessment.

"Is that a thing?"

"Fuck if I know. It should be." She looks over the table. "So, do they have any recs?"

"You know they do. These women are like the Illuminati of Clitorises."

"Ah. Cliterati. I get it now. Why not Illumirises?"

My brow furrows. "That sounds more like an energy drink instead of a group of highly read women." I bat my hand through the air. "Plus, I already have like twenty recs."

"Sounds like you'll be busy tonight." She chuckles, "In more ways than four." She pats herself on the back. "That's what I have to say to you now. No longer can I say more ways than one... because you're a fucking overachiever."

"I love you and you will always be my one."

Her head falls to the side as she clutches her chest. "Boo boo."

I glance at my watch because I have to get back to work to prepare for a meeting.

"How much time do you have?"

"A few minutes."

She bends down and starts digging through her purse. "Here." She hands me a thick envelope. "Open it."

I'm confused. We typically don't get each other Easter cards. Is that even a thing? I'm getting sidetracked. I open the card and it explodes into butterflies springing into the air, causing me to scream and nearly topple backwards.

"Will you be my maid of honor?" she squeals, ignoring the mess all over me and the table.

I smile and grab her hands. "It would be my honor."

She claps her hands gleefully.

"But did you need to do this?" I ask, picking at the small flecks of confetti.

"No. But I just love them."

I wipe as much of the confetti from the table into my hand as possible, dumping it on my plate. Fortunately, most of it ended up on the table and on me, but I still hate leaving a mess. Ignoring the looks from others in the restaurant, I walk to the front counter and ask for a broom. The lady behind the register gives me a weird look, so I explain what happened and she just smiles and tells me she'll get it, and gives me a cookie for offering. So win-win.

Lizzy is gathering up our things when I get back to the table. "No broom?"

"No. She appreciated the offer, but said she'll get it."

"So, are you seeing them tonight?"

"I don't know. I know they eat at Bo's tonight. So I'm not sure. We have to talk about our future tomorrow. They said to really think about it. Like what it will mean living with them. Kids, marriage, family trips, and so on."

"That's tough. Maybe you should find some poly support groups and see what they do," she says without a hint of humor.

"That's a good idea."

My phone dings again.

"Hey." She grabs my arm before walking in the opposite direction of me.

"What's up?"

"Did you post in your smutty groups anonymously?"

"No. Why?"

"Did you see if anyone you know was in there first?"

"Fuck. No. But… you don't think. Shit." My mind is trying to figure out who I would know that could be in there. "Maybe I could change my name on my profile."

"Then people would still know."

"Yea, but only those who I'm friends with."

She bobbles her head from side to side.

"Damn it Lizzy. Now you have me freaked out."

"Sorry."

"I'm going to delete the post."

"After you take some screenshots."

"Of course." I give her a hug, then pull my phone out of my purse and quickly delete my posts after taking a few screen shots. Amateur hour.

EMMETT - ALL IS FINE WHEN YOU SIXTY-NINE

NERVES PRICKLE UNDER MY skin as my head swivels for the hundredth time between the clock on the dash and the front door of the tall office building. Another minute passes and I step out of the car and stand beside the passenger door. The office door pushes open and a string of men and women file out. My eyes quickly scan them, looking for the only face that matters, and then I see her.

I give a quick whistle and I'm reminded of Mrs. Mary when we were kids. She would send us outside to play in the neighborhood if we were old enough and then at night, she'd let out an ear-piercing whistle, her version of a dinner bell, and we'd all come running back. My whistle just now wasn't as loud.

Everlee looks at me, and a smile spreads across her face. She jogs over to meet me, throwing her arms around my neck.

"Hey Trouble." I plant a quick kiss on her cheek.

"You know. If you were to put on some plaid, you could be a super sexy lumberjack." Her hands pass over my beard, then give it a gentle tug.

"You don't like the super sexy chef?" I ask, opening the passenger door.

She climbs in without asking where we're going or what we're doing.

I jog around to the driver's side and when I climb in, she answers my question.

"Of course I love the super sexy chef." Her cheeks flush a shade of pink.

I pull onto the road and take the turn to her apartment.

"Did you just want to drive me down the block to my house?"

"Maybe." I find some on-street parking and turn the car off. Before she can get out, I dart out of the driver's seat and run around to open her door.

"This is a pleasant surprise."

"I'm glad you think so."

"Do you want to come up?"

"Very much so." I've wanted to see her every second of today since I didn't get a chance to see her this morning before she left. This afternoon I got an invitation to a special dinner honoring my recent accomplishment with Bo's and I wanted to invite her to come with us. On a date. I guess it wouldn't be a typical date, but...

She pushes her door open and slips out of her shoes. "If you want a drink or a snack, help yourself." She points to the kitchen. "I'll be right back."

My heart races in my chest as I watch her walk into her bedroom, fighting the urge to follow her and press her against the wall and take her mouth in mine, because that's what I want to do. I fucking missed her with every ounce of my being. It's why I got my cock pierced. I had to do something. It doesn't make much sense, but I needed to get my mind off her. When Sophie left, I got my nipple pierced, but Everlee felt different. I get it. We weren't together for a long time, but damn... like when you know, you know. I let myself believe for a moment she could be- would be- different. At least that's what I wanted. Want. Still want.

When I got the invitation for the dinner, I was extremely excited. Obviously for the event and honor itself, but also because I feel like it's an opportunity to show her what we could be like. We had put ourselves in this bubble and always said if we tried to go outside of it, then it would pop. Our world, our life, would pop. That's where we went wrong last time. We created a world inside of a bubble instead of learning how to live within the world. With Everlee, we have to take it slow and learn how to survive together in the world.

She walks back into the living room wearing a pair of joggers and a t-shirt that grips her tits and torso beautifully.

She takes the drink I'm offering and smells it.

"Oh stop. You'll like it."

"Sex on the beach?"

I wink. "I would have made you an old-fashioned, but you don't have any Luxardo."

She smiles innocently. "I know. I thought about buying it several times, but it hurt, so I didn't." She takes a sip of her drink. "But this is good."

"I know."

The air changes and she studies my face. "I missed you."

"I missed you."

She walks over and sits her glass on the counter and wraps her arms around me, pressing her head to my chest and looks up at me with those beautiful eyes of hers. I brush her hair back from her face. "A couple of things." I place a soft kiss on her forehead and she moans, closing her eyes. "Will you come to a dinner honoring me on Wednesday night? All the guys will be there. It will be like a date."

"A date?"

Her brows raise on her forehead, and I wonder if I've overstepped. We have *the* talk tomorrow, but... I guess it's just wishful thinking. Maybe if we make plans, then every-thing will work out.

"With all four of you?"

"Yes." I don't know if that helps or hurts.

Her hands travel up around my neck as she stands on her tiptoes, placing a soft kiss on my lips. "Yes. I would love to go."

"Do you want to go dress shopping tomorrow?"

"I can just use my dress from Valentine's Day."

I attempt to mask my disappointment, keeping my expression neutral and composed.

With her arms still clasped around my neck, and her body pressed to mine, she asks, "Did *you* want to go dress shopping tomorrow?"

"Kind of. Maybe I wanted to help you pick out a dress and buy it for you."

"You don't need to buy me a dress."

"I know. But..." My hands slide down her arms, over her shoulders, around her back and rest on her hips, just under her shirt. "But I want to. Plus, we should all match." He smiles.

"Yea?" she asks in a soft and flirtatious voice.

"Yes." I nod slowly.

"Ok then."

Unable to withstand the miniscule distance between us any longer, I press her hips into mine. "Let me kiss you now."

"Ok." She smiles.

Slowly, I lean down and take her lips with mine, soft, delicate. She has a hint of pineapple on her tongue from her drink that makes me want more. My hands rake up her back, under her shirt.

"You need to come to dinner with us tonight," I say between kissing her, because stopping for even a second is too long.

"At Bo's?"

"Mmhmm." I move to her jawline.

"So I should change?"

"I can help." I slowly lift her shirt up, pulling it over her head and tossing it to the ground. She's already braless and her nipples are hard and asking to be sucked.

"You are perfection." I run the backs of my fingers over her breast, watching goosebumps erupt in their wake, before leaning in and taking one in my mouth.

Her hands tangle in my hair as she holds me to her.

Taking her other breast, I stroke her nipple between my teeth, careful to apply the right amount of pressure, while I hook my fingers inside of her pants, sliding them down.

Standing back up, I lift her with ease and her legs wrap around me. "Where are you taking me?"

"Where do you want to go?" I ask, continuing to plant kisses on her neck.

"I don't care." She moans.

Desire swells with each step I take, and the overwhelming need to be inside of her trumps everything else, so we make it as far as her couch.

I sit her down and, without waiting, I pull her panties off, tossing them over my shoulder and rub the side of my face up the inside of her leg.

"I love when you lick my pussy," she says, fingers gliding through my hair.

"I love licking your pussy." My hands reach around the back of her hips and pull her to the edge of the couch. I inhale her sweet scent and slowly run my tongue up the middle.

"Yes," she moans out, shifting her hips into my face.

I've barely touched her, and she's already glistening. Her responsiveness to me, to us, is like a drug. I run my tongue in circles before sucking on her clit, causing a groan to escape.

Rocking back on my hind legs, I look up at her. "I want you to ride my face." I don't wait for an answer, pulling her off the couch, at the same time I roll onto my back. She quickly crawls up my body and sits on my face. My hands clamp on her thighs as I hold her to me as she rocks her hips, her hands running over her breasts.

"Wait. Wait. Wait," she says, lifting off my face.

"What's wrong?"

"Can we try something?"

"Sure?"

"I want to sixty-nine. I want to suck you off while you eat me out." She doesn't wait for an answer as she undresses me, freeing my hard cock.

"Well, I've never been one to say no to what a lady wants."

She shimmies down my body, her perfect ass up in the air, as she takes me in her mouth. There is no teasing, no hesitation. She's hungry and knows exactly what she wants. Her hand clamps around the base of my cock as she squeezes hard enough to remind me of those frozen popsicle treats you eat in the summer. Her mouth feels like heaven as her tongue flicks the ring at the end.

"Do you like that?" I ask, lifting my head slightly to watch her.

Her tongue licks up the underside of my shaft and swirls around the tip and the ring, causing it to flip back and forth. "Very much," she whispers before taking me in deep.

I buck in her mouth, losing control with the way she's sucking. I have to stop, though. When she comes back up, I use my fingers on the underside of her jaw to get her to pause, and her eyes flicker with a hint of confusion.

"I thought you wanted to sixty-nine. If you keep going, I'm going to come and then keep eating you out."

She smiles. "Well, we can't have that then. I should also mention I want you in my pussy. I want to feel you, just you."

"Ask and ye shall receive."

"Oh. I'm asking."

She pushes up and leans across my body as her wet pussy glides over my cock, almost making it impossible to focus. I want to give her the sixty-nine she wants, but feeling her there. So close. It's all I can do to not flip her over and fuck her. Her nipples brush across the small hairs on my chest as her lips find mine, causing my stomach to clench.

"I love your mouth," she moans.

Her tongue presses in as her hips slowly rock against my cock. A tightness coils in my stomach and a heat flashes across my skin. "Damn, Trouble. You're making me ache with the need to fuck you so bad right now."

A smile curls on her lips as she swings a leg over, turning around. "Then we should do this, so you can fuck me properly." She lines her pussy up with my mouth and lowers herself as her hand wraps around my length.

A moan escapes as I lap up her arousal. She's so fucking wet. Wet for me. Because of me. And now she's sucking me off. She sinks lower and takes me in deep, her tongue ravenously licking along the top of my shaft, before she sucks on my head, pushing it back in again. My hips buck off the ground and I hit the back of her throat, feeling a slight twitch in her mouth.

As I run my tongue across her clit and circle it around, I run my fingers through her pussy, getting them wet, pumping them in a few times until she's moaning and rocking her hips.

I don't mind sharing her with the boys, because that's what we do, who we are, but I also love that it's me and her right now. I can fully pleasure her and the moans she's giving me, just me, are almost as much of a turn on as her bobbing on me.

With her arousal slick on my fingers, I run them over her perfect little hole and press in just a little, until she bucks and moans, eager for more. With each gentle push, I go a little deeper, preparing her.

She bucks off my cock and screams out, "Fuck. Shit. Mother ass!"

Chuckling, I press my finger in as my tongue fucks her pussy.

She pants out in quick shallow breaths. "Can't. Focus. On. Cock." Her breath shudders. "I want to come. With you inside me. But. Oh God. I'm. Fucking. Close."

"Do you want me to stop?" Praying she says no.

"No. Never. Oh God, Emmett." She rocks her hips back into me, on all fours, my dick abandoned, but I don't care.

She doesn't slow down, so I just keep my finger and mouth still while she fucks me. Taking what she wants. Letting me give her what I can.

She's getting close, because her pussy starts to quiver.

A low guttural moan escapes from deep inside her and I know she's feeling it. An intense orgasm. The deeper her groans, the more intense. She rocks a few more times, then grabs my cock like a fiend, taking it fast and hard. My muscles stiffen as I'm about to come, but I can't. Not like this.

I pat her ass, but she doesn't stop.

"Trouble," I warn playfully.

She continues and I'm getting close, too close, to that point where my body takes over and finishes.

"Everlee," I say more sternly.

Fuck. She doesn't stop.

Pressing my hands under both of her hips, I time the lift when she's at the head of my cock. I can bench three hundred, so she's nothing but a feather.

She squeals and wobbles around in the air, looking at me. Fortunately, I'm able to hold her up.

"What are you doing?" She laughs.

"I want to fuck you, and you're about to make me explode in your mouth."

The mischievous twinkle in her eyes pulls at places inside of my chest. I shut it down and lower her to the floor beside me.

"Bend me over the couch?" she asks innocently.

"I love the way you ask for what you want."

Her lips curl into a reckless smile as she stands up, walking over to the couch and placing her hands on the back of it.

Stroking my shaft slowly, I walk over and line up at her entrance. After the near explosion I just had, I take my time, because I want to feel her. Savor her. I lean over, letting my length run between her glistening lips of desire as I plant kisses along her spine, starting at the top of her neck and working my way down. She shifts from side to side, trying to inch closer to my cock, but I move it out of the way. A frustrated sigh escapes her lips, causing me to chuckle. Saying nothing, she continues to sway gently as I kiss around her hip bones and then proceed to her ass. "I love your ass," I murmur breathlessly against her skin.

"I love your cock inside of me," she whispers, all too subtly.

Smiling, I bite her ass, then lick over the marks before planting a soft kiss, carrying it up her spine. Hands on her hips, I slowly push into her. Slower and slower, to elongate the sound of her moans. It feeds the want and desire within me. Fully seated inside of her, I hold her there, pressing deeper with everything I have. She feels so fucking good. I withdraw gradually, until the tip hovers teasingly at her entrance, and then ease back in with excruciating slowness, relishing the intense warmth of her pussy. Tired of waiting, she tries to take over, rocking her hips more. She's aching for my dick. Aching to be fucked.

So I give her what she wants. I unleash on her, sending my cock inside of her, using her hips to pull her onto me at the same time I push into her.

A heat rises inside of me, lighting me like a torch, the faster I press into her. Sweat beads on my chest, rolling down the crevices of my muscles and tickling my skin.

She whips her head back. "Harder E."

E. I smile, then fuck her. I relentlessly thrust into her, so hard I'm scared I'm going to break her, but she doesn't whimper or wince. She yells. Screams. Begs for more.

"Your ring feels fucking amazing," she rasps, her hands gripping tighter onto the couch. "Come inside of me. Please. Fill me."

Her words are my undoing. My mind goes hazy as we move together. Me pushing. Her pushing. Wet slaps of my balls hitting her pussy echo around the room and it's a glorious sound. A tingle shoots down my spine and hovers there, causing my balls to tighten. I pick up speed, if that's even possible, and she knows. She stops moving and lets me fuck her. Lets me have control.

My orgasm hits me hard. Like a fucking rocket shooting into the sky. Fuck, it feels amazing as my warmth mingles with her come.

She lets out a grunt as I press into her one more time and stop. My cock pulses and I just savor the feeling. This feeling. Her. And me.

After a few minutes pass, I pull out and we collapse on the couch. I roll her over so she's laying on top of me, her body blanketing me. She rests her hands on my chest and places her chin on them, staring at me and after a moment she giggles.

"What?" A smile tugs on my lips as I lazily stroke her back, savoring in this moment.

"I can feel your seed leaking out of me." She chuckles again.

"My seed, huh?" My brow peaks with humor.

She nods her head slowly.

"I see seed in the books I read and find the word so funny."

A familiar ache squeezes in my chest, so I fight back the words that threaten to spill out and reveal my feelings to her. I try to reason it's because I'm in a bliss filled post coital place, but I don't know if that will work anymore. Or much longer, at least.

"Do you want to come shower with me?" she asks. "My shower is nowhere close to the size of y'all's and we likely won't fit in there together, but I'm willing to try."

We cuddle on the couch a little longer until she becomes a wiggle worm with constant giggles. "It sort of tickles as it trickles." She throws her head back in a cackle. "I'm a poet and didn't know it!"

"Let's get you cleaned up." I playfully pat her butt, then push her off the couch so she lands with a thump on the floor.

"Ass."

"Yes, I do love yours." I pinch it as we walk into the bathroom.

An overwhelming urge to tell her about me surfaces. About my orientation. It never really came up before because I didn't think it mattered. But I want her to know me. Know all of me. Know the parts of me I keep tucked away and hidden from most.

I knew when I was in my late teens that I found boys attractive and had thoughts and dreams of them. Sexual dreams. It was a weird time in my life because things were going ok at Mary's and I didn't want to rock the boat with the guys. They were my guys. But not like that. Never like that.

I was scared they could sense something was different with me, so I started distancing myself. I felt it was better if I did it before they learned the truth and did it on their own. After about six months, they threw a bag on my head and whisked me away in a car. Not their best idea since I nearly shit my pants, but they ended up taking me to a lake and forced me to tell them what was going on.

I was so scared. Probably the most scared I'd ever been, but they didn't care. They sat there, staring at me with furrowed brows. They were mad. Mad that I thought they would leave me. Not giving them credit is what they barked. The bonds we had created went deeper than blood. We were a brotherhood in every sense of the word.

It was a year later when I had my first threesome with Jax. There was this girl Jax was seeing, and she had mentioned wanting a threesome with another guy. We'd met a few times, and she was flirtatious with me, so they asked me. Jax trusted me and he was giving me the opportunity to have both of them. I'd been watching a lot of male on male porn and pulled him aside before we met up with her and asked if he had a problem fucking me while I fucked her. He thought about it for a minute and then gave some quip on how a hole is just a hole. But I didn't think it was that simple and felt it was more for me than for him, but we agreed and that's what we did. I loved fucking her, but equally loved the feeling of him inside of me. We told the guys what happened because we figured they'd find out and they were accepting. Jax and I knew it wasn't a thing. He had no desire to fuck other men or be fucked by them, but it was our thing.

A couple of months later, we went our own ways, Knox and Jax to the military, Callum to business school, and me to culinary school. I had dated several men while in school, but always felt like there was something missing.

We talked as often as we could, and would meet up for short stints when Knox and Jax came home. It was like no time had passed, when in reality several years had passed. Callum and I graduated from our schools, and Jax and Knox both called their last tour.

We had our own places for a while, but had ideas for the future.

Big ideas.

We decided to rent a place together, each of us pulling jobs to contribute and storing away as much money as possible until we could make our dreams happen. Our first business was a sex club.

It made sense, because we had questions, thoughts, feelings we wanted answers to, but didn't know where to find them. Rather, more importantly, find them safely. It was a tremendous success. Slow at first, but then it really took off.

We called her Allure.

Even with its success, there were a lot of things we did wrong with it or things we wanted to change as we learned more, but it was cost prohibitive. A buyer from Dallas came to us, wanting to buy us out, offering a deal that was hard to refuse.

It didn't take long for us to agree to the sale. It's what gave us the capital to open Bo's, Vixen and to purchase a clothing store we renamed and rebranded to Loveuz.

"You coming?" she calls from the bathroom, pulling me away from my thoughts.

"Yea." I step into the bathroom. "There's something I want to tell you."

EVERLEE - MOUTH YOGA AND SQUATS

EMMETT AND I ARRIVE at Bo's a few hours later. The shower was a bust. I knew he was big, but didn't realize how big. We were standing in the shower tub combo and had no room to move around. Our arms were tucked by our chest and we spun a few times, feeling like we were those floppy sponges at a car wash. He eventually climbed out and let me finish, while he stayed and just talked to me.

Talked is an understatement.

He unloaded so much on me. But it was nice. There were a lot of questions I'd been wondering about and I think part of it was him wanting to show me a peek behind the curtain. To show he wanted this. Us.

After I got out of the shower, we ended up cuddling on my bed, staring at my shelf of dildos. I went through the story of each, recounting it with the same pride and love as one would speak about their own children - sharing where they came from and the reasons behind their existence. So that wasn't super awkward. He especially found my green monster dildo the most interesting and offered next time we should use it. I had to assume he meant when we were just one on one, because there's no way in hell I could take five cocks. The thought made my skin shiver.

No.

But then that damn kinky ass bitch hiding in the corner of my mind is like, well... maybe we could. I shut her down. Shoved her back in the corner.

When we walk into Bo's, the hostess gives me the once over then directs us upstairs. I figure she's not used to seeing someone else with *them*, especially a woman who has her arm linked with Emmett's.

"There they are." Callum stands, holding his arms out wide. He looks delicious as sin, with his dark jeans and a light blue button down that hugs him in all the right places. "I was beginning to think you two ran away together."

"Thought about it," Emmett teases.

I walk over to Callum, giving him a hug and a kiss on the cheek, stealing the corner of his lips. "Leave you boys? Never again."

Jax stands up and walks over, wearing a thin black sweater that hugs his body like a condom hugs a banana. I pinch my eyes together. Most random ass thought ever. I'm hungry and I blame it on my stomach, especially after my sexcapades earlier, coupled by the fact it's so late. Well, later than I'm used to. Cut a woman's food supply off and her brain does funky things. Cut a cock supply off... and well, same thing.

I kiss him the same as Callum, but at the last second he turns his head just quick enough that I get more than the corner.

"Yep. Your lips taste like Emmett's cock." He chuckles and I blush.

Based on the in-depth conversation Emmett and I just had, I know Jax has never tasted Emmett's cock and he's just teasing.

I walk over to Knox, who is wearing a pair of khaki shorts and a white short-sleeve button down. He looks like he's ready for the beach. "Hey love," he says, wrapping his arm around me and planting a kiss on my cheek.

"Hey yourself." I'm smiling so much my cheeks hurt. I look around and notice most of the upper floor is empty, with only a few tables that have people at them. From what I can tell, it seems to be more private parties and business meetings. I can't help but wonder if this is on purpose or not. The downstairs, as usual, is very busy. Every table is full.

They all take their seats. Callum at the head, Jax to his right, Emmett across from Jax and Knox to Emmett's left. Jax pulls out the seat beside him, but I walk past it and sit at the other end of the table across from Callum. I don't know why, but I feel like pushing him tonight. To see how he'll react. I don't know what it is about stoking the flames in his eyes that turns me on, but they do.

Jax blows out a cool breath with a chuckle and pushes the seat back in while Callum stares at me, his eyes unwavering. Before he can say anything, the server comes over and greets them all and asks me what I'd like to drink.

Callum answers unflinching. "She'll have what we're having."

She casts a weary glance at me and waits for me to correct him, then after a beat, nods and walks away.

"You think you can sit at the end of the table?" he asks, perching his chin on his clasped hands.

"I didn't know there were assigned seats. Maybe I wanted to sit by Knox," I clap back.

Knox places his hand over mine. "You can always sit beside me or on me. Lap, face. I have no preference."

I cast him a lopsided grin, then blow a kiss.

"If you two are done."

I shrug, then feel a heat stir when he throws a 'be careful' look that excites me more than it scares me. "So, are we talking shop tonight?" I gently slam both of my fists on the table.

"Shop?"

"I don't know what you all do up here. I figured it was business related."

"Usually. But not tonight," Callum says.

"No?"

"Nope. Just wanted to go out with you. Like a date."

My heart flutters a bit at the one word. Date. Only instead of it being one person, it's four people. Totally normal, right? God, I want this so badly. Of course, instead of being the mature adult I strive to be on most days, I say something stupid. Jokes, the mortar to the brick wall surrounding my feelings. "Hmmm. No strings. No hallway tango. No-" I use my thumb and forefinger to create a circle and then insert my other finger inside of it.

"Not tonight."

"Are you cutting me off?" I moan.

"Fucking sex fiend," Jax mumbles under his breath as the server walks back over with our drinks.

Old Fashioned's. I assumed that's what he ordered, which is why I didn't correct Callum. I trust him. Trust all these men. They are my home, but how could I tell them that? What would I be giving up? Marriage? Kids?

Marriage is just a paper and a ring. We'd have all the important stuff without that. Kids? That's a little harder to swallow. I don't know if I've ever wanted them or just been made to believe I should want them. Kids aren't for everyone, and it doesn't make you selfish if they're not for you. I imagine in some ways the men felt their little poly pod prevented the conversation of kids from coming up because they probably feared they wouldn't be wonderful parents because of their past.

But I've seen them.

I saw them at the Easter events. They were right in there with the children and the smiles on their face and pure joy they were radiating warmed my heart. I think they'd be great parents, but then that begs the question in a poly pod how does that work? Who's the father? I chuckle to myself. Fuck. If Nick Cannon can do it, why can't I? Call me Nicki

Cannon. I could have kids with all of them, they could all be fathers... The longer I think about it and look at their faces, the more it continues to develop. What if–

My phone dings three times in a row and we all look at it. I flip it over and chuckle. "Lizzy."

Lizzy: *What's up bee-atch!*

Lizzy: *Did you figure out how to please your harem?*

Lizzy: *That's what the cool kids call it these days.*

Everlee: *At Bo's with them now, about to eat dinner.*

Everlee: *And haven't had a chance too.*

Everlee: *Emmett came over.*

Lizzy: *The mountain man with his schmexy beard.*

She sends a GIF of a sexy mountain man chopping wood. "Lizzy thinks your beard is sexy," I tell Emmett.

"I've always liked her." He smiles, casually stroking his beard.

Everlee: *Text you later.*

Lizzy: *I feel like you're lying to me because you're going to be four dicks deep.*

Lizzy: *Sounds like a country song.*

Lizzy trying to sing a song about four dicks deep in a deep southern accent, swirls around in my mind. Or maybe that's me? I have this horrible tendency to hear words, then break off into song. I'm sure there's some country remake of four dicks deep and a tractor or a dog that ran away.

> **Everlee:** *Love you boo.*

I sit my phone down and see the guys looking around at each other, talking with their eyes. "Everything ok?" I ask hesitantly.

Callum nods slowly, then looks at me. "Would you like to invite Lizzy to dinner?"

My eyes widen in shock. "Really?" I whisper out, heart pounding through my chest with excitement. It isn't so much to have Lizzy at dinner, but to *have* her at dinner. She's never met the guys all at the same time. Sure, she'd seen them here and there or talked to them one off, but she'll be stepping into this world. My world. Our world.

"Yes," he intones.

My hand glides across the table, resting on my phone, giving him the opportunity to change his mind. Their genuine attempts to create a normal relationship with me are palpable and appreciated. It helps Lizzy knows and Beckett likely knows. Is this all to prepare for our talk tomorrow? Is this their way of showing me it can work? We can work?

Jax nods the approval at me again, so I flip my phone over and begin typing out the text.

> **Everlee:** *Would you like to come to Bo's and have dinner with us?*

> **Lizzy:** *Are you trying to initiate me into the harem?*

> **Everlee:** *Ha. No.*

Lizzy: *Son of a bitch.*

Lizzy: *I already started doing squats and mouth yoga.*

Everlee: *Squats?*

Lizzy: *You don't question the mouth yoga?*

Everlee: *You mean the thing you recently made up?*

Lizzy: *Ehh. Squats. I don't know.*

Lizzy: *It couldn't hurt when popping on that cock.*

Everlee: *I retract the invite.*

Lizzy: *Already walking that way.*

Everlee: *Cannot compute.*

Lizzy: *Shut it, hussy. I'm excited!!!*

Lizzy: *I'll be on my best behavior.*

Everlee: *I doubt it.*

Lizzy: *You know me so well.*

Lizzy: *Should I greet them with Sir? Harem? The 4 D's?*

I literally have no response. Anything I type will encourage her, and she doesn't need help. I put the phone back down and sigh. "She'll be here in a few minutes. I'm going to apologize for anything inappropriate she says now, so I don't spend the entire dinner doing it."

They all chuckle like I'm kidding, but they don't know the little tornado they invited to dinner. My tornado, but still a fucking tornado.

Lizzy is walking up the stairs a few minutes later, escorted by the hostess, who now looks thoroughly perturbed and confused, before she walks back down. I hold my breath and grip the table when Lizzy awkwardly clasps her hands in front of her and nods into a small bow. "Greetings and Salutations, gentleman." She pops up and looks at me. "Boo."

"Lizzy," I say, walking over to her and giving her a hug.

"How did I do? I thought 4Ds was a little too informal for Bo La Vie."

"A little?" I stifle a laugh.

"Well, you know. First time meeting them and all. Want to make a good impression. Not because I want in the harem. Obvi. I mean, who would get who? And Tony's great." She beams and grabs my shoulders. "They're much more handsome when they're all together at the same time," she whispers. "So maybe I *will* need an application for hot man harem master."

"Please behave," I implore softly.

"Boo boo. You don't have to tell me three times."

I cast a weary glance at her and lead her over to the table, officially introducing her to the other part of my life. The part that's been mostly off limits until tonight.

Each guy stands up and gives her a hug, and she's fanning herself as she takes the seat by Jax. She makes small talk about how handsome they are and how pleased she is to see me happy again.

The server walks over and gets Lizzy's drink order- a lemon drop martini, then takes our order.

Emmett chooses several appetizers for the table before handing it over to us to order our entrée. Lizzy passes, since she's already eaten dinner and says she'll just nibble on the apps, but couldn't pass up an invitation to dine with all of us.

Dinner goes by unexpectedly smooth and normal. Lizzy surprises me by being on her best behavior and not saying anything embarrassing, even though there were moments when she clearly stored away some comments for later. I could see that look in her eyes like a crazy gremlin after getting wet.

After dinner, the guys try to convince me to come home with them, but I tell them no. If tomorrow is our big talk, then I need to take the night to compile a list of pros and cons, then convince myself why the cons don't matter. If I went to their house, we'd end up having mind blowing sex and I wouldn't put the thought needed into this it deserved. I messed up one time already. I won't do it again. I can't.

Lizzy offers to take me home, but I decline her too, opting for my good pal Betty.

She's at Bo's ten minutes later with a smile plastered on her face, wearing what looks to be a nightgown with rubber ducks on it.

"Well, slap me silly darling," she says, peeking through her passenger window.

I give each of the guys a hug since they refuse to leave until they see me off and then give Lizzy a hug, who doesn't leave because I'm sure she's gathering more intel for whatever crazy thoughts she's thinking.

As we pull away, I toss them a wave.

When we get to the light, Betty turns around and looks at me. "Have a good night? I hope you don't mind what I'm wearing. I was going to change then thought, well shit, why? It's my girl, Everlee."

I chuckle. "What you're wearing is totally fine. I wish I was wearing it, too."

"I put on a bra if that makes you feel better."

She pulls down the road and I notice the clothing store Emmett mentioned a few shops down and chuckle to myself. All three businesses lined up along in a row.

I let out a satisfied sigh, feeling a wave of contentment wash over me.

"Have a good night?"

"The best."

"I've been wanting to try that place out, but it's so expensive for sandwiches."

"Betty. When I tell you they are orgasmic...." I blow out a satisfied puff of air. "It's worth it."

"Orgasmic you say?" her voice ticks up an octave.

"Orgasmic."

"I was talking to Lizzy the other night after her engagement, and she said she wanted to have the reception there. So who knows? Maybe I'll get to try it then."

I nod. "It would be a great venue."

"She was so darn fa-lute-en happy that night. She was trying to call you in the car, but she couldn't between her squealing and kissing that man."

"I'm really excited for her."

"When are you getting married? I'm sure one of those handsome men you were with tonight would love to make an honest woman out of you."

"Betty!" I snap playfully. "Why do you assume I want to be an honest woman?"

She throws her head back in a fit of laughter and hits the steering wheel. "You kids these days."

"I don't know if I will ever get married." Am I saying this because I believe it or because I'm preparing myself for tomorrow night?

I yawn and rest my head on the window.

"Well, here we are, deary. You try to get some rest tonight."

"Thanks Betty. Good seeing you."

"You too, darling. Glad to see you out and about again." She pats my knee.

I tip her through the app, then step out. I have a feeling that even though the sandman is banging on my door, I won't get any sleep. Tomorrow is a big day... and probably night.

EVERLEE - DEVIL IN A DRESS

THOUGHTS RACED THROUGH MY mind all night and I didn't get to sleep until close to midnight. I decided to go old-school and grab a piece of paper and write out the pros and cons, but in a fit, scribbled it all out and balled it up. The logical part of me wanted to take a systematic approach to this important decision, but my gut was telling me my mind was already made up. I'd just have to go into the conversation with my concerns and worries and just talk to them.

I don't want to get hurt. They don't want to get hurt. We have a mutual desire to protect ourselves, even if it means making the hard decision now to not pursue this any further.

This morning, Emmett sent me a text notifying me of our appointment at La Belle's at five thirty tonight and also mentioned he would be picking me up from work.

Checking my phone for the hundredth time, I flip it over and try to ignore the fact I still have fifteen minutes before they get here. My fingers tap tap tap impatiently on my desk as my eyes dart over the spreadsheet in front of me. I've been staring at it for close to an hour now and haven't made a bit of progress since I can't focus. My stomach is a bundle of nerves and excitement and everything else in between. I feel like this conversation is damn near a marriage proposal, but I know it's not. Duh. But it feels like it in some ways.

We aren't going into this saying we're going to spend the rest of our lives together and something won't happen where we mutually walk away. We're just saying the reasons for us walking away won't be reasons that are avoidable now.

Same reason I fully believe on the third date you should ask your date if they want kids. Seems a little too soon in the relationship, but I think it's better to know something like that upfront. If you aren't on the same page, why waste your time? You'll get to a point much later down the line where one of you will try to convince yourself of something you don't want and eventually, years later, there will be anger and resentment. Just saying.

I walk over to the window and look down at the street and see a limo parked out front and a smile curves across my lips and a flutter spreads in my belly.

He's here.

In a limo.

That has to be him, right? It would be kind of embarrassing if it's not.

Scurrying to my desk, I pick up my phone and text to see if he's here, to which he responds immediately, confirming my suspicion.

Pulse hammering in my chest, I turn my computer off, because honestly, I'm not starting anything new with eleven minutes left in the day and I have been useless for the last sixty.

Tossing my bag over my shoulder, I make my way downstairs. By the time I get outside, Brady is standing by the back door with his hand on the handle.

"Good day, Ms. Everlee."

"Brady." I nod, smiling.

When I climb in, I'm shocked to see all the guys sitting in the car. The few butterflies I had before turn into hundreds! "Well, hello there," I say in a somewhat awkwardly sultry voice.

They all nod, saying their forms of hello.

"How was your day?" Knox asks, planting a kiss on my cheek as I sit beside him.

"Better now."

Emmett leans forward and pats my leg, asking for me to put it in his lap, so I do. He slips my shoe off and starts rubbing the arch of my foot, and I slowly melt into the seat.

"You're moaning," Jax whispers.

"Sorry."

"Damn it, Jax," Knox whines. "Why do you always have to tell her?"

"I don't need you ejaculating in your pants," he snaps back.

Knox puckers his lips. "I didn't realize you had so much cock awareness."

Emmett has the hands of the Gods. And the mouth... My mind flashes back to every time his lips are on me, causing my pussy to flutter. Trying not to lose it on the ride to the dress shop, I close my eyes and let my head rest on the back of the seat. I don't know how much time passes, but when he hit a bump, my heart lurches in my throat and I sit up, hands pressed to the seat.

"We're here." Jax gently pats my leg, pulling me out of whatever blissful state I was in.

A few more minutes and he would have had to wake me up.

We walk in and Andre is wearing a flamboyant gold sequin top with a small poof at the bottom and tight, black leather pants, holding a tray of champagne in his hand.

A huge smile lights his face when he sees me and then his eyes grow wide as they travel to the four man-gods behind me. His hand wobbles and he does a full circle, somehow managing to hold up the tray of glasses without spilling a drop.

"Wow," he breathes and leans over to whisper loudly to me. "Girl. Who are these delicious men?"

"They're my friends." I chuckle, not knowing what else to call them. Although, we'd have to think of something, because why would four hotter than hell men go dress shopping with a girl?

"I want some friends like yours." He fans himself before taking a long sigh before offering us champagne. "I was so excited when I saw your name on the appointment list. Easiest client I've had all year and your body. Perfection." He kisses the tips of his fingers.

The guys shift out of the corner of my eye and I catch their looks of agreement, which sends a fire through my core.

"What can I do for you today?"

Emmett steps forward slightly. "She needs a formal dress, preferably in the gray family. We'd also like our vests to match her dress and this will all be on one bill."

Andre lifts his brow and looks over his shoulder at me, and I just smile and shrug.

"We have several dresses that will look fantastic on you." He throws his fingers in the air like he's capturing a light-ning bug, but in a super artistic way. "Let's see if we can find your vests first since you all are... well... large chested. I'll have to get measurements."

I chuckle under my breath at Andre's face and general super giddy demeanor.

"Sounds good," Callum says, cutting his eyes at me with a playful smirk.

Andre directs us to a private room in the back that has a changing room and mirrors for walls. In the center of the room is a raised platform with several light gray tufted chairs in a semicircle around it with a dressing room in the corner.

"I'll give you all this room, if that's ok with you?" Andre asks, ushering us in. "If you'd like some more champagne, let me know." When no one speaks, he whips the measuring tape off his shoulder. "Who's my first victim?"

They all look at each other before Callum stands up, removing his jacket. He's wearing his typical long sleeve button down, in a dark blue today.

Andre gulps loudly, then walks over. "Arms out please." He pulls a notepad and pencil out of his pocket and tucks it in his mouth, measuring around Callum's arms, chest, and the length of his torso, jotting them down each time. "When is your event?"

"Tomorrow." Emmett pulls his lips in apology.

Andre grabs his chest, flabbergasted, then cuts his eyes at me. "Give a man some time, why don't you? Are you going to be the one who gets their wedding dress a few days before you get married too!" he teases.

With a laugh, I avert my gaze, trying to find something else to grab my attention. "I'm going to look for dresses while you boys are getting measured."

Disregarding the concerned look that Callum gives me, I respond with a cheeky wink. I'm not leaving because of the wedding comment, but because I'm finding it difficult to see them all looking so delicious in a room like that.

Andre finds me thirty minutes later. "Girlfriend. Please tell me one, or all of them, is gay."

I let out a light-hearted chuckle, shaking my head in amusement.

"That's a damn shame," he huffs, then looks around. "Well, we've found a vest for them. They must be the luckiest men in the world."

"Because they know me?"

"Yes, darling, and because I happen to have vests here for them in two different colors."

"Two?" I tease. "How did we get so lucky?"

"Girllll."

"What colors are we working with?"

"We got a light silver or a slate gray. Men said whichever dress you find you like in those colors is the vest they'll go with."

I found a few dresses that caught my eye while I was walking around, so we go through the racks to see if they were the right colors. Three of them are but four are not, and one of the four was my favorite. Oh well! The others are still beautiful.

He grabs them off the rack and walks them back to the room, and hangs them on several hooks. The guys are sitting casually in their seats, ankles propped on their knee, laughing and chatting while drinking their champagne. I wish I could take a picture of this moment and keep it with me forever.

"Which one do you want me to try on first?" I ask them and they all give a different answer.

Andre suggests the lightest gray one, so I grab it and head into the changing room while Andre leaves to look for more options. He isn't super thrilled with any of the choices we picked and thinks he can do better. Which doesn't bother me at all. In fact, I appreciate it.

I listen to the men talk about some baseball game they recently watched while I slip on the dress. It's a light gray one shoulder satin a-frame dress with a slit up my left leg. When I walk out, the men's heads turn to look at me, breathing fire into my bones.

Their looks.

The way it makes me feel. Untouchable.

I'd say it's better than an orgasm. Maybe the orgasms with Rich, but with them... nothing is better than their orgasms. They have taken me to new heights, new places, I didn't think was possible. They've reached into the depths of my soul to pull those suckers out like a pirate plundering for treasure deep in Atlantis. That's how far they've traveled to extract those tingly, mind numbing, pussy throbbing moments of bliss.

"Well?" I ask, tossing my hip to the side and throwing my hands in the air.

"Do that again," Callum commands, nodding in my direction.

"This?" I ask, knocking my hip out again.

He strokes his chin approvingly while Jax's teeth scrape over his bottom lip.

"I don't know," Knox says. "I feel like it's missing something." He stands up and walks around me. "Back too high." He runs his hand down my side. "And no pockets."

I cut my eyes at him, failing to hold back a laugh. "Pockets? What do you know about pockets in dresses?"

"I see pictures online of girls losing their minds over dresses with pockets."

"Shut the fuck up," Jax says, wiping his hand over his face.

"What?" Knox sighs, sitting back down. "It's a legitimate thing. Just because you aren't as in touch with women as I am..."

Andre knocks on the door before bustling in with the vests and another dress. "Here are the vests. You can try these on and make sure they fit. Our seamstress is here right now and for a premium fee, we can get them altered quickly if needed. And then I found this dress. We had it on hold for a woman, but she called this morning and said she no longer needed it. It's absolutely stunning and matches these perfectly." He shimmies his shoulders.

The dress is stunning. It's a lighter gray, floor length dress with a beaded plunging neckline, full slit up the left side with a soft light gray layered tulle skirt.

"Wow." I rub my hand down the front of the dress. It's a thing I do. I have to feel things and smell things. Gets me in trouble occasionally, but mostly it works out.

I grab the dress and head into the changing room. Andre says he'll give us a few minutes in private while he has to work on some things. I slip it on and give a quick turn in the single mirror in the small changing room and fall in love. I didn't realize before it's also backless. My stomach tightens into knots with anticipation. When the men see this, I have a feeling they're going to lose their minds.

"Ready?" I ask, my clammy palm gripping the curtain.

"Yes," they all say in unison.

I step out and their jaws drop.

"No," Jax and Callum say in unison after their tongues roll back into their mouth.

"Agree. Nope. That's not the one," Emmett adds, nearly standing out of his seat.

"The fuck it isn't!" Knox nearly shouts, actually leaping from his chair.

The guy's eyes are on fire, and the bulge in their pants is growing. There's no way.

"I thought you all would like this one," I say, turning around to show them the back.

"Fuck me," Jax whimpers.

Callum walks over to me, slipping his hand around my waist, pressing his cheek to mine, and I nervously glance at the door.

"Don't worry about him. I don't give a damn if he sees me." He pulls me closer so his hard erection is pressed against my hips. "If you wear this dress, men will look at you. And if they look at you, the way I know they will, you will lose all of us. We will be in jail for plucking out their eyes."

"Why is that so sexy?" I breathe out.

"Can you feel my cock? That is from you turning around. Simply walking out and turning around. Do you want me to have a hard on the entire night?"

"Can't you think of something that is super gross?"

His chuckle is low and gravelly, reverberating through my every bone. "Love. There is nothing in this world that could compete with the way you look in this dress."

"It doesn't have pockets." Jax chides.

Knox walks over. "Fuck the pockets. It has a slit to her clit. A clit slit!" he says, running his hand up my leg all the way to my pussy, causing a breath to escape my lips.

There's a knock at the door, but Emmett snaps. "Not now." And the door quietly closes.

A minute later, Jax and Emmett are surrounding me and all four of them have their hands on me.

"Another reason you can't choose this dress is because you'd have to wear underwear with it and we all know how much you hate that," Callum says, his hand snaking up the slit and curving around my ass.

I look down and swish my hips from side to side. "No. I don't."

"The fuck you won't." Jax's eyes blaze. I've seen this dark possessive side of him several times, usually in the heat of sex, when he grabs my throat and presses me against the wall and this is no less hot. His words are like a hand around my throat and a red hot iron in my cunt. I wince briefly at the image of the red-hot iron being shoved into my pussy, because I, unfortunately, am also a very visual person, but I push past it. Because that is what I feel. On fire.

"Squid in a ball of sagebrush!" I blurt.

"What?"

"I don't know. It was the first thing I could think of to help all your erections go away. We can't fuck in the middle of the store. One of you sure. Four of you? No fucking way. I love this store and I have a fondness for Andre, so I don't want to get kicked out."

"Come up with something better than squid in sage-brush," Jax huffs.

"Roadkill." Their eyes raise. "In a porta-potty." They grimace. "Covered in maggots."

"That's just sick," Knox says.

"Well?" I shrug.

There's another soft knock on the door and the boys take their seat, trying to cross their legs, but their hard daddy dongs won't let them. They each grab a magazine, brochure, or pamphlet off the tables between their seats and open it on their laps.

"Come in," I say, eyes nervously glancing around the room, like a parent has walked in and caught me doing something I shouldn't have been doing.

Andre hesitantly pushes the door open and looks around the room cautiously. I think he knows the game, but is still playing along, and then his eyes land on me. "Stunning. I knew when I saw it, it'd be the one." He turns to the guys. "What do you all think?" He's asking to be nice, because it's obvious by the way they are sitting what they think.

Callum flippantly tosses his hand in the air. "It's nice."

Andre clutches his chest, "Nice?" As if the simple word doesn't do me justice.

I decide in this moment if I ever need a pick me up and Lizzy isn't around, then I will make an appointment to come try on dresses with Andre. Not to buy, but to let him dress me.

"We're taking it," Knox blurts out.

Jax, Callum, and Emmett's heads all turn slowly to Knox like he just threatened them to a duel, rather, a quadel. Is that what you would call a four-way duel?

"Do you men want to see how your vests look with the dress?" He flicks his fingers between us all.

"Nope. We're good," Jax blurts out.

A knowing smile curves on Andre's lips. "Yes. I suppose you are. Well, I will let you all get changed back into your clothes while I prepare to check you all out."

"Sounds lovely," Emmett squeezes out, tucking the pageant pamphlet back into its acrylic holder.

"Very well. See you all soon."

He turns quickly and exits, closing the door behind him.

"Well, I don't think you fooled him," I tease.

"No shit!" Jax claps back.

I throw him a playful snarl.

He jerks his arm, pointing towards the dressing room. "Go change."

Callum adds, "Now."

"I don't like being told what to do."

"You will change right now or we will never be able to come back here again because we *will* destroy that dress, tearing it off your body and fucking you until you can't walk. Now go. Please," Callum pleads.

I smile a wicked smile, and his eyes narrow on me, waiting. "Yes, Sir." I turn without waiting to see the look in his eyes, knowing that I got exactly what I wanted.

Happy with myself, I take my time removing the dress and placing it back on its hanger. I toss it over my arm and walk out to the seating area and see that all have left except Jax.

"Waiting on me?"

He stalks over towards me in three heavy strides and clamps his hands around my jaw, pushing me backwards against the mirror. "You." The one word speaks volumes. His lips crash to mine in an unforgivingly passionate kiss. He pulls off. "You will learn to listen to us." He goes back in for another kiss, his tongue pressing its way in. "You will learn to obey." He presses his nose against the base of my neck, inhaling. "Or you will suffer the punishment."

My head is in a complete daze, high in the clouds. After a second, I steady my gaze and push him away. "Get the whips and handcuffs ready then, because I will not comply." I step around him and start to walk out of the door when I feel a hand grab my wrist and spin me around.

His hands cup my cheeks, pressing his forehead against mine. "You're the devil in a dress."

It takes me a minute to process what he's saying. It's a line from a Teddy Swims song. One of my new favorite songs, actually. "Are you in peril?" I whisper back with a heady breath, continuing the lyric.

He nods and whispers, "I'm a masochist." He takes my lips softly, kissing me in one of the most passionate kisses I've ever experienced. His words and kiss are laced with a level of emotion that robs me of my breath. That causes an ache to stir deep within my chest. A feeling I've been trying to push away for a long time. He pulls away and then walks around me, leaving me standing there speechless, breathless, and wetter than a bloat of hippos in the mating season.

I huff and walk out.

EVERLEE - WHEN YOU ENJOY BEING PUNISHED

WE CLIMB BACK INTO the car with my dress and their vests in the trunk. I sit on the seat on the right side, while Jax and Knox sit across from me, and Emmett and Callum sit along the back.

"I hope you're happy," Callum says. "You've doomed us to a life in prison," he continues dryly.

I chuckle, my gaze shifting back to Jax, my head still unable to move on from the private moment we had earlier, trying to decipher what his words meant. I know what I think they mean. What I want them to mean, but it's kind of crazy. Right?

I shake my head to clear my thoughts. "Well, I love the dress and would still like to pay you for it."

"Not going to happen," Emmett says, resting his hand on my leg.

"Get the whips and handcuffs ready," Jax mumbles under his breath.

I cast a flirtatious side eye at him, and he shakes his head, not offering even a hint of a smile.

"She will not comply," he says coolly, enunciating the last word.

"Comply?" Callum echoes, dripping sex, like it's more of a challenge.

Jax rubs his hands over his face like he's frustrated. "No."

I thought they were kidding earlier, but now I'm beginning to wonder. I know they honestly wouldn't do the eye thing, but they seemed slightly worried about tomorrow night. Perhaps I should make a concession and wear underwear... but also... should I? They'd have to learn if we're together, they aren't always going to get their way. They've always been so in control, but I don't like being controlled. Sure, I *will* make concessions. Relationships are give and take, but I won't let them dictate what I wear.

"Is Brady dropping me off?" I ask, turning to look out of the window.

"No," They all say in unison like it was planned.

"Excuse me?" I say with a flair of sass, naturally bucking their attempted control. Admittedly, I do like it sometimes and it turns me on, but I will always fight it because I believe they like that too. They don't strike me as the types to want a yes person and I'm never going to be that. A fact which should be stated in our talk later.

"You aren't going home. You are going to be punished," Jax says.

"You say that like it's a bad thing, but I love being punished by you." I snipe back. A smile curls at the edge of Knox's lips and I feel like Emmett's too, but his beard hides most of it. Callum and Jax keep with their grumpy faces. I continue, "I don't have clothes at your house."

"You do," Jax says matter-of-factly.

"I don't."

"We got you a few outfits from Loveuz and put them in a closet for you."

"You bought me clothes and gave me a closet?"

"Yes," Jax says simply.

"Are you still mad at me?" I tilt my head to the side, trying to be cutesy, but he only glares at me.

"I thought you would like the dress."

"We fucking love the dress!" Knox chimes like a puppy, waiting for his turn to play.

"Just not on you. In public," Jax adds.

"It's not that bad."

Jax rubs his hands on his pants. "Everlee." My name from his lips slices through the car. "You..." he struggles. "You are going to be the hottest woman by far in that room tomorrow night. You are going to have so many eyes on you. Men and women alike. You're going to have men jacking off in the bathroom to images of you in that dress." He leans forward, resting his forearms on his legs. "You are ours. Ours alone. We share you. But we don't want to share you with anyone else. In no way. Physically or mentally."

The rawness of his words causes a ball to form in my throat, making it difficult to swallow. Well, fuck. Now I feel guilty for wanting to wear the dress. "Fine. But now I have no dress," I resolve.

Jax sighs. "You can wear the dress, but you will not leave our side the entire night."

"That's all well and fine, but you aren't going into the bathroom with me."

"Want to bet?"

I sigh, wanting to change the topic. "Can we have our talk now?"

"No!" Knox blurts. Almost like he's scared it's going to be bad.

I wink at him. "It's not bad. I'm not going anywhere. I don't have to be married, and kids." I hesitate on this one because this is the one I'm still on the fence about, but like a person who tries to climb over a chain linked fence and gets their pants stuck on a point at the top and are now hanging over the side. I'm mostly on one side with a flailing ankle on the other. "I'll be ok with no kids because I'll have Knox."

"Mama."

"Call me mommy," I tease, trying to keep the conversation as light as possible. Then another thought creeps in. Why are there never any mommy kinks? Always the daddy, but never the mommy. I will have to reach out to the Cliterati.

I shake my head, getting back to the conversation. "I'll be honest. This is the one that I was stuck on the longest, for several reasons. I think I'll be ok without kids. I will be the best auntie to Lizzy's brood, because she'll likely have no less than twelve. But," I pause, looking at them all. "Is that something you're ok with?"

They look confused.

"I saw you at the Easter event. I watched you all, and your faces lit up around the kids. And I've seen it repeatedly."

Callum chimes in. "We can't have kids."

I feel a small punch in the chest. "Can't?"

"Physically we can, but we just *can't.*"

"Because of your childhood?" This is getting deeper than I meant it to go.

"Yes, and our lifestyle."

"Nick Cannon does it," I retort playfully.

Callum tilts his head at me with an amused smile.

"It's not the exact same, but damn. Imagine if he had one big ass mansion, and they all had a wing. It would be so much easier for him. Maybe he does. I don't know." I clasp my hands together. "Look, I'm not trying to change your minds about kids. I'm not naïve to think it can happen in the back of a limo and in one conversation. I just want to make sure you all are thinking about the long term, too. I'm sure you have, but..." I shake my head. "I don't know. You all would just make excellent fathers, and I don't want you to let what happened in your childhood dictate your future."

"What about your family?" Knox asks, knowing that was-is- a big thing for me.

Taking a deep sigh, I glance out of the window, trying to put all the random thoughts into a string of words. "I don't have an answer for that one yet. Marriage was easy, kids was a little more difficult, but my family. That's tough. Lizzy and Beckett know. At some point, I will have to come out to my parents, but I don't know when or how. I won't push them away, but I will need to tell them. At the end of the day, you all will be my life. While I love my family and they love me, they will eventually pass on and I don't want what could be with us to be pushed aside for them. My hope is that over time, I will figure out a way to tell them- show them- that this is good. We are good. And hope their love for me outweighs their thoughts on our relationship." My hands fidget in my lap as I continue to watch the cars pass us by. I count them for a moment, just to get out of my head. My parents accepted Beckett, and I hope they will accept me. It will just take some time.

"Anything else?" Callum asks after a minute.

Taking a deep breath, I refocus and sit back in the seat. "Yes. Actually. You will not control me. I don't know how this has worked for you in the past, but I'm my own person. We can discuss things, but you will not demand."

The air seems to lift in the car some and Emmett leans forward. "So I can't demand you to come?"

"And I can't demand you to sit on my cock?" Callum says.

"Or suck me off?" Jax adds.

"Or..." Knox fumbles, then throws his hands in the air. "Man! I was unprepared. Y'all should have told me!"

We all laugh, and just like that, the heavy mood in the car lifts. In some ways, I feel this decision required more time, but in other ways, it's something I've been toying with for months. I left, but they were never gone for me. Sure, I avoided them for almost two months, but they were never not on my mind. Every. Damn. Day.

Always wondering what it would be like. What it could be like. What we could do differently.

"Now, where do we go?" I ask.

"Like from here, emotionally or physically?" Knox asks.

"Shut the fuck up!" Jax shoves him over.

"What? I thought it was a valid question."

"Come here, baby." I pat the seat beside me, and Knox steps across the car and lays his head on my bosom. My bosom, not my breasts. It sounds more motherly and less erotic to say bosom unless they are bouncing. Bouncing bosoms sounds like it would be in a smut book written by a man. Or maybe her heaving, supple, satin smooth, 72DDD breasts that bounced joyfully whilst she popped up and down on my fifteen-inch-long cock that measures nine inches in diameter whilst my gigantic biceps with a circumference of sixty-nine inches holds her upright. That would definitely be written by a man in a book. *So many measurements.*

"Thank you, mommy." He cuts his eyes up at me, so I rub his head.

"Is this going to be a thing now?" Jax chomps. "If so, we may need to revise this arrangement."

"I've got two bosoms." I hold my arm out.

"Cupid," he states simply, using my safe word.

"Can we get some dinner? I'm starving," I say after my stomach rumbles.

"It's like a sound machine down here," Knox says, sitting up.

Callum presses the intercom button for the front. "Brady, can you please take us to McCrory's?"

"Sure thing."

Another date. Us just going out. Simple. Easy peasy, lemon squeezy. I'm so happy right now I feel like I could burst at the seams. Like a rainbow would literally split me in half and shoot out of me.

This is going to be good. We are going to be good.

EVERLEE - WHEN YOU'RE A PUPPET MASTER WITH A MARIONETTE OF COCKS

DINNER WAS SUPERB. THE last two hours were filled with amazing food and conversation. We talked about any and everything under the sun and really just enjoyed each other's company. It was nice. Like a little slice of what could be.

"We really need to figure out sleeping arrangements, though," I say, walking into their house.

"You aren't going to want to sleep with all of us every night," Callum says. "You may want one of us, or none of us."

"Maybe down the road I won't, but right now... I do. I just want to be around you all, all the time. I know that's silly and chemical reactions and all in my head. But I just want to make up for all that lost time."

Callum's hand brushes over my cheek. "We have all the time in the world." He kisses my temple.

"What do you want to do tonight?" I ask in a semi-seductive voice. Ever since seeing their reactions at the dress store, I've been itching to try what my little wonder women cliterati groups came up with.

"Nothing. You're being punished," Jax shoots. He was quiet at dinner and on the ride home. Really, ever since his semi-confession in the dress store.

"Aren't you also punishing yourself?" I retort.

"It's why I'm so pissed."

"So no takers then?" I ask, and they all look awkwardly around at each other. I laugh. "Well then. You've all seen my wall of dildos, so you know I have no qualms about pleasing myself. I was just hoping to please you all first, but I guess we have all the time in the world," I say lackadaisically. With my finger pressed against my chin, I raise my eyes to the ceiling and let my mind wander. "Where should I get myself off at? Hot tub? The voyeur room? The shower? The living room? Here, in the kitchen?" The guys shift, so I smile and start slowly unbuttoning my shirt.

"Everlee," Jax warns.

Ignoring him, I toss my shirt on the floor and slowly unzip the back of my skirt, letting it fall to the ground so I'm only standing in my bra, panties, and high-heeled shoes.

"She..." Knox chokes out, pointing at me, before shoving his fist in his mouth, whining. "The heels."

I unhook my bra and let it slide down my arm, letting it fall to the floor.

"Mother, may I?" Knox asks, killing all my sultry passion, because I laugh.

"Yes, you may."

He runs over and bends down, wrapping his hands around my waist, pulling my hips to him while he takes a breast in his mouth. I run my fingers through his hair, arching my back and moaning out. One because it feels good, but also a little for show.

"Knox. You pussy whipped dick!" Jax lashes out with a hint of humor playing on his words, grabbing Knox away from my breast. Knox was in the middle of sucking, so part of my nipple is pulled away with him and I let out a yelp.

"Sorry love. That wasn't my fault."

Jax watches me for a second to make sure I'm ok before moving.

"All good." I slip my underwear down, wiggling my legs to get them to slide down, then flick them off, aiming straight for Jax. They hit him in his chest and he catches them. For a moment, I think he's going to lift them to his nose, but then he tilts his head and drops them. I know I'm wearing him down, chipping away at his walls, and it has become my mission tonight to do just that.

Grabbing the closest chair to me, I pull it out and turn it around, sitting down in it. The guy's intense gaze lands on me, flicking between my face and my pussy. Slowly, I drag my finger to my mouth, sucking on it, then glide it down my body. Their breaths are short and shallow, the hunger ignited in their eyes.

With a tantalizing slowness, I trace my fingers down to my clit, caressing it softly before sliding them deep inside. I tilt my hips up just a little, granting me more access and giving them a better view.

Knowing how they react, I let out a moan and arch my back while my other hand reaches up to run over my breasts and around my neck. I continue to rub my finger on my clit, circling it, dipping it inside to get it wetter and wetter, spreading it around. I close my eyes, enjoying the touch as my teeth bite down on my bottom lip and I add a second finger.

Peeking through one eye, I look at them, smiling when I see the bulge in their pants and the flush across their skin. With each passing moment, my breaths match theirs in shallowness, amplifying the ecstasy building inside me. It's a potent mix of their longing stares and the pleasure coursing inside of me. My finger moves faster and faster as I inch ever closer to the glorious release. My hips slide down in the chair, my breath hitches, my eyes snap shut and my head drops back. I'm... so... cl-

A hand snatches at my wrist, and everything comes halting to a stop. I already know whose it is based on the firmness of the grip.

Slowly opening my eyes, I tilt my head up to find Jax staring at me, his eyes pure fire and lust.

"You aren't finishing."

"I'd rather finish you first, anyway," I say. That was my plan the entire night until they tried to put guardrails on me. Then I made a pivot!

"Not going to happen, princess."

"We'll see." I rub my hand over his pants, pressing my palm against his hard erection.

He lets out a puff of breath that tells me I'm close.

"No." He grabs my hand and pulls it away.

I press my other hand against him at the same time I rise on my tiptoes and plant kisses on his neck, inhaling his citrusy, musky scent. His hand holds on mine, but he doesn't move it away, standing there letting me grip and rub while I gently suck on his neck. After a moment, I take it a step further and start unbuckling his pants, sliding them down, freeing his cock.

I look up at him through my lashes, pulling my hand out of his grip and running them down his chest as I drop to my knees. Grabbing his cock, I pump my hand up and down gently, rubbing my thumb over the arousal on his tip before licking a stripe down the bottom side of his cock, coating it in my saliva.

His arms are still crossed on his chest as he fights against what he wants. I plant kisses down his shaft, twirling my tongue around the crown before taking it in my mouth, sucking it a few times before swallowing him down in one quick burst. He hits the back of my throat and my throat tightens as he hits my gag reflex.

"Fuck," he sighs and his hands fly to my head, gripping my scalp tightly as he shoves his cock into my mouth.

I smile in satisfaction, tearing down the last of his walls.

I let him fuck my face. A silent apology for pushing him earlier and he takes it.

"Goddamn squirt," he groans, a long, low, and needy groan that lights my soul on fire. Squirt. His affectionate name for me. My insides burst with glee. Like fireworks exploding inside of my body as tingles race across my skin. His grunts and moans, the way he takes, and the breaths he makes, give me power. Confidence. Need. The need to please him, to please all of them.

When he slows, he lets me push off, but only for a second. "I want all of you. Now." My request turns into a command, followed with a low rumble that sparks the men into action.

As Knox is ripping off his pants, he's running out of the room and returns a moment later with a pillow in his hands. "For your knees, Ali."

My heart nearly bursts, both from Knox and because I have all my men around me in a semicircle. I move from one to the other, taking them in my mouth for a few tugs, getting them wet, alternating, pumping two others at the same time. I feel like a puppet master with my marionette of cocks. Like a master organist at the grandest pipe hall, although a master trombonist would probably be more fitting.

"I want..." I say between switching cocks. "To take..." I move to Knox. "Two of you in my mouth."

"I will sacrifice my cock for this dangerous, yet worthy undertaking," Knox chimes.

As I look up, Emmett's presence towers over me, standing in front of me alongside Knox.

"Well, twist my cock," he mumbles, with a smile curling on his lips.

I grab both of them, sucking them in my mouth a few times each, then press them together, pumping them as one. The hungry expressions in their eyes, the sight of their cocks rubbing together slick with my saliva, and the breaths they suck in light my pussy on fire. I'm so wet and ready to be touched, but tonight's not about me. It's about pleasing them.

Slowly, I pull them to my mouth, flicking my tongue between both their dicks before pressing their heads together and circling my tongue around them before taking them in as much as I can. My mouth is so full and burning at the edges and the only thing I can think about, albeit, briefly, is mouth yoga. Should have done more mouth yoga.

I grip them tightly and rock my head back and forth on their cocks, before moving between each of them individually, taking them deeper, before pressing them together again and taking them as one. Once I have it under control, I grab each of their hands and place them on their cocks, so they can hold them together while I slowly pump on Jax and Callum, who have been stroking themselves, watching me take two dicks.

"You're a fucking Queen Ev," someone says. I can't tell who it is, because they mumble, and the hums and moans from everyone else filters it out.

Emmett and Knox continue to pump into my mouth as we all move in unison. I've never gotten off before without anyone touching me, but tonight could be the night.

"Hold on," Callum breathes out and everyone stops. Emmett and Knox pull out of my mouth, and while missing their cocks, my mouth also welcomes the reprieve.

"What's going on?" I ask.

Callum grabs my hand, lifting me to stand. "Knox, grab her."

Knox obeys, throwing me over his shoulder, with my ass up in the air. I smack Knox's back, screaming and laughing. "This is not how tonight is supposed to go!"

"In your opinion. In our opinion, *this* is how tonight is *not* supposed to go," Callum retorts. "You're stubborn, so we gave in for a little while, but you will learn we always win."

I pop my head up to glare at him, and he throws his head back in a laugh, then boops my nose.

"Ass," I mumble.

"No. But I'm going to get yours in a few minutes," he says, causing a flush to sweep over my skin.

When we get in the voyeur room- which really doesn't seem like the right name anymore- Knox flops me onto the bed.

"This is more like it," Callum says, running a finger up my side, past my ribcage and to the underside of my arm. Like a reverse Dirty Dancing move. Is that what we're doing? A little dirty dancing? A little horizontal mambo? God, I hope so. These men have me turned on all the time and when I saw them today at La Belle, it was everything I could do not to jump them. A moment later, I feel the familiar fuzzy handcuffs being clasped around my wrists. "Now. What to do with you?"

I watch them all walk around the bed, eyeing me like a piece of prey and excitement bubbles in my belly.

"Knox?" I moan out, knowing he will feel the need I have right now.

He climbs on the bed, pressing a knee between my legs. "Yes, Ali?"

"Will you fill me with your cock and fuck me until you come?"

His eyes do this sort of flutter thing as a heady breath escapes his lips. "How can I say no to you, love?"

"I was hoping you wouldn't," I drawl out slowly, rubbing my calf up his leg.

"Higher." He urges and I move my leg higher. "Higher," he says again. "Now the other." He clasps a hand around my shin, rubbing his hand down, and plants kisses, while I bring my other leg up to sit on his shoulder. He moves to my right leg, mixing in little nibbles, causing goosebumps to spread along my skin, and my back to arch off the bed.

"Knox," I warn.

"You didn't say when, love, and if I recall, you're still being punished."

I narrow my gaze at him, the ache from within driving me crazy with lust and desire. "Please fuck me. Please."

"Begging? I love it when you beg for my cock." He smiles, grabbing my legs and thrusts in quickly without hesitation.

The first push sends my body reeling as tingles travel up my spine. "Yes! Give me more, Knox!" He holds my legs to the ceiling and pounds into me repeatedly. Nothing fancy, no more taunting. Just pure sex. His need consuming him and wrapping us up in our own cocoon. Taking and giving. My legs begin to shake as Knox moves even faster, edging closer to his own release as I'm coming to mine. I feel like I'm about to explode and I do. I scream out as pleasure tears a seam straight through me and rolls over me in wave after delicious wave.

Knox lets out a grunt, and I can feel his cock throbbing inside of me before he slows. He lets my legs fall to the side as he leans over and takes my mouth with his. "Always misbehave, because I love punishing you." His lips softly press to mine before he slides his tongue in.

I love kissing this man. The way he makes me feel. To say like I'm the only one seems trite or cliche, but it's the truth. Like he's searching for something and he finds it with me. Like he's testing the waters, scared to get in, but then gets lost.

I'm breathless when he pulls away and I'm left panting.

He climbs backwards off the bed and I see Jax walking over, taking long strokes of his cock, causing his tattoos to dance on his chest and arms.

He grabs my ankles and flips me over on my stomach. His roughness electrifying my skin. I'd never been one for rough sex, but with him, it's... exciting. Thrilling. I trust him with every part of my body, knowing he'll push it to the very edge, but is always in complete control.

"Move up to the headboard," he commands.

I awkwardly push up, sliding my body to the headboard, waiting for my next instruction.

"Grab it."

I grab it and look over my shoulder.

He presses two fingers to my cheeks and pushes my head away.

"Jax," I whisper.

He brings his head down beside mine, but doesn't speak.

"Earlier…" I whisper.

His breath hitches, like he knows what I'm going to say. What I'm going to ask. He slides my hair to the side and presses his lips against my ear. My pulse nearly beats out of my chest with anticipation of what he's going to say.

His next words come out in a low growl that shakes me to my very core, nearly making me come. "I'm going to need you to shut the fuck up and take our cocks like a good girl."

A puff of air leaves my lungs, and I slowly turn my head to look at him. It's like he just stepped out of one of my smutty books and holy fuck, is it hot.

He rarely calls me a good girl, mostly Callum, but hearing the words on his lips… A fire sweeps across my skin, igniting it, causing my eyes to flutter and my legs to shake.

His finger glides down my spine, causing my back to arch up like a cat in heat. His hands brush along both of my ass cheeks, rubbing them, grabbing them. Something cool glides over my forbidden place and I know what's happening next. He presses a finger in and begins prepping me, sliding it in and out. He adds more lube and another finger, continuing to pulse and swirl, stretching me wider and wider. His fingers curve in a come-hither sort of move eliciting a low groan. "Jax," I cry out, dropping my head and shoulders to the bed so my ass is still sticking up in the air, begging for him.

He pulls his fingers out and I hear him squirt a little more lube, no doubt coating his length to help it easily glide in. The head of his cock slowly presses into my opening and pauses, allowing me to stretch around him. He pulls out, then presses in again, going a little further, causing my eyes to roll into the back of my head and my stomach to tighten.

"Yes," I grind out, face in the bed.

He pumps faster and faster, filling me to the hilt. When he pulls out, I rock back into him, needing more. Taking more.

He slides his hand up between my shoulder blades and grips the back of my neck, his other hand on my ass, and presses down as he unleashes his thrusts into me. Anger. Frustration. Lust. Need.

I bow my back, pressing my ass up higher, as he hits every nerve, every sweet spot, within my ass. This is fucking insane. My orgasm builds, slower this time, like a tsunami, ready to wipe out an entire village, and I don't want it to stop.

"Jax," I moan as I'm getting closer, but he says nothing.

His hands and his cock claim me.

I am his, and he is mine.

"Yes! Yes! Yes!" I howl out, my body nearly ripping in two. This orgasm is so much more than before and lasts longer until my body is quaking around his cock. He thrusts one, two, three times and then stills. He pulsates inside of me just before he collapses, his chest pressing to my back.

He moves my hair aside and plants a kiss on my cheek and just stays there for a moment like he wants to say something, but can't find the words or perhaps the courage. I turn my head towards him and take his lips. It isn't a rough or super passionate kiss, but there are unspoken words woven within it.

He pulls out, leaving me empty, and I crumple to the bed, rolling over.

"Have you had enough?" Callum asks.

My gaze fixates on him and Emmett stroking their cocks and while I don't know if I can have another orgasm or give anymore; I feel a stirring inside of me. I *want* to give these men everything. Every part of me I can.

"Never," I murmur.

Callum stretches onto the bed, unlocking the handcuffs, and lies on his back. "We're going to take you together." He pats his chest, inviting me to climb on top.

It takes me a minute to move because my muscles and bones feel like jelly. This moment feels a little surreal, as it reminds me of the first time I was in this room. Straddling him while the others watched.

I look down at him, watching him breathe, as I trace his tattoos with my fingers. He is a beautiful man. A beautiful canvas, painted with black ink and a story. I'm so thankful I get to learn what every one of those tattoos means to him, when he got it, and why.

Our hands mindlessly roam each other as we soak one another in, and then I feel a soft kiss on the back of my neck and my head lolls backwards.

"Hey Trouble," Emmett says, as his lips travel up my neck and around to mine. His tongue slowly pulses in, causing my head to swim.

This man.

These men.

I lift my body up and sink onto Callum. His hands travel to my hips and hold me there while I continue to kiss Emmett. Both of them moving slow for me, only giving what I can take.

The kiss with Emmett deepens, and I want more. Need more. Like it's oxygen breathing fire back inside of me and my hips respond gyrating slowly on Callum. Emmett's hands slide up my back and around my waist, grabbing my breasts as he continues to kiss my mouth in a slow and passionate kiss. I place my hands over his as he plays with my nipples, intertwining us as one.

"Emmett," I whisper out, and he knows exactly what I need.

He slides his hands on my back, gently pressing me forward. I don't need as much prep this time, but I still hear the lube being squirted and feel its cool slickness slide along my backside.

"If it's too much, you say the word Trouble." Emmett sweeps the hair along my back and presses his lips to my ear.

"Never."

Callum chuckles. "Never say never, love. There's only one of you and four of us."

"Never," I whisper, pressing my lips to his. A puff of air escapes when Emmett slowly pushes in where Jax was. "I feel so full."

"You have two cocks inside of you." Callum plants kisses along my jaw.

My hands press to the bed and rock back on both of them, slowly at first as I get used to their fullness. Once they are completely seated inside of me, they begin to push and thrust. They've waited the longest and I want to make it good for them, even though I feel like my body can't give anything else.

"Fuck me, please," I whimper.

"Everlee," Callum says, his hands cupping my cheeks with concern spread across his face. "We can stop."

"Please don't. I need you. I want you."

I catch Callum look over my shoulder at Emmett and a moment later they both move fast. Fucking me with a gentle ferocity. Their moves in complete sync. Moving, rubbing, hitting every sweet spot in my body.

We are one.

A pile of heat, sweat, and pleasure.

No words. Just connectedness.

Wet slaps fill the room, along with grunts, sighs, and moans. Each of us lost in our own world.

A moment later, they still inside of me, their cocks pulsing and I collapse on Callum's chest. Emmett pulls out and rolls over on the bed and I turn my head, looking at him.

"You are so fucking amazing, Trouble." His fingers dance on my heated, sweaty skin.

He lays there for a moment, stroking my back before rolling off the bed so it's just Callum and me. His cock continues to get softer inside of me with each passing minute, but I don't want to move. Even if I had the strength right now, I don't want to. This connectedness. Tonight felt different in so many ways. It's like all the worry of the what ifs evaporated.

We are together.

All of us.

And I'm not leaving.

The walls they had built started to come down tonight. Like they gave a part of themselves to me and I gave a part of myself to them. It had been happening all week, little things here and there.

I must have fallen asleep on Callum, because my head feels like it's in a daze as my body is being carried. "Sorry," I mumble into his chest. "I didn't mean to fall asleep on your dick."

His chest shakes with a low chuckle. "I kind of liked it," he whispers, kissing my forehead. "We're going to take care of you now."

I hum in delight and promise to only close my eyes until I get in the water.

EVERLEE - POWER TO THE PUSSY

I LIED TO MYSELF.

I didn't just close my eyes until I hit the water. In fact, I don't even remember the water.

I open my eyes and I'm in a tangle of arms and legs and I wonder if this could be my bedroom. Part of me shudders at the thought, only because I know I'm not the only girl that's been in this room, or in this bed, which causes jealousy to spike within. I try to shove it away, because I'm here now and I will be in the future.

They picked me and I picked them.

Knox stirs beside me, so I roll over to face him. His eyes flutter open, the sleep still stinging them, but when he sees me, a smile curls his lips. His hand brushes through my hair and he presses his lips to my forehead. "Good morning, beautiful."

A smile of pure joy lights up my face.

"You want to get some breakfast and let them sleep?"

I nod slowly.

He rolls out of the bed and I slide out from under Emmett's arm, grabbing Knox's hand as I stand. My muscles are a little sore, like if you ran five miles when you're used to running five feet, but nothing too bad. I will just do some stretching today to see if that helps.

Knox shows me to the room where my closet is and I slip on a pair of some of the softest joggers I've ever felt and a loose-fitting t-shirt. The bathroom has all the essentials, so I quickly brush my teeth and hair and then put it back in a ponytail.

When I walk downstairs, Knox is waiting for me, wearing gray sweatpants and a gray hoodie, looking so damn delicious. How is this my life?

"You ready?" he asks, holding his hand out.

"Yes." I smile, reaching to grab it.

He writes a quick note and leaves it on the counter, letting them know we'll be back soon.

We walk down the sidewalk hand in hand to a small bakery on the corner and grab coffees and teas and an assortment of bagels, donuts, and muffins.

"How do you feel?" he asks.

"Fine."

He cuts his eyes at me. "Ali?"

"I'm a little sore, but overall, I'm good."

He shifts the bag of baked goodies to his other arm and reaches for my hand. It's a gentle gesture that melts my heart.

"Are you ok?" I ask.

He looks at me and there is a brief flicker of something behind his eyes and then it's gone, replaced by a chuckle and a smile. "I'm always good." He squeezes my hand.

And with that, I don't push, but continue to walk with him, squeezing his hand, giving him whatever silent encouragement he needs.

We get back to the house and all the guys are in the kitchen waiting for us. They sport disheveled hair, wearing joggers or sweats low on their hips, and no shirts. I swear I can hear a fucking choir singing in my head.

My gaze falls to Emmett. "I'm sure this won't be anywhere close to what you could make, but it's my kind of cooking." I laugh.

"It's perfect." He slips his arm around me and kisses my temple.

"I can cook a few excellent dishes, though. Maybe one night this week, I'll cook for you all. We can have an early dinner before you have to head out to Vixen."

"I like the sound of you here and cooking dinner," Emmett says, then corrects. "Not the whole domestic woman cooking dinner thing, just that you'll be here. I'm all for woman's rights. Power to the pussy." He thrusts both fists in the air.

"Way to make it fucking awkward," Jax chimes, grabbing some syrups and creamers for the coffees.

Callum digs into the cabinet and pulls out a long serving dish while Knox and I unload our cakey spoils. We all sit around the island, talking, eating breakfast, and just enjoying the casual conversation and it's at this moment I know this is how I want every morning. I knew it before on some other level, but now... it's entwined in every fiber of my being, like it's been baked within my DNA to be here with them.

Waking up in their arms. Eating breakfast with them. Getting ready for work with them. I want it all.

JAX - AVOIDANCE

I'VE NOT BEEN LOOKING forward to tonight ever since we left the dress shop. I'm excited to celebrate Emmett because he deserves all the successes and accolades he's going to get, but Everlee. That dress.

Unclenching my fist, I give myself one more look in the mirror, fixing the one piece of hair that refuses to stay in place. I straighten my bowtie, and head downstairs where I can tell Everlee is, because the men are losing their minds.

She faces away from me, and I can't help but notice the lines of the dress, tracing them down to where it rests just above the curve of her perfect ass. One wrong bend and a glance from a guy that's not us will result in me losing my ever-loving shit.

Why does she have to be so goddamn stubborn? I love that part of her, but equally hate it.

Love? No. That's not what I meant.

Obviously.

To love her now would be crazy. Stupid. Reckless. And I'm not reckless. I'm cool, calculated, and a bit of an ass most of the time, but it's usually for a good reason.

She turns to look at me over her shoulder and her eyes twinkle with lust and her lips part ever so slightly. Fuck this dinner. I just want to take her mouth and make her mine. Ours.

She turns towards me and poses, sticking her leg through the slit and my eyes drink up every delicious drop of her, from her painted toes all the way up her leg where the dress barely covers her delicious pussy. Is it wet? The flush on her cheeks and the shallow pants in her chest tell me she probably is, and the thought of that causes my dick to twitch.

Damn her.

But I will not give her the satisfaction of knowing what she does to me.

That's a lie. I always say that then want overcomes logic and I lose control with her, and the fact it turns her on only makes it worse. It's like she's awakened the beast inside of me I've tried so hard to keep pressed down. He was created and unleashed when I was in the SEALs. It's what made me good. Made me lethal. But I had to stuff him back down when I left. That part of me growing again, and it scares me.

"Don't you look handsome, Jax." She smiles, likely because she's reading my face and body language and knows what she's done. What she does.

I put my hands in my pockets to act nonchalant, but really it's to make sure my dick is behaving. "Everlee."

She puckers her lips into an o face with humor in her eyes. "I see we are still a crabby patty about this dress."

I shrug and brush past her.

Avoidance. That will be the name of the game tonight.

"Well, I think you look delicious," Knox chimes, bouncing over and wrapping his arm around her, tilting her back into a kiss.

He doesn't understand. He was there with me at some of our darkest times and while I leaned into the rage, he built walls and pretended like it never existed. Monsters live in the world and tonight they will have their eyes on our woman and I'm not ok with that.

There's a knock on the back door.

It's time.

God help me get through this night without ending up in jail or killing someone.

Callum guides Everlee out, followed by Knox, Emmett, and then lastly me. After locking the door, I climb into the back of the limo and purposefully choose to take the seat by Emmett instead of the one by Everlee.

The gray taffeta is falling to either side of her leg and I'm sure if I tried hard enough, I'd be able to see she isn't wearing panties. Because why would she?

"You ok man?" Emmett whispers, nudging my shoulder.

I cut my eyes at him, wondering why he'd ask such a stupid question, and he just chuckles.

"You can't break her."

"Watch me."

"Oh. I have. I rather enjoy it. She gives you a run for your money."

"She's infuriating."

"Is that what you call it?"

My gaze narrows at him, ignoring his innuendo. "I'm going to try not to ruin your night by attacking someone."

"If they lay hands on her, then I'll have your back. But if they're looking, then let them. She's ours, not theirs."

I shrug.

I'm not always a possessive son of a bitch, but there's something about her which brings out that side of me and I hate it. It makes me feel things I don't want to feel.

The limo stops several minutes later, and we climb out of the car. It's a large cream-colored building with a few black and white banners strewn across the front for decoration with a red carpet rolled out.

"Looks the same as last time. Well, almost," Everlee says to Callum.

This must have been where they came in February.

Knox is leading the group, with Everlee behind him and Emmett and Callum to her side, with me behind them. The watchful eye.

She loops her arm in Emmett's and I tense. Not because it's Emmett, but because we're in public. I try to squash down the worry and tell myself no one will know we're a unit. She's on a date with her man, who's here receiving an award for his restaurant and his friends. Easy. Simple.

We walk into the enormous building and they have several camera stations set up. Knox and Everlee both jump at the chance to get our picture taken, so we walk over and wait in the short line. The photographer is a little confused at first, so Everlee, being Everlee, dictates the order of pictures. First Emmett by himself, then all five of us, then just the four guys.

We follow the music and the crowd to the main dining room, where they have assigned seating. As we snake our way to the front, there are two people sitting at our table, and again, I tense.

This is going to be the worst fucking night of my life.

Knox reaches the table first, and a smile spreads across his face. He leans down to give the woman a hug. When she stands up, I recognize her petite frame. Sophie and her husband, Jacques.

She turns to look at each of us and then her eyes land on Everlee. She throws her arms out and brings her into a hug. "Darling. You look stunning and this dress." She grabs the skirt and lifts it. My pulse quickens in a panic and I let out a low growl. "How have you been, my sweet?"

"Good." Everlee smiles, her gaze catching mine.

"You look good."

Emmett steps in, giving her a hug. "What are you doing here?"

"I couldn't miss this dinner to celebrate with you, my friend. Callum called me and told me the good news, and Jacques and I were already talking about taking a brief trip to the States. So voila!" She exclaims, throwing out her hands.

"Thank you so much for being here," Emmett says, shaking Jacques' hand.

"We'd be nowhere else," Jacques says with a smile.

We take our seats at the table. Everlee sits beside Sophie, and then Emmett sits beside her, and the rest of us fill in, so Knox is left sitting on the other side of Jacques.

"I can't wait to dance tonight," Sophie says, shaking her shoulders.

"Me either." Everlee smiles.

"It's a shame Vixen isn't open tonight. I'd love to show Jacques your club."

"You can come tomorrow night," Callum offers.

"We won't be here. We leave tomorrow morning to travel out west."

"Ooh. Where are you going?" Everlee asks, clasping her hands together.

She is breathtakingly beautiful without ever trying. The twinkle in her eyes lights up her soul. I can't believe that dickface, Richard, ever cheated on her and then would be stupid enough to try to win her back. The fact he keeps showing up at her place is infuriating and makes me want to ram his head through a fucking wall until he gets the picture. Although, I wouldn't do that.

I think.

Dinner and the awards go by. Emmett is called on stage and gives a small speech about his vision and what it's taken for him to get to where he is, thanking all of us for our love and support. It's a wonderful speech.

They remove the accordion style wall, folding it into its wall cubby, revealing a dance floor. My stomach sinks. I was hopeful when I didn't see one in the main room, that perhaps the Gods had smiled on me.

Nay.

They smite me.

Of course, Everlee and Sophie are the first two up, hand in hand, moving to the dance floor. I sit back for a minute, watching them. Perhaps if I'm not around her to see the eyes traveling all over her body, I won't be tempted to protect her. That lasts all of three minutes until Knox and Emmett pull Callum and me onto the dance floor. Jacques gets up reluctantly and follows us over, standing behind Sophie, putting his hands on her hips.

My gaze flickers to Everlee, who is swaying her hips and my eyes lock in on her split, dancing dangerously close to her pussy. I move to the side, blocking any view, and try to settle my shoulders since I can feel knots forming in them.

"This isn't so bad, is it?" she asks me, interlacing her fingers in mine.

Without speaking, I cut my eyes at her and she chuckles, releasing my hand and rubbing down my arm.

I don't know how much time has passed before the women decide to sit down, but I'm so thankful.

"You should try to smile a little or your face will get stuck like that," a singsong voice whispers over my shoulder.

I turn to look at Sophie and she smiles.

"Things are good?" she asks, sitting down.

Emmett, Knox, and Everlee have gone to get some drinks from the bar.

"They are."

"I'm glad to see you all have found your way back to one another. She was very sad when she left."

"She shouldn't have left."

Sophie tilts her head to the side.

"I know why she did. I get it. But it doesn't matter any-more. We're going to try."

"I'm thrilled for you all. I've gotten to know her over the last several months and she is pretty fantastic."

"Yes. She is." My gaze catches her as they walk back over to the table.

Sophie pats my shoulder, vacating the seat. "I think we're going to head out," she says, giving Emmett another hug. "We have an early flight tomorrow morning."

"It was so good seeing you again." Everlee steps forward, giving her a hug.

"Perhaps next time we see each other, you can let Jacques and I host!"

"France?"

"Oui."

"Oui oui," Everlee says, shaking her shoulders and I can't help but smile.

"Congratulations to you again," Sophie and Jacques say to Emmett before leaving.

"Well." Everlee looks at us. "Should we go to? It's been several hours and Jax hasn't killed anyone, even though I was worried a couple of times while we were dancing. I'd hate to press my luck."

"Somehow, I don't believe you. Pressing your luck seems to be what you enjoy doing most of all," I retort.

A wicked grin curls on her lips and her eyes twinkle mischievously.

"That's what I thought," I say, curling my arm around her waist. And just like that, I'm doing what I said I wasn't going to do. Give in to her. She's like a siren.

"Yes!" Emmett claps. "It's been a fantastic night and I don't want to ruin it." He knocks back the rest of his bourbon neat and places the glass on the table.

As we're leaving, I allow myself to finally exhale my breath and let my shoulders relax.

We get in the car and Everlee looks over at me. "That wasn't so bad, was it?" She rubs my leg up and down, then slides her slit to the side. "And I even bought nude panties to wear for you."

"You couldn't have told me that earlier?" I growl in irritation.

"Where would be the fun in that?"

She smiles and I take her lips, gripping her neck with my hand. She fights at first, but it only takes seconds before I can feel her melt into it. Into me. One of the things I find most intoxicating about her is that she's so easy to read. There's never any guessing. Well, if she's wearing panties with a dress, maybe. But her feelings, thoughts, emotions... what she likes. What gets her off. Open book, and I want to give it all to her.

EVERLEE - JUST SAY YES

IT'S ONLY BEEN JUST over twenty-four hours since I've seen them. Last night, I was at work late and didn't feel like going to Vixen. My body needed to recover, and I just needed a me night, even though when bedtime rolled around, I was really missing them and very much wanted an us night.

Waking up tangled in their arms is one of my favorite things.

I spent most of last night talking to Lizzy, and she kept me entertained, as usual, with all of her craziness. She told me she has a meeting with Emmett Tuesday to talk about plans for renting out Bo's for her reception. She doesn't have a date yet, and it's just a preliminary meeting to discuss potential costs and requirements, but I could tell by her voice it doesn't matter. It's just items on a checklist for her. She's going to have her beautiful wedding that will be way over the top, and I will be there supporting her every single step of the way. Enjoying and living vicariously through her.

Knox formed a group chat with all of us this morning, so I've spent most of my morning staring at my phone. These men are horrible for my work ethic.

I force myself to put my phone back in my purse and ignore it while I hustle through several reports and wrap up three presentations for the next week. My stomach grumbles and knows it's almost time for lunch, so I grab my phone to call Lizzy, but before I can, I find five texts and two missed calls.

The guys.

I called the last number that called me. Emmett.

"There she is," he says jovially.

"Hey there."

"Come downstairs."

"Why?"

"Just come down now!" he says, super excited.

I can't help the smile spreading across my face as I walk through the cubes and to the elevator. When I get downstairs, I see the sleek black Audi parked out front with Jax's head and arms on the passenger side door, Knox driving and Emmett standing by the back door. Callum is sitting in the seat behind the driver, looking at me.

"What's going on?" I ask, drawing nearer.

"Don't freak out," Emmett says, leaning in to give me a hug and pressing a quick kiss to my cheek.

"Ok," I say cautiously.

"We have a surprise for you and hope you'll say yes."

He ushers me into the middle of the back seat and I look at all of my guys, cheeks hurting from smiling. "Ok. What is it?"

"It wouldn't be a surprise if we told you," Jax says dryly from the front without turning around.

"Glad to see you're in a good mood," I say, squeezing his shoulder.

He grabs my hand and presses his lips to it. "I'm in a great mood."

Sitting back, I rub a hand on Emmett's and Callum's thighs and look out of the window. "I missed you all last night."

"We missed you too," Callum says.

Buildings turn into trees, and I notice we're getting closer and closer to their house. "Where are we going?"

"You'll see."

My heart is nearly pounding out of my chest with excitement.

We're on their road and I'm completely confused. "We're going to your house? If you guys wanted a midafternoon bang, you could have just asked me."

"We would, but this is not that."

We drive past their house to the next unit and pull into the driveway. My stomach gets tight. "Where are we?"

No one speaks as they climb out of the car.

"Hello?" I ask cautiously, excited.

Callum pulls a set of keys out of his pocket and walks up the back steps to open the door.

Inside is an open floor plan, with bits of furniture placed around the space. Decorated, but not furnished. It's a similar design to their house, but not nearly as big.

"Whose house is this?"

Knox is beaming like a light-bright, bouncing up and down, so Callum nods to him and he nearly explodes. "Yours!"

"I'm sorry. What?" Shock takes me back.

Jax steps forward in his typical calm and collected self. "What he meant to say is yours if you want it. We've had it for a while and we aren't doing anything with it. We'd ask you to move in, but know you still like your space. So we thought you'd like this, instead. You can get out of your apartment, be closer to us so we can see you and you can see us whenever you want, and you can be closer to Lizzy."

"I can't afford this."

"You don't have to. It's already paid for."

"I can't take this. It's too much."

Knox frowns. "Do you not like it?"

"I love it," I say, walking around. It's exactly what I pictured for myself after I got married. Lots of natural light, a small garden in the back, open floor plan.

"You can walk to Lizzy's," Knox chimes.

"That's a long walk," Jax says.

"Not super long."

I laugh. It would be nice to get out of the apartment and be closer to them, but still have my space. I can't believe I'm even thinking about this.

"I will have to buy a car to take to work."

"We can-" Knox starts, but I hold my hand up.

"You aren't buying me a car."

"I was going to say we can help you pick out one." His eyes give away his lie.

I smile, cupping his cheeks, pressing my lips to his.

"So is that a yes?" he asks tentatively.

"We will have to work out some sort of arrangement. I can't in good conscious just live here for free."

"I can think of ways you can pay us back," Emmett says, stepping forward.

"Like dinner? Lots and lots of dinner?"

"Yes dinner. I do love to eat." He winks.

A flush ignites my skin.

"Is that a yes?" Knox chirps, stepping closer.

I slowly nod.

"I need to hear your words," Callum commands, tilting my chin up with his fingers.

"Yes."

Emmett picks me up and spins me around, and I squeal out in glee.

Lizzy is going to shit a complete brick when I tell her.

Emmett puts me down. "But I'm serious. We need to find some sort of payment."

Jax swoops in. "We will."

I press on his hard chest. "I'm not talking about sex."

"Me either." His eyes twinkle, and he picks me up into a kiss, then puts me down.

"Now let's introduce you to your new house." Callum grabs my hand and leads me around.

I'm so happy I'm scared I'm going to burst. My heart feels so full. Like impossibly full.

I call out the rest of the afternoon, because I'd be completely useless. Emmett orders some take out and we get some blankets and lay them on the floor for a picnic in what will be my dining room.

When we finish, we all lay on our backs staring at the ceiling, making a human star on the floor, completely content and happy. My pulse races. Races with the possibility of what our future looks like. Together.

"Hey guys..." I breathe. The words that I want to say get stuck in my throat and the only thing I can think to say are the words from Teddy Swims, who I listened to all last night. "So if you're going to leave me... leave me in the middle of the night and set the bed on fire."

I love them with every fiber of my being, even if I'm still too chicken shit to say the three words out loud.

They roll over on their stomachs and look at me, so I reluctantly roll over, scared of what I'll find. But in my defense, they have all but just bought me a house, so that seems like a pretty big fucking deal.

"Everlee," Callum says quietly.

"We won't leave you. You are ours. And we can't wait to see what our future holds with you."

"Samesies," Jax coos.

I scoot forward and wrap my arms around their necks as we all press our foreheads together, letting the emotions pass.

"So, when can I move in?"

"Any time you want, love."

I sit up and place my hands on my knees. "Maybe I'll bring some things over this weekend, then see if my brother can come help in a couple of weeks. I have to give the apartment some notice."

"You have us four," Jax retorts. "You don't need your brother's help."

"I know. But he's been talking about coming up, anyway." I hesitate asking the next question because I feel like I've already pressed my luck with these guys.

"Yes," Callum answers.

"Yes?"

"He likely already knows about us. We kind of did a piss-poor job of hiding it."

My lips twist into a smile. "I'll tell him in person, not over the phone."

"Whatever you decide. Let's just not get too crazy." He chuckles.

I notice Emmett and Jax checking their watches.

"I need to head to Bo's," Emmett says, sticking out his bottom lip.

"And we need to head to Vixen," Jax echoes.

I frown.

"But you can stay here or at our place." He rolls his eyes. "Or we can have Brady drive you home."

I smile. So many options. "I'll call Lizzy and tell her the good news and will probably wait for you in your living room when you get home."

"We love the sound of that," Emmett says.

The guys stand up and try to help clean up, but I scoot them out of the door. Callum runs back up, handing me the keys, and gives me a quick kiss. "See you later, love."

As I watch my guys walk to Jax's car, my stomach feels like it's literally bubbling with happiness.

After I watch them drive away, I close the door, pressing my back against it.

I don't know how long I will stay here before I end up at their house. Maybe we could add a bridge connecting the two houses with secret entryways. I laugh at myself, but still think through ways I can convince them.

After I clean up the containers and plates, and fold up the blanket, I video chat Lizzy.

She picks up on the second ring and immediately is swiveling her head around. "Where are you?"

"I did a thing."

"You did a thing? If you've added another dick to your bouquet of man dicks, I'm going to lose my mind."

I laugh, "No."

"So what is it? Which sexual origami did you achieve this time? I swear my body hurts for you."

"Nothing."

"Tell me."

"Well, I'm trying to find the words, but you keep talking."

"That's not like me."

"I'm moving... closer to you."

"YOU MOVED IN WITH THEM?" Her tone is somewhere between excited and shocked.

"Not exactly. They have a house beside theirs and they are giving it to me."

"THEY GAVE YOU A HOUSE! Fuck, I need to climb on that donkey dick. Shit. Do you have a rainbow twat? That shit is magical."

"Lizzy," I repeat, trying to stop her from talking. "Do you want to come over?"

"Duh."

"Street number is 15069."

"No, the fuck it isn't."

"Would I kid you?"

"I'd hope you'd never kid about something as sacred as the sixty-nine."

"Never," I say, putting my hand over my heart.

"Be there in a few."

She hangs up and I sit the phone down and just explore again. This time on my own and at my pace. This is my new place, right beside my guys. I love how they know me so well. Giving me the space if I need it, with all of us knowing I'll be at their house most every night. I love them so much and can't wait to see what our future holds.

I let out a scream of happiness, then call my brother.

EVERLEE - FAMILY

A MONTH LATER...

"Holy shit Ev. This is nice," Beckett says, walking into the foyer, holding Will's hand. I look down and he rolls his eyes. "Shocker. You already knew."

"Well, I strongly suspected." They sit their bags down and continue to look around.

It's not fully decorated or furnished yet, but that will come with time- it's only been a month. I got rid of a lot of my stuff instead of moving it because it was older and needed to be replaced, anyway.

The guys kicked me out of the house two days after they gave it to me and said they were working on a surprise. When they let me back in a few days later, they had converted one of the rooms to *our* bedroom. There was a large circular bed which filled up the entire space so we could all sleep together. I screamed with excitement and ran and flipped on the bed. It's too big to sleep in when they aren't with me, but that's only been a few nights in the last month.

They worked on it during the day when I was at work, and at the same time, created a special shrine to my dildos. It was a joke thought up by Knox, and Jax, being the smartass he is, built it. So now there is a little cut-out in my closet with electric candles and beaded necklaces for my dildos.

"Well, as I'm sure you also suspected..." he looks at me, but doesn't speak. "Those guys... are... my..."

"Oh my God. Just spit it out, you little Pollyanna."

I smile. "You knew?"

"Yea." Will nods. "It was pretty impossible not to know. Those guys looked like they wanted to eat you for breakfast, lunch, and dinner."

"Gross. I'm standing right here."

"I know," Will says, patting his chest and clawing at the air.

"Just please don't say anything to anyone," I implore.

"Who would I tell? Mom and dad? Could you imagine? A gay and a poly." He laughs.

The doorbell rings and we all turn around and I open the door.

"Betty?" I ask, shocked.

"Girl! I hope you don't mind. I seen you updated your address in the app and I had to come see for myself what all this hubbub was about." She looks over my shoulder. "Oh, I'm sorry."

"Come in Betty. This is my brother and..." I pause, unsure how to introduce him.

"His boyfriend, Will," Will chimes in, saving me.

"I was going to watch her panic a little longer," Beckett adds, and I smack his chest.

"Guys. This is Betty. Share driver extraordinaire."

"Well, if the apron fits," she says, bouncing her hair a little. "I don't want to stay long since I just popped over uninvited. But I bought you a little house plant."

"Betty. You are always welcome and thank you so much for this. It's my first plant and I know just where to put it." Placing it on the table by the front window, I admire how the light filters through the curtains, casting a soft glow on its petals.

There is another knock at the door.

"My goodness, are you always this popular?" Beckett teases.

"Not usually."

I open the door and Lizzy and Tony are standing there.

Lizzy looks at all of us, then settles on Betty. "Betty! You sassy minx, what are you doing here?"

"Came to give Everlee a house plant."

"Well, this is perfect timing! We're having an engagement party at none other than… drum roll, please." Tony pats the door. "Bo's!"

I already knew, but I didn't say anything. "So exciting. When?"

"Like you don't know." She cuts her eyes at me, and I wink.

"In a couple of weeks. The weekend before Memorial Day. Please say you can come Betty! I'd love to meet the man who made an honest woman out of you."

Betty chuckles. "Honest woman may be taking it a little too far," she says, shimmying her shoulders.

"That's why you're our sassy minx!"

"Meow. Call me kitty cat."

My eyes grow wide as I look around the room for reactions. I love this woman. Absolutely fucking love this woman.

"Well, I have to go. People are waiting."

"We'll see you soon, ok?" I lean over and give her a hug.

"Nice meeting you," Beckett calls after her.

Once the door closes, Lizzy turns to look at Beckett. "Come over here and give me a hug, you big ol' gay firefighter."

"I don't think that was all needed." He smiles, lifting her into his arms.

"Who's your handsome plus one?" she asks, even though she already knows since I told her all about them when I came back after Easter.

"This is Will."

"His boyfriend," I chime, pumping my eyebrows.

"Ooh la la."

"Well, are we ready to go grab some dinner?" I ask.

"Yes," everyone says in unison.

Unfortunately, it's just us five tonight. They guys couldn't get off work, but we told them we're going to swing by Vixen's later, so they reserved our table in VIP for us. Emmett's bartending tonight, so it will be nice to have us all together under one roof. All the people I love.

What's Next?

After this page is a Bonus Scene from Beckett's POV if you want some MM. Will and Beckett will get their own spinoff this year. :)

There are a few bloopers/deleted scenes that I thought were too funny to delete and also a note about Knox.

If you want to skip all of that and dive into the next book in the series, Rainbows and Unicorns, click here!

Everlee and her men are back!

Everything is going great for them, but when a woman from the men's past enters the scene with a proposition that is hard to refuse, how will things change for our favorite quintet?

BONUS SCENE FROM BECKETT'S POV (AFTER EASTER EGG HUNT)

BECKETT – BEING A BIT TABOO, NEVER HURT ANYONE

I DROP MY PHONE on the counter and tilt my head. "I think she knows."

Will chuckles. "Knows what?" he asks, walking across the kitchen, like a tiger stalking its prey. "How I tried to get you off in the car?"

I laugh. "No. But what was that about?"

He shrugs. "I don't know. I guess being around those men and knowing, rather, strongly suspecting, they are a taboo little poly pod, made me want to be a bit taboo, too."

"You've always said you wanted to keep us on the down low." I run my hands up his chest and over his shoulders.

"I do. It makes it a little more exciting, don't you think? Once the guys at the firehouse know, then we'll get shit and be treated differently because we would be two *gay* fire-fighters. Anytime we walk off together, their only thought will be that we're having sex."

"Won't that be what we're doing?"

"Stop. You know what I mean."

"But, seriously, is that what we'll be doing? If so, I need to call the captain right now!" I tease, leaning over to grab my phone.

He reaches across me, his chest brushing against mine, to hold my hand down. "You wouldn't." His eyes hold a note of fear and panic behind the playful flirtation.

"Of course... not." My smile drops, "I wouldn't out you. That's your secret to tell when you're ready."

His eyes narrow on me. "I can't tell if you're being sarcastic." He steps back cautiously.

Cupping his cheeks in my hands, I stare into his deep brown eyes. "About that? Never. I was outed when I wasn't ready and dealt with a lot of blowback. I may tease you about it, but would never follow through." Leaning in, I place my lips on his.

He pushes away and stares at me, his gaze still questioning.

I laugh. "What?" A flurry of emotions flitter through me. The panic in his eyes triggers something in me. The part of me that wants to protect him, to put his worries and fears at ease. The part that wants to fight all of his dragons for him.

Fuck.

He shrugs before leaning back in for the kiss. It's different this time. A soft kiss, which quickly turns into a lust-filled hunger as his tongue pushes its way in like a dog searching for a bone. Need grips him. Grips me as he presses his hips against mine, sending us toward the counter. His hands travel down my chest and land on the waistband of my pants, pausing. Waiting for permission? No. Teasing? He's always been the more reserved one between the two of us, but today. Now. He's almost feral, making me wild with lust.

I pull my head out of the kiss and grab his hands. "We're in my parent's kitchen."

He looks around and whispers, "I don't see anyone here." He places his lips under my jaw and starts gently kissing. His lips feel like fire on my skin as his hand slips inside my pants and grabs my hardening cock.

He hums as his fingers clasp around it, pumping a few times. "I want to taste you so bad." He nips at my neck and sucks on my fevered skin.

My head rolls to the side as a groan escapes. "Who are you right now?"

A low, gravelly chuckle reverberates from his chest.

Will is still a mystery to me in a lot of ways. We'd been seeing each other unofficially for almost two months and any time I try to make it more official, he pushes away. He has a lot of reservations around the firehouse knowing he's gay and the only reason I found out was because I ran into him, literally, at a notoriously spicy gay bar on blackout night. They turned the lights off, and the name of the game was to move around like a bunch of zombies and kiss the first person who grabs on you and you grab on them. My lips connected with him, and it was like an explosion of fireworks. The kiss was deep, intense, passionate. I didn't want it to end. When the lights came back on, I was shocked and he was mortified. We ended up at the bar and grabbed a couple of shots and talked.

He wasn't at all what I expected. I thought he was your average southern, strait laced, heterosexual, brown hair, brown-eyed, quiet boy who always followed the rules. Instead, I got... so not that. The only thing I nailed was the brown hair and brown eyes.

He pulls his hand out of my pants and grabs the hem of my shirt, slipping it over my head. "I love your chest," he murmurs against my pecs as he trails kisses down, following the edges and lines of my muscles, to the top of my pants.

With bated breath and my heart threatening to burst from my chest, I can't help but keep my eyes glued to the driveway. Am I really about to let this happen? Am I about to get sucked off in my parent's kitchen with the possibility they will be home any minute?

He pulls down my pants, freeing my hard cock, and drops to his knees. My eyes fall on him kneeling before me like he's kneeling to the God's at the altar and my cock twitches with excitement. A smile curves on his lips as he runs his mouth along the length of my cock, but not touching it. He's so close, though. So close I can feel his warm breath flowing over it like a morning fog over a mountain. I can almost feel the moisture from his tongue and have to fight with every muscle I have not to move towards him.

"Fuck!" I cry out, my cock aching to be touched. "Stop playing and take me. Take me in your mouth and make me fucking come." My stomach tightens as desire swells inside of me. He wraps his hand around the base of my cock and swirls his tongue over the tip, eagerly lapping the arousal that has beaded there. My head falls back and my legs quake as I fight the urge to push into his mouth and take what I so desperately want right now. He's toying with me and I fucking love it. Payback for teasing him the other day at the firehouse.

Running my fingers through his hair, I grip them on his scalp tighter and tighter, as he slowly takes me in, further and further, until I hit the back of his throat and feel it constrict around me. His cheeks hollow before he drags me out, his tongue sliding along the length of my cock.

A shiver starts at the base of my spine and runs up my back as a heady breath escapes.

"Do you like that?"

"Mmhmm," I moan, running my fingers through his hair.

His hand works at the base of my cock, while his head bobs a few times, coating it in his saliva. "Damn Will, you suck cock so good." And he does. He's the best I've had.

He smiles under my praise before he sucks me hard and deep into this mouth, working it like it's a fucking popsicle melting in the sun. My hands drop from his head as I latch them onto the side of the counter to help hold me up. Lust filled sighs and grunts escape from my lips as I watch my cock disappear into his mouth repeatedly. It's so fucking hot, causing my stomach to tighten.

I force myself to look out of the window as dread fills me. My parents are accepting, but seeing me get sucked off in their kitchen would probably be too much for them to handle.

He grabs my balls and begins massaging them while my cock continues to punch into his mouth, hitting the back of his throat.

"I'm about to come."

His hands drop as he reaches up to grab my ass, like he's trying to press me further into his mouth. I go, wanting to give him every inch of me.

"Goddamn," I grunt, as his throat is nearly pulsating around my cock. "Oh. My. Will," I cry out, my orgasm hitting me fast, shooting down his throat.

He lets out a moan as he swallows and swallows, his tongue pressing my cock tighter in his mouth each time.

I shudder out a breath at the same time he's standing up. I grip my hand around the back of his neck and bring him to my mouth, parting his lips with my tongue. Claiming him. I tug his bottom lip between my teeth, sucking, as another moan uncontrollably escapes. I would be so fucked right now if my parents came home, because I'm cock out in their kitchen and if I saw them pull up right now, I wouldn't move away from this kiss. From him.

His hard shaft is pressing through his pants as we push them closer together. *Needing* to feel them together.

He pushes me back, both hands on my chest. "Take me to your bedroom. I need you. I need your cock."

Studying him for a second, I try to figure out what exactly he's asking. Is this it? I give him a quick kiss, grab my shirt, pull my pants back up, then grab his hand and dart up the stairs. I'm so excited. Beyond excited. I've wanted to fit my cock in his perfectly tight ass since the second I met him and have him do the same, but we decided to take things slowly. Part of me wonders how experienced in the lifestyle he is, because I know he's not out to most, and every time his family comes up, he gets skittish.

We walk into my bedroom, and I close and lock the door. I can feel his nerves from across the room. "Are you sure you want to do this?"

He nods.

"Have you had sex before?" The question is out before I can stop myself.

He chokes out a laugh but doesn't answer.

"Will?"

He nods. "With a woman."

My brows raise.

"Once. I was trying to convince myself I wasn't gay. You can see how well that turned out."

I move across the room in two gigantic steps, wrapping my hands around the back of his head, bringing his lips to mine. I nearly melt into his kiss. It's hot. Passionate. I love kissing him. I pull away from his mouth and plant kisses on the corners of his lips, on his jawline, on his earlobes. His moans only drive me crazier with want and desire to give him everything. I'm falling for this man against all my better judgement. Damn it.

It's in this moment I realize we can't have sex. At least not like this. Not at my parent's house when they could be home any minute. No. His first time - our first time - needs to be special. Not rushed.

I grab his shoulders and his dizzied gaze lands on me.

"We can't have sex."

His head recoils in shock, like I've slapped him.

"My parents could be home any second and your first time, our first time, needs to be more special. We need to take our time. You aren't a quick fuck kind of guy for me."

His gaze softens.

"I want to do this, us, right."

"You do?"

"Yes." I laugh. "I've been trying to tell you for a while that I like you."

He slowly shakes his head like he knows where this conversation is going.

"Look. I'm not forcing anything. I just think we should wait. I'd hate for my parents to come home... it's just... not right."

"So you don't want..." He can't finish the sentence.

"Oh. No. I definitely want. I want your cock so fucking bad I ache. I want to taste it. I want to ride it. I want it to fuck me. I want everything."

He smiles.

"Ok?" I question, making sure we're in a good spot.

He nods. "I get it. I just... I'm... I'm so hot for you."

I smile, grabbing the hem of his pants. "I said we couldn't have sex. This isn't sex," I say, pulling his pants and boxers down in one swift motion. I stare, admiring his bouncing cock and his bulging thighs. I've never been with another man that is the same size as me. As muscular as me. What would it feel like to have his weight on me? For me to press into him? Into me? I'm getting hard again, so I pull down my pants.

Dropping to my knees in front of him, I wrap my hand around his length. There is a bead of arousal glistening at the tip, so I run my thumb across it, then lick it off. His hands tangle in my hair, guiding me to his cock. I smile. "You want me to suck you off?"

He nods, nibbling on his lower lip.

I run my tongue down the underside of his shaft, all the way to his balls and then back up, before sucking his cock in with a heady groan.

"Oh, my..." his chest rumbles out, pressing his hips into me and causing him to hit the back of my throat.

I moan around him, pleasure seeping out of every pore, as he takes what he wants. Takes me. My mouth. My hand plays with his balls, while I continue to bob on him, taking him faster with each thrust.

"You feel so fucking good," he pants. "But..."

I pause, looking up at him. "What's up, babe?"

"I want to feel your body on me, beside me. I need to feel your cock pressed against me."

He's so fucking sexy.

I stand up and push him backwards until he falls on the bed. His eyes go wide with surprise and excitement as he slides himself into the center. As I crawl over the top of him, my cock bounces on his stomach. Starting with gentle kisses on his chest, I slowly make my way up to his neck before finally reaching his mouth. The kiss is deep, hot, passionate. I could kiss him forever. If I had one last breath, I would spend it kissing him.

Fuck. I shouldn't be thinking about that. Feeling that.

It's all I can do to stop from fucking him right now, the way he's looking at me with those eyes. His dick pokes me in the stomach and I can feel dribbles of his arousal brush against my skin. My head is swimming in want. The want to have him in my mouth, in my hand, in my ass.

The want to have him. Period.

As I lower my hips onto him, our cocks press up against each other and I grind, feeling the friction between them as they rub between our bodies. I lean forward and take his mouth, devouring it with mine. Our tongues tangle in the art of seduction, heat, dominance. I may be on top right now, but he wants control. I fight him for it, as our hands explore each other's bodies. Arms, ass, face. I want to feel every part of him with every part of me.

His hands grip my ass, holding me to him as he rocks his hips up into me. "God. I want you so fucking bad."

"You have me. You have all of me," I pant out before sitting up. Reaching across the bed to my nightstand, I grab the lube out of the drawer. I'm straddling him as I squirt some into my palm and rub my hands together before reaching down to coat our cocks.

In one swift motion, he rolls us over so he's straddling me. "My turn." He smiles wickedly, taking both cocks in his hand and cupping the other around it and strokes us while our cocks rub together.

My eyes roll into the back of my head.

A moment later, he presses both hands on my chest and begins rocking, the base of our cocks rubbing together, before he leans over and sucks on my neck. "I'm going to mark you."

The friction between our bodies intensifies as I tangle my fingers in his hair, pulling tightly as sighs and slaps fill the air.

With our bodies still pressed tightly together, I roll him to the side and eagerly grab our cocks, pumping them with a feverish rhythm. Our legs tangle as one. I want his come all over me. I want to bathe in it.

"Yes," he urges, watching our dicks sliding through my fingers.

My balls tighten as pleasure starts to boil over. "Will?"

"I'm about to come."

"Come for me, baby."

His hips shift as he loses control and fucks my hand. I squeeze harder and he lets out a sigh of appreciation. His hips thrust up, sending his cock through my hand, pulsing as he shoots his come all over us. A second later, tingles shoot through my body and I release, coating both of us in white streams of need. Come and sweat covers our chests as our breathing steadies and our pulse slows.

I want nothing more than to lie here with him and bask in our post orgasm glow, but it's getting late and the lingering dread of my parents showing up and finding him here is still weighing on me.

"Join me in the shower?"

He looks at me.

"Quick shower. In and out. My parents are going to be home soon."

"You really need to get your own place."

"Ok. Everlee."

He smacks my chest. "She's right."

I roll my eyes. "Shower?"

"Yes, please."

Note about Knox

NOTE: WE NEVER HEAR from Knox's POV because he's never really spoken to me. I have to dig deeper into him, but I feel like he's a little more broken on the inside and uses jokes as a cover because he's scared of getting hurt. He keeps a lot of things private, unwilling to let himself dig it. Jax and Callum are so easy to write because what you see is what you get with them. Alpha males in every sense of the word and Emmett... he is slowly coming out of his shell. I feel like in some ways he was, and still is, a little guarded, but is letting his walls down with Everlee.

BLOOPERS

OUTTAKES:

<u>BECKETT AND WILL</u>

Will quickly pulls my pants and boxers with such force, my cock swings back up, knocking him in the chin.

"Did I just get dick wapped?"

"What can I say? Cock knows what the cock wants."

<u>LIZZY MEETS GUYS AT BO'S</u>

Lizzy gives all the guys a hug and is fanning herself as she takes a seat by Jax. "You guys are so much hotter than your dick pics."

Callum spits out his drink in shock.

"Fuck Lizzy," I turn to the boys. "She's kidding. I don't show her the pics."

"So there are pics?" She taps the tips of her fingers together mischievously.

I cast a hard stare at Lizzy and she rolls her eyes.

<u>WHEN EVERLEE WANTS TO TAKE CARE OF THE GUYS AFTER THE DRESS SHOP. WHEN CALLUM TELLS EVERYONE TO HOLD ON.</u>

Callum walks into the office and grabs something out of the desk drawer, then walks back into the room and I laugh while he walks over to the sink. "What is that?"

"Well, if Lizzy can buy you dildos, so can we."

"A confetti dildo?"

"For celebrating taking our relationship to the next level."

My cheeks are hurting from laughing as I watch him nearly jack the dildo off with warm water and soap.

"We need it extra clean for our pussy." He smiles coyly.

Knox tears out of the room and is coming back a moment later with another pillow. "For your other knee. The dildo can suction to the middle of the floor... between your knees!"

"Knox thought the suction cup would come in handy."

"You guys bought me a dildo?" I say in an awe-too-sweet voice.

"We know how much you love being gifted dildos," Emmett says matter-of-factly.

"I don't know if 'love being gifted' are the words I'd use. They're almost like a sympathy gift." I laugh. "But this is the first dildo someone has ever bought me that wasn't a sympathy gift... and it has confetti."

Callum walks over and has me rise on my knees so he can position the dildo below me. I sink down on it, letting its girth fill me. Not as full as the guys, but it will do.

"Now where were we?" I ask lining myself with the dildo and the men's cocks.

I suck each of them in my mouth a few times to coat their cocks before I resume Knox and Emmett. Once I find my rhythm, I lift myself up and down on the dildo. I have no idea how in the fuck I'm tetrising this shit, but it's working. It's almost like patting your head and rubbing your belly at the same time. It just takes time and concentration.

I bounce faster as Emmett and Knox pump into me. Between the bouncing, pumping, and sucking, I lose my rhythm and start taking them one at a time, sucking a few times, pumping a few times while still bouncing. It becomes a frenzy of cocks and hands and everything else in between.

About the Author

Hi friends! Follow me below for all the updates, behind the scenes and bonus content! I will be launching some merch too. Just finalizing plans and details for that!

You can always email me at authorsnmoor [at] gmail.com or message me below. I will say I have a newsletter and have been horrible with it... to the point where I hardly send one out. I do rely more on facebook, Insta and TT for most of my communication. I do plan on working on the newsletter this year so who knows haha... But I can guarantee that you will not get bombarded with a lot of emails haha! If anything, quite the opposite.

Newsletter
Etsy Shop AuthorSNMoor
Tiktok@authorsnmoor
Instagramsn_moor
FacebookSN Moor Author — Author SN Moor Fan Group
GoodreadsS.N. Moor
Amazon